JOE R. LANSDALE

BUMPER CROP

GOLDEN GRYPHON PRESS • 2004

Foreword: "The Remains of My Days . . ." copyright © 2004, by Joe R. Lansdale.
"God of the Razor," first published in *Grue #5*, 1987.
"The Dump," first published in *Rod Serling's The Twilight Zone Magazine*, July 1981.
"Fish Night," first published in *Specter!*, Arbor House, 1982.
"Chompers," first published in *Rod Serling's The Twilight Zone Magazine*, July 1982.
"The Fat Man," first published in *The Horror Show*, January 1987.
"On a Dark October," first published in *The Horror Show*, Spring 1984.
"The Shaggy House," first published in *The Horror Show*, Fall 1986.
"The Man Who Dreamed," first published in *The Horror Show*, 1984.
"Walks," first published in *Cemetery Dance*, Fall 1997.
"Last of the Hopeful," first published in *The Good, the Bad, and the Indifferent*, Subterranean Press, 1999.
"Duck Hunt," first published in *After Midnight*, Tor, 1986.
"Down by the Sea Near the Great Big Rock," first published in *Masques*, Maclay & Associates, 1984.
"I Tell You It's Love," *Modern Stories*, 1983.
"Pilots," first published in *Stalkers*, Dark Harvest, 1989.
"In the Cold, Dark Time," first published in *Dark Harvest Summer/Fall Preview: 1990*, Dark Harvest, 1990.
"Bar Talk," first published in *New Blood #7*, 1990.
"Listen," first published in *Rod Serling's The Twilight Zone Magazine*, May/June 1983.
"Personality Problem," first published in *Rod Serling's The Twilight Zone Magazine*, February 1983.
"A Change of Lifestyle," first published in *Rod Serling's The Twilight Zone Magazine*, Nov/Dec 1984.
"The Companion," first published in *Great Writers & Kids Write Spooky Stories*, Random House, 1995.
"Old Charlie," first published in *The Saint Magazine*, August 1984.
"Billie Sue," first published in *A Fist Full of Stories (and Articles)*, CD Publications, 1996.
"Bestsellers Guaranteed," first published in *Espionage Magazine*, May 1985.
"Fire Dog," first published in *The Silver Gryphon*, Golden Gryphon Press, 2003.
"Cowboy," first published in *The Good, the Bad, and the Indifferent*, Subterranean Press, 1999.
"Master of Misery, first published in *Warriors of Blood and Dream*, AvoNova, 1995.

Copyright © 2004 by Joe R. Lansdale

Cover illustration copyright © 2004 by John Picacio

LIBRARY OF CONGRESS CATALOGING-IN-PUBLICATION DATA

Lasdale, Joe R., 1951–
    Bumper Crop / Joe R. Lansdale. — 1st ed.
       p.   cm.
    ISBN 1-930846-24-X (hardcover : alk. paper)
    1. Horror tales, American.   I. Title.
PS3562.A557   B86   2004
813'.54—dc21   2003019750

First Edition.

Contents

To my son, Keith

Foreword

The Remains of My Days . . .

*H*IGH COTTON, PREVIOUSLY PUBLISHED BY Golden Gryphon Press, contained what I believe to be among the best of the best stories I've written. What follows is *Bumper Crop*. In Southern terminology, High Cotton is when the cotton is growing well and growing high. Bumper Crop refers to when your crops give an added splurge, usually referring to vegetables, not cotton, but it's a kind of surprise crop. An added treat.

Therefore, the title.

Many of these stories are favorites of mine, and if they are not my very best, they are among the best of my shorter works. In fact, most are very short. A few, like "God of the Razor," have added greatly to my career. Primarily in the novel *The Nightrunners*. But I've also written about the razor character in comics and other stories. An anthology of God of the Razor stories written by others, as well as myself, will soon be forthcoming from Subterranean Press under the title *Lords of the Razor*.

Numerous writers have told me how much they like my story "Bestsellers Guaranteed," because they understand the frustration of the main character.

But I won't discuss them all. I'll just say a number of readers have picked one or more of these stories as their favorites, and I've been asked repeatedly, when will they all be collected. Many were collected in *Bestsellers Guaranteed*, but it is long out of print and hard to find used. Some stories have never been collected, or were collected in a very limited manner.

Therefore, my reasoning for this collection.

Although some stories have not been collected before, most have been reprinted again and again. Here and overseas. A few I gleaned from two collections I did for Subterranean that contained early work. Most of the stories in those collections were not great and this was known up front. That was the fun part of those collections.

The books were limited and designed for fans who wanted to see how I was "birthed" as a writer, so they were a perfect and fun showcase for that kind of thing, and, they contained a lot of introductory material on how I became a writer, for those who care about such things, and that, in many ways, was more the drawing card for the collections than the stories themselves.

But, a few of the tales in those books weren't bad at all, so I borrowed the best of those. I also added a few from lesser-known collections, like *A Fist Full of Stories*, and one, "Fire Dog" is very recent, and is a favorite of mine. It came from a Golden Gryphon anthology.

A large number of the stories in this book are what I call catchy.

Once you read them, you remember them, and may even find yourself telling them to others, the way you find yourself humming a catchy tune. It's what makes them memorable. Their simplicity, and that catchy element.

In spite of the fact that many of them can be told quite well, I prefer you read them. I like to think the prose adds considerably to the flavor of the tales, and that's how I butter my bread, you buying the stories and me spending the money.

High Cotton and *Bumper Crop* are, to date, the definitive volumes of my short work.

Of course, new work, new collections come out all the time. But, if you like what I do, then these two books are a good way to introduce others to my work, or if you would like to have collected the largest part of my worthwhile short work, these are the books to do it.

Each book represents a different take on the short story. The former, *High Cotton*, is pretty Southern Gothic, though not exclusively, and this one is much more of the twist and surprise and ain't that damn weird school.

So, as I said, these two books are my best short story representatives.

Now, in the next few years that may change.

I hope it does.

I hope I have many short stories left to write. Many more volumes to provide readers.

These tales have certainly added greatly to my life, in pleasure, finance, and, hopefully, since they entertained me while writing, they will entertain you.

Joe R. Lansdale (hisownself)
Nacogdoches, Texas
June, 2003

Bumper Crop

In 1980, while holding down a full-time job, I began a novel called The Night of the Goblins. I had just written Act of Love and Dead in the West *in the same year! Not to mention numerous other things. (God, how did I do it?) I thought it might be nice to try and write a novel proposal—fifty pages and an outline—and try to sell from that.*

I wrote the proposal, sent it to my then incompetent and highly irritable agent, and waited. Act of Love *sold before the proposal went out, I believe, then* The Night of the Goblins *went to the same publisher. They thought it was too violent, too strange, and basically, they didn't understand it.*

I thought, gee, what's to understand?

I finished the novel in 1982 in a four-month blitz, sent it to my new agent, and he said it didn't fit in any box he could find. It wasn't horror. It wasn't mystery. It wasn't suspense. It wasn't exactly mainstream.

I told him thank you, fired him, marketed the novel around, got the most savage rejects you could imagine, none of them really complaints about the writing, but complaints about the fact that I was trying to write something that shouldn't be talked about. Some of the written rejects practically stuttered.

At least they were paying attention. That was a good sign.

I put the novel away and now and then, assuming it was never going to sell, I borrowed from it. I took a portion out of it, revised it, and came up with this story, "God of the Razor." I felt I could at least make some profit out of the time I had invested in the book.

Nope. No one wanted the short story.

Until Peggy Nadramia at Grue *bought it. Thanks, Peggy.*

The story was later picked up for The Second Black Lizard Anthology of Crime Fiction *and a mystery best-of-the year volume as well. Editors who rejected it the first time out, and don't remember they did, love to tell me how much they liked it. Uh huh.*

By the way, the book it was stolen and revised from, as were a number of other stories, did sell and came out in 1987, five years after it was finished, seven years after it was conceived. The title was changed. It was called The Nightrunners.

God of the Razor

RICHARDS ARRIVED AT THE HOUSE ABOUT eight.

The moon was full and it was a very bright night, in spite of occasional cloud cover; bright enough that he could get a good look at the place. It was just as the owner had described it. Run down. Old. And very ugly.

The style was sort of Gothic, sort of plantation, sort of cracker box. Like maybe the architect had been unable to decide on a game plan, or had been drunkenly in love with impossible angles.

Digging the key loaned him from his pocket, he hoped this would turn out worth the trip. More than once his search for antiques had turned into a wild goose chase. And this time, it was really a long shot. The owner, a sick old man named Klein, hadn't been inside the house in twenty years. A lot of things could happen to antiques in that time, even if the place was locked and boarded up. Theft. Insects. Rats. Leaks. Any one of those, or a combination of, could turn the finest of furniture into rubble and sawdust in no time. But it was worth the gamble. On occasion, his luck had been phenomenal.

As a thick, dark cloud rolled across the moon, Richards, guided by his flashlight, mounted the rickety porch, squeaked the screen, and groaned the door open.

Inside, he flashed the light around. Dust and darkness seemed to crawl in there until the cloud passed and the lunar light fell through the boarded windows in a speckled and slatted design akin to camouflaged netting. In places, Richards could see that the wallpaper had fallen from the wall in big sheets that dangled halfway down to the floor like the drooping branches of weeping willows.

To his left was a wide, spiraling staircase, and following its ascent with his light, he could see there were places where the railing hung brokenly askew.

Directly across from this was a door. A narrow, recessed one. As there was nothing in the present room to command his attention, he decided to begin his investigation there. It was as good a place as any.

Using his flashlight to bat his way through a skin of cobwebs, he went over to the door and opened it. Cold air embraced him, brought with it a sour smell, like a freezer full of ruined meat. It was almost enough to turn Richards's stomach, and for a moment he started to close the door and forget it. But an image of wall-to-wall antiques clustered in the shadows came to mind, and he pushed forward, determined. If he were going to go to all the trouble to get the key and drive way out here in search of old furniture to buy, then he ought to make sure he had a good look, smell or no smell.

Using his flash, and helped by the moonlight, he could tell that he had discovered a basement. The steps leading down into it looked aged and precarious, and the floor appeared oddly glasslike in the beam of his light.

So he could examine every nook and cranny of the basement, Richards decided to descend the stairs. He put one foot carefully on the first step, and slowly settled his weight on it. Nothing collapsed. He went down three more steps, cautiously, and though they moaned and squeaked, they held.

When Richards reached the sixth step, for some reason he could not define, he felt oddly uncomfortable, had a chill. It was as if someone with ice-cold water in their kidneys had taken a piss down the back of his coat collar.

Now he could see that the floor was not glassy at all. In fact, the floor was not visible. The reason it had looked glassy from above was because it was flooded with water. From the overall size of the basement, Richards determined that the water was most likely six or seven feet deep. Maybe more.

There was movement at the edge of Richards's flashlight beam, and he followed it. A huge rat was swimming away from him, pushing something before it; an old partially deflated volleyball perhaps. He could not tell for sure. Nor could he decide if the rat was trying to mount the object or bite it.

And he didn't care. Two things that gave him the willies were rats and water, and here were both. To make it worse, the rats were the biggest he'd ever seen, and the water was the dirtiest imaginable. It looked to have a lot of oil and sludge mixed in with it, as well as being stagnant.

It grew darker, and Richards realized the moon had been hazed by a cloud again. He let that be his signal. There was nothing more to see here, so he turned and started up. Stopped. The very large shape of a man filled the doorway.

Richards jerked the light up, saw that the shadows had been playing tricks on him. The man was not as large as he'd first thought. And he wasn't wearing a hat. He had been certain before that he was, but he could see now that he was mistaken. The fellow was bareheaded, and his features, though youthful, were undistinguished; any character he might have had seemed to retreat into the flesh of his face or find sanctuary within the dark folds of his shaggy hair. As he lowered the light, Richards thought he saw the wink of braces on the young man's teeth.

"Basements aren't worth a damn in this part of the country," the young man said. "Must have been some Yankees come down here and built this. Someone who didn't know about the water table, the weather and all."

"I didn't know anyone else was here," Richards said. "Klein send you?"

"Don't know a Klein."

"He owns the place. Loaned me a key."

The young man was silent a moment. "Did you know the moon is behind a cloud? A cloud across the moon can change the entire face of the night. Change it the way some people change their clothes, their moods, their expressions."

Richards shifted uncomfortably.

"You know," the young man said, "I couldn't shave this morning."

"Beg pardon?"

"When I tried to put a blade in my razor, I saw that it had an eye on it, and it was blinking at me, very fast. Like this . . . oh, you can't see from down there, can you? Well, it was very fast. I dropped it and it slid along the sink, dove off on the floor, crawled up the side of the bathtub and got in the soap dish. It closed its eye then, but it started mewing like a kitten wanting milk. Ooooowwwwaaa, oooowwwaa, was more the way it sounded really, but it reminded me of a kitten. I knew what it wanted, of course. What it always wants. What all the sharp things want.

"Knowing what it wanted made me sick and I threw up in the toilet. Vomited up a razor blade. It was so fat it might have been pregnant. Its eye was blinking at me as I flushed it. When it was gone the blade in the soap dish started to sing high and sillylike.

"The blade I vomited, I know how it got inside of me." The young man raised his fingers to his throat. "There was a little red mark right here this morning, and it was starting to scab over. One or two of them always find a way in. Sometimes it's nails that get in me. They used to come in through the soles of my feet while I slept, but I stopped that pretty good by wearing my shoes to bed."

In spite of the cool of the basement, Richards had started to sweat. He considered the possibility of rushing the guy or just trying to push past him, but dismissed it. The stairs might be too weak for sudden movement, and maybe the fruitcake might just have his say and go on his way.

"It really doesn't matter how hard I try to trick them," the young man continued, "they always win out in the end. Always."

"I think I'll come up now," Richards said, trying very hard to sound casual.

The young man flexed his legs. The stairs shook and squealed in protest. Richards nearly toppled backward into the water.

"Hey!" Richards yelled.

"Bad shape," the young man said. "Need a lot of work. Rebuilt entirely would be the ticket."

Richards regained both his balance and his composure. He couldn't decide if he was angry or scared, but he wasn't about to move. Going up he had rotten stairs and Mr. Looney Tunes. Behind him he had the rats and water. The proverbial rock and a hard place.

"Maybe it's going to cloud up and rain," the young man said. "What do you think? Will it rain tonight?"

"I don't know," Richards managed.

"Lot of dark clouds floating about. Maybe they're rain clouds. Did I tell you about the God of the Razor? I really meant to. He rules the sharp things. He's the god of those who live by the blade. He was my friend Donny's god. Did you know he was Jack the Ripper's god?"

The young man dipped his hand into his coat pocket, pulled it out quickly and whipped his arm across his body twice, very fast. Richards caught a glimpse of something long and metal in his hand. Even the cloud-veiled moonlight managed to give it a dull, silver spark.

Richards put the light on him again. The young man was holding the object in front of him, as if he wished it to be examined. It was an impossibly large straight razor.

"I got this from Donny," the young man said. "He got it in an old shop somewhere. Gladewater, I think. It comes from a barber kit, and the kit originally came from England. Says so in the case. You should see the handle on this baby. Ivory. With a lot of little designs and symbols carved into it. Donny looked the symbols up. They're geometric patterns used for calling up a demon. Know what else? Jack the Ripper was no surgeon. He was a barber. I know, because Donny got the razor and started having these visions where Jack the Ripper and the God of the Razor came to talk to him. They explained what the razor was for. Donny said the reason they could talk to him was because he tried to shave with the razor and cut himself. The blood on the blade, and those symbols on the handle, they opened the gate. Opened it so the God of the Razor could come and live inside Donny's head. The Ripper told him that the metal in the blade goes all the way back to a sacrificial altar the Druids used."

The young man stopped talking, dropped the blade to his side. He looked over his shoulder. "That cloud is very dark . . . slow moving. I sort of bet on rain." He turned back to Richards. "Did I ask you if you thought it would rain tonight?"

Richards found he couldn't say a word. It was as if his tongue had turned to cork in his mouth. The young man didn't seem to notice or care.

"After Donny had the visions, he just talked and talked about this house. We used to play here when we were kids. Had the boards on the back window rigged so they'd slide like a trap door. They're still that way . . . Donny used to say this house had angles that sharpened the dull edges of your mind. I know what he means now. It is comfortable, don't you think?"

Richards, who was anything but comfortable, said nothing. Just stood very still, sweating, fearing, listening, aiming the light.

"Donny said the angles were honed best during the full moon. I didn't know what he was talking about then. I didn't understand about the sacrifices. Maybe you know about them? Been all over the papers and on the TV. The Decapitator they called him.

"It was Donny doing it, and from the way he started acting, talking about the God of the Razor, Jack the Ripper, this old house and its angles, I got suspicious. He got so he wouldn't even come around near or during a full moon, and when the moon started waning, he was different. Peaceful. I followed him a few times, but didn't have any luck. He drove to the Safeway, left his car there and walked. He was as quick and sneaky as a cat. He'd lose me right off. But then I got to figuring . . . him talking about this old house and all . . . and one full moon I came here and waited for him, and he showed up. You know what he was doing? He was bringing the heads here, tossing them down there in the water like those South American Indians used to toss bodies and stuff in sacrificial pools . . . It's the angles in the house, you see."

Richards had that sensation like ice-cold piss down his collar again, and suddenly he knew what that swimming rat had been pursuing, and what it was trying to do.

"He threw all seven heads down there, I figure," the young man said. "I saw him toss one." He pointed with the razor. "He was standing about where you are now when he did it. When he turned and saw me, he ran up after me. I froze, couldn't move a muscle. Every step he took, closer he got to me, the stranger he looked . . . he slashed me with the razor, across the chest, real deep. I fell down and he stood over me, the razor cocked," the young man cocked the razor to show Richards. "I think I screamed. But he didn't cut me again. It was like the rest of him was warring with the razor in his hand. He stood up, and walking stiff as one of those wind-up toy soldiers, he went back down the stairs, stood about where you are now, looked up at me, and drew that razor straight across his throat so hard and deep he damn near cut his head off. He fell back in the water there, sunk like an anvil. The razor landed on the last step.

"Wasn't any use; I tried to get him out of there, but he was gone, like he'd never been. I couldn't see a ripple. But the razor was lying there and I could hear it. Hear it sucking up Donny's blood like a kid sucking the sweet out of a sucker. Pretty soon there wasn't a drop of blood on it. I picked it up . . . so shiny, so damned shiny. I came upstairs, passed out on the floor from the loss of blood.

"At first I thought I was dreaming, or maybe delirious, because I was lying at the end of this dark alley between these trash cans with my back against the wall. There were legs sticking out of the trash cans, like tossed mannequins. Only they weren't mannequins. There were razor blades and nails sticking out of the soles of the feet and blood was running down the ankles and legs, swirling so that they looked like giant peppermint sticks. Then I heard a noise like someone trying to dribble a medicine ball across a hardwood floor. *Plop, plop, plop.* And then I saw the God of the Razor.

"First there's nothing in front of me but stewing shadows, and the next instant he's there. Tall and black . . . not Negro . . . but black like obsidian rock. Had eyes like smashed windshield glass and teeth like polished stickpins. Was wearing a top hat with this shiny band made out of chrome razor blades. His coat and pants looked like they were made out of human flesh, and sticking out of the pockets of his coat were gnawed fingers, like after-dinner treats. And he had this big old turnip pocket watch dangling out of his pants pocket on a strand of gut. The watch swung between his legs as he walked. And that plopping sound, know what that was? His shoes. He had these tiny, tiny feet and they were fitted right into the mouths of these human heads. One of the heads was a woman's and it dragged long black hair behind it when the God walked.

"Kept telling myself to wake up. But I couldn't. The God pulled this chair out of nowhere—it was made out of leg bones and the seat looked like scraps of flesh and hunks of hair—and he sat down, crossed his legs and dangled one of those ragged-head shoes in my face. Next thing he does is whip this ventriloquist dummy out of the air, and it looked like Donny, and was dressed like Donny had been last time I'd seen him, down there on the stair. The God put the dummy on his knee and Donny opened his eyes and spoke. 'Hey, buddy boy,' he said, 'how goes it? What do you think of the razor's bite? You see, pal, if you don't die from it, it's like a vampire's bite. Get my drift? You got to keep passing it on. The sharp things will tell you when, and if you don't want to do it, they'll bother you until you do, or you slice yourself bad enough to come over here on the Darkside with me and Jack and the others. Well, got to go back now, join the gang. Be talking with you real soon, moving into your head.'

"Then he just sort of went limp on the God's knee, and the God took off his hat and he had this zipper running along the middle of his bald head. A goddamned zipper! He pulled it open. Smoke and fire and noises like screaming and car wrecks happening came out of there. He picked up the Donny dummy, which was real small now, and tossed him into the hole in his head way you'd toss a treat into a Great Dane's mouth. Then he zipped up again and put on his hat. Never said a word. But he leaned forward and held his turnip watch so I could see it. The watch hands were skeleton fingers, and there was a face in there, pressing its nose in little smudged circles against the glass, and though I couldn't hear it, the face had its mouth open and it was screaming, and *that face was mine.* Then the God and the alley and the legs in the trash cans were gone. And so was the cut on my chest. Healed completely. Not even a mark.

"I left out of there and didn't tell a soul. And Donny, just like he said, came to live in my head, and the razor started singing to me nights, probably a song sort of like those sirens sang for that Ulysses fellow. And come near and on the full moon, the blades act up, mew and get inside of me. Then I know what I need to do . . . I did it tonight. Maybe if it had rained I wouldn't have had to do it . . . but it was clear enough for me to be busy."

The young man stopped talking, turned, stepped inside the house, out of sight. Richards sighed, but his relief was short-lived. The young man returned and came down a couple of steps. In one hand, by the long blond hair, he was holding a teenage girl's head. The other clutched the razor.

The cloud veil fell away from the moon, and it became quite bright.

The young man, with a flick of his wrist, tossed the head at Richards, striking him in the chest, causing him to drop the light. The head bounced between Richards's legs and into the water with a flat splash.

"Listen . . ." Richards started, but anything he might have said aged, died, and turned to dust in his mouth.

Fully outlined in the moonlight, the young man started down the steps, holding the razor before him like a battle flag.

Richards blinked. For a moment it looked as if the guy were wearing a . . . He was wearing a hat. A tall, black one with a shiny, metal band. And he was much larger now, and between his lips was a shimmer of wet, silver teeth like thirty-two polished stickpins.

Plop, plop came the sound of his feet on the steps, and in the lower and deeper shadows of the stairs, it looked as if the young man had not only grown in size and found a hat, but had darkened his face and stomped his feet into pumpkins . . . But one of the pumpkins streamed long, dark hair.

Plop, plop . . . Richards screamed and the sound of it rebounded against the basement walls like a superball.

Shattered starlight eyes beneath the hat. A Cheshire smile of argentine needles in a carbon face. A big dark hand holding the razor, whipping it back and forth like a lion's talon snatching at warm, soft prey.

Swish, swish, swish.

Richards's scream was dying in his throat, if not in the echoing basement, when the razor flashed for him. He avoided it by stepping briskly backward. His foot went underwater, but found a step there. Momentarily. The rotting wood gave way, twisted his ankle, sent him plunging into the cold, foul wetness.

Just before his eyes, like portholes on a sinking ship, were covered by the liquid darkness, he saw the God of the Razor—now manifest in all his horrid form—lift a splitting head shoe and step into the water after him.

Richards torqued his body, swam long, hard strokes, coasted bottom; his hand touched something cold and clammy down there and a piece of it came away in his fingers.

Flipping it from him with a fan of his hand, he fought his way to the surface and broke water as the blonde girl's head bobbed in front of him, two rat passengers aboard, gnawing viciously at the eye sockets.

Suddenly, the girl's head rose, perched on the crown of the tall hat of the God of the Razor, then it tumbled off, rats and all, into the greasy water.

Now there was the jet face of the God of the Razor and his mouth was open and the teeth blinked briefly before the lips drew tight, and the other hand, like an eggplant sprouting fingers, clutched Richards's coat collar and plucked him forward and Richards—the charnel breath of the God in his face, the sight of the lips slashing wide to once again reveal brilliant dental grill work— went limp as a pelt. And the God raised the razor to strike.

And the moon tumbled behind a thick, dark cloud.

White face, shaggy hair, no hat, a fading glint of silver teeth . . . the young man holding the razor, clutching Richards's coat collar.

The juice back in his heart, Richards knocked the man's hand free, and the guy went under. Came up thrashing. Went under again. And when he rose this time, the razor was frantically flaying the air.

"Can't swim," he bellowed, "can't—" Under he went, and this time he did not come up. But Richards felt something touch his foot from below. He kicked out savagely, dog paddling wildly all the while. Then the touch was gone and the sloshing water went immediately calm.

Richards swam toward the broken stairway, tried to ignore the blond head that lurched by, now manned by a four-rat crew. He got hold of the loose, dangling stair rail and began to pull himself up.

The old board screeched on its loosening nail, but held until Richards gained a hand on the door ledge, then it gave way with a groan and went to join the rest of the rotting lumber, the heads, the bodies, the faded stigmata of the God of the Razor.

Pulling himself up, Richards crawled into the room on his hands and knees, rolled over on his back . . . and something flashed between his legs . . . It was the razor. It was stuck to the bottom of his shoe . . . That had been the touch he had felt from below; the young guy still trying to cut him, or perhaps accidentally striking him during his desperate thrashings to regain the surface.

Sitting up, Richards took hold of the ivory handle and freed the blade. He got to his feet and stumbled toward the door. His ankle and foot hurt like hell where the step had given way beneath him, hurt him so badly he could hardly walk.

Then he felt the sticky, warm wetness oozing out of his foot to join the cold water in his shoe, and he knew that he had been cut by the razor.

But then he wasn't thinking anymore. He wasn't hurting anymore. The moon rolled out from behind a cloud like a colorless eye and he just stood there looking at his shadow on the lawn. The shadow of an impossibly large man wearing a top hat and balls on his feet, holding a monstrous razor in his hand.

I have a soft spot in my heart—or maybe it's my head—for this one, though I hated it when I wrote it. It's a simple little Fred Brown/ Robert Bloch sort of story, and it was the result of a popcorn dream, as well as the fact that I was listening to a lot of old radio shows my friend Jeff Banks had loaned me.

About the popcorn dreams. The nuttiness in many of my stories, especially stories of this period, was the result of popcorn. I avoid the stuff most of the time, but when the urge hits, or when the bank account looks low, my wife makes up a huge batch. Her popcorn is the only popcorn that does it to me. She has her own special method of popping it up, and I tend to overeat. I go to bed. I have weird dreams. I get up and write the dreams and sell them. So far, every popcorn dream I've ever written down—a few were just too nonsensical— has sold. I guess it could be said I owe my career to my wife and her popcorn.

Radio shows. Bloch. Brown. Popcorn dreams. It all came together. I woke up in the middle of the night and wrote this story down. (I seldom do any writing in the middle of the night, by the way, but then I was working full time and wrote when I could manage it.) When I finished, I thought it was, to put it mildly, dumb. I didn't even make a copy. I folded it immediately, put it in an envelope so I wouldn't change my mind, went back to bed, and next day mailed it off to the then new Rod Serling's Twilight Zone Magazine, *a magazine I badly wanted to appear in.*

More I thought about the story, dumber I felt. Boy was I an idiot, and I didn't even have a copy of the story to look over and see how big an idiot I was.

Couple of days later, one night actually, Ted Klein, then editor of Twilight Zone Magazine, *phoned to say he loved it and wanted to buy it for the magazine. Later it appeared in* Best of the Twilight Zone, *a magazine anthology. I suddenly began to like it better.*

The Dump

ME, I LIKE IT HERE JUST FINE. DON'T SEE NO call for me to move on. Dump's been my home nigh on twenty years, and I don't think no high-falutin' city sanitation law should make me have to pack up and move on. If I'm gonna work here, I ought to be able to live here.

Me and Otto . . . where is that sucker anyway? I let him wander about some on Sundays. Rest of the time I keep him chained inside the hut there, out of sight. Wouldn't want him bitin' folks.

Well, as I was sayin', the dump's my home. Best damn home I ever had. I'm not a college man, but I got some education. I read a lot. Ought to look inside that shack and see my bookshelves. I may be a dump-yard supervisor, but I'm no fool.

Besides, there's more to this dump than meets the eye.

'Scuse me. Otto! Otto. Here, boy. Dadburn his hide, he's gotten bad about not comin' when I call.

Now, I was sayin' about the dump. There's more here than meets the eye. You ever thought about all that garbage, boy? They bring anything and everything here, and I 'doze her under. There's animal bodies—that's one of the things that interests old Otto— paint cans, all manner of chemical containers, lumber, straw, brush, you name it. I 'doze all that stuff under and it heats up. Why, if you could put a thermometer under that earth, check the heat that stuff puts out while it's breakin' down and turnin' to compost, it would be up *there*, boy, way up *there*. Sometimes over a hundred degrees. I've plowed that stuff open and seen the steam flow out of there like a cloud. Could feel the heat of it. It was like bein' in one of them fancy baths. Saunas, they call 'em. Hot, boy, real hot. Now you think about it. All that heat. All those chemicals and dead bodies and such. Makes an awful mess, a weird blend of nature's refuse. Real weird. And with all that incubatin' heat . . . Well, you consider it.

I'll tell you somethin' I ain't told nobody else. Somethin' that happened to me a couple years ago.

One night me and Pearly, that was a friend of mine, and we called him that on account of he had the whitest teeth you ever seen. Darn things looked *painted* they were so white . . . Let's see, now where was I? Oh, yeah, yeah, me and Pearly. Well, we were sittin' around out here one night shootin' the breeze, you know, sharin' a pint. Pearly, he used to come around from time to time and we'd always split a bottle. He used to be a legit, old-time hobo. Rode the rails all over this country. Why, I reckon he was goin' on seventy years if not better, but he acted twenty years younger.

He'd come around and we'd talk and sit and snort and roll us some of that Prince Albert, which we'd smoke. We had some good laughs, we did, and I miss old Pearly sometimes.

So that night we let the bottle leak out pretty good, and Pearly, he's tellin' me about this time down in Texas in a boxcar with a river trash whore, and he stops in midsentence, right at the good part, and says: "You hear that?"

I said, "I don't hear nothin'. Go on with your story."

He nodded and told the tale, and I laughed, and he laughed. He could laugh better at his own stories and jokes than anyone I'd ever seen.

After a bit Pearly gets up and walks out beyond the firelight to relieve himself, you know. And he comes back right quick, zippin' his fly, and walkin' as fast as them old stiff legs of his will take him.

"There's somethin' out there," he says.

"Sure," I say. "Armadillos, coons, possums, maybe a stray dog."

"No," he says. "Something else."

"Awww."

"I been a lot of places, boy," he says—he always called me boy on account of I was twenty years younger than he was—"and I'm used to hearin' critters walk about. That don't sound like no damn possum or stray dog to me. Somethin' bigger."

I start to tell him that he's full of it, you know—and then I hear it too. And a stench like you wouldn't believe floats into camp here. A stench like a grave opened on a decomposin' body, one full of maggots and the smell of earth and death. It was so strong I got a little sick, what with all the rotgut in me.

Pearly says, "You hear it?"

And I did. It was the sound of somethin' heavy, crunchin' down that garbage out there, movin' closer and closer to the camp, like it was afeared of the fire, you know.

I got the heebie-jeebies, and I went into the hut there and got my double-barrel. When I came out Pearly had pulled a little old thirty-two Colt out of his waistband and a brand from the fire, and he was headin' out there in the dark.

"Wait a minute," I called.

"You just stay put, boy. I'll see to this, and I'll see that whatever it is gets a hole in it. Maybe six."

So I waited. The wind picked up and that horrible stench drifted in again, very strong this time. Strong enough so I puked up that hooch I'd drunk. And then suddenly from the dark, while I'm leanin' over throwin' my guts out on the ground, I hear a shot. Another one. Another.

I got up and started callin' for Pearly.

"Stay the hell where you are," he called. "I'm comin' back." Another shot, and then Pearly seemed to fold out of the darkness and come into the light of the fire.

"What is it, Pearly?" I said. "What is it?"

Pearly's face was as white as his teeth. He shook his head. "Ain't never seen nothin' like it . . . Listen, boy, we got to get the hell out of Dodge. That sucker, it's—" He let his voice trail off, and he looked toward the darkness beyond the firelight.

"Come on, Pearly, what is it?"

"I tell you, I don't know. I couldn't see real good with that there firebrand, and it went out before too long. I heard it down there crunchin' around, over there by that big hill of garbage."

I nodded. That was a pile I'd had heaped up with dirt for a long time. I intended to break it open next time I 'dozed, push some new stuff in with it.

"It—it was comin' out of that pile," Pearly said. "It was wrigglin' like a great gray worm, but . . . there were legs all over it. Fuzzy legs. And the body—it was jellylike. Lumber, fence wire, and all manner of crap was stickin' out of it, stickin' out of it like it belonged there, just as natural as a shell on a turtle's back or the whiskers on a cougar's face. It had a mouth, a big mouth, like a railway tunnel, and what looked like teeth . . . But the brand went out then. I fired some shots. It was still wrigglin' out of that garbage heap. It was too dark to stay there—"

He cut in midsentence. The smell was strong now, solid as a wall of bricks.

"It's movin' into camp," I said.

"Must've come from all that garbage," Pearly said. "Must've been born in all that heat and slime."

"Or come up from the center of the Earth," I said, though I figured Pearly was a mite near closer to right.

Pearly put some fresh loads in his revolver. "This is all I got," he said.

"I want to see it eat buckshot," I said.

Then we heard it. Very loud, crunchin' down those mounds of garbage like they was peanut hulls. And then there was silence.

Pearly, he moved back a few steps from the double-barrel toward the shack. I aimed the double-barrel toward the dark.

Silence went on for a while. Why, you could've heard yourself blink. But I wasn't blinkin'. I was a-watchin' out for that critter.

Then I heard it—but it was behind me! I turned just in time to see a fuzzylike tentacle slither out from behind the shack and grab old Pearly. He screamed, and the gun fell out of his hand. And from the shadows a head showed. A huge, wormlike head with slitted eyes and a mouth large enough to swallow a man. Which is what it did. Pearly didn't make that thing two gulps. Wasn't nothin' left of him but a scrap of flesh hangin' on the thing's teeth.

I emptied a load of buckshot in it, slammed the gun open and loaded her again. By that time it was gone. I could hear it crashin' off in the dark.

I got the keys to the 'dozer and walked around back of the shack on tiptoe. It didn't come out of the dark after me. I cranked the 'dozer, turned on the spotlights, and went out there after it.

It didn't take long to find it. It was movin' across the dump like a snake, slitherin' and a-loopin' as fast as it could go—which wasn't too fast right then. It had a lump in its belly, an undigested lump . . . Poor old Pearly!

I ran it down, pinned it to the chainlink fence on the far side of the dump, and used my 'dozer blade to mash it up against it. I was just fixin' to gun the motor and cut that sucker's head off when I changed my mind.

Its head was stickin' up over the blade, those slitted eyes lookin' at me . . . and there, buried in that wormlike face, was the face of a puppy. You get a lot of them here. Well, it was alive now. Head was still mashed in like it was the first time I saw it, but it was movin'. The head was wrigglin' right there in the center of that worm's head.

I took a chance and backed off from that thing. I dropped to the ground and didn't move. I flashed the lights over it.

Pearly was seepin' out of that thing. I don't know how else to describe it, but he seemed to be driftin' out of that jellylike hide; and when his face and body were halfway out of it, he stopped movin' and just hung there. I realized somethin' then. It was not only created by the garbage and the heat—it lived off of it, and whatever became its food became a part of it. That puppy and old Pearly were now a part of it.

Now don't misunderstand me. Pearly, he didn't know nothin' about it. He was alive, in a fashion, he moved and squirmed, but like that puppy, he no longer thought. He was just a hair on that thing's body. Same as the lumber and wire and such that stuck out of it.

And the beast—well, it wasn't too hard to tame. I named it Otto. It ain't no trouble at all. Gettin' so it don't come when I call, but that's on account of I ain't had nothin' to reward it with, until you showed up. Before that, I had to kind of help it root dead critters out of the heaps . . . Sit down! I've got Pearly's thirty-two here, and if you move I'll plug you.

Oh, here comes Otto now.

"Fish Night" has echoes of Bradbury, but it was the first story I ever wrote that struck me as a complete story in the way I wanted to write a story. It had the obligatory twist ending, as many horror stories had, but it had a thematic depth and point to it that my work before had not possessed. It had more than one layer. It was evenly written. It had some style, if it was slightly borrowed in that department.

I moved on rapidly from that story, began to write a series of stories that had more texture, and eventually my own style jumped out. It really didn't have far to jump. It had been there all the time. I just didn't know it. I moved out of the California school of horror (Bradbury, Nolan, Matheson, etc.) shortly after this story, and into the Lansdale school of . . . well, of whatever. But this story, at least in my mind, is one of the more pivotal stories in my career.

It is a favorite of many readers. It was filmed once by the university here in Nacogdoches, but never edited to completion. It was optioned for a short film for a while, but nothing came of that either. It still gets reprinted quite a lot. Here, and abroad.

It was inspired by a fish mobile my wife had. I fell asleep on the couch, where I could see it hanging, and when I woke up, I had dreamed this story. I was geared to write a story, and was subconsciously looking for ideas. Bill Pronzini was doing an anthology called Specter! and he wanted something from me. I decided to attack the ghost idea from a different angle.

I hope you like reading it as much as I enjoyed writing it. It was written quickly, and came out pretty much as I envisioned. It's nice when that happens.

Fish Night

IT WAS A BLEACHED-BONE AFTERNOON WITH A cloudless sky and a monstrous sun. The air trembled like a mass of gelatinous ectoplasm. No wind blew.

Through the swelter came a worn, black Plymouth, coughing and belching white smoke from beneath its hood. It wheezed twice, backfired loudly, died by the side of the road.

The driver got out and went around to the hood. He was a man in the hard winter years of life, with dead, brown hair and a heavy belly riding his hips. His shirt was open to the navel, the sleeves rolled up past his elbows. The hair on his chest and arms was gray.

A younger man climbed out on the passenger side, went around front too. Yellow sweat-explosions stained the pits of his white shirt. An unfastened, striped tie was draped over his neck like a pet snake that had died in its sleep.

"Well?" the younger man asked.

The old man said nothing. He opened the hood. A calliope note of steam blew out from the radiator in a white puff, rose to the sky, turned clear.

"Damn," the old man said, and he kicked the bumper of the Plymouth as if he were kicking a foe in the teeth. He got little satisfaction out of the action, just a nasty scuff on his brown wingtip and a jar to his ankle that hurt like hell.

"Well?" the young man repeated.

"Well what? What do you think? Dead as the can-opener trade this week. Deader. The radiator's chickenpocked with holes."

"Maybe someone will come by and give us a hand."

"Sure."

"A ride anyway."

"Keep thinking that, college boy."

"Someone is bound to come along," the young man said.

"Maybe. Maybe not. Who else takes these cutoffs? The main highway, that's where everyone is. Not this little no-account shortcut." He finished by glaring at the young man.

"I didn't make you take it," the young man snapped. "It was on the map. I told you about it, that's all. You chose it. You're the one that decided to take it. It's not my fault. Besides, who'd have expected the car to die?"

"I did tell you to check the water in the radiator, didn't I? Wasn't that back as far as El Paso?"

"I checked. It had water then. I tell you, it's not my fault. You're the one that's done all the Arizona driving."

"Yeah, yeah," the old man said, as if this were something he didn't want to hear. He turned to look up the highway.

No cars. No trucks. Just heat waves and miles of empty concrete in sight.

They seated themselves on the hot ground with their backs to the car. That way it provided some shade—but not much. They sipped on a jug of lukewarm water from the Plymouth and spoke little until the sun fell down. By then they had both mellowed a bit. The heat had vacated the sands and the desert chill had settled in. Where the warmth had made the pair snappy, the cold drew them together.

The old man buttoned his shirt and rolled down his sleeves while the young man rummaged a sweater out of the back seat. He put the sweater on, sat back down. "I'm sorry about this," he said suddenly.

"Wasn't your fault. Wasn't anyone's fault. I just get to yelling sometime, taking out the can-opener trade on everything but the can openers and myself. The days of the door-to-door salesman are gone, son."

"And I thought I was going to have an easy summer job," the young man said.

The old man laughed. "Bet you did. They talk a good line, don't they?"

"I'll say!"

"Make it sound like found money, but there ain't no found money, boy. Ain't nothing simple in this world. The company is the only one ever makes any money. We just get tireder and older with more holes in our shoes. If I had any sense I'd have quit years ago. All you got to make is this summer—"

"Maybe not that long."

"Well, this is all I know. Just town after town, motel after motel, house after house, looking at people through screen wire while they shake their heads No. Even the cockroaches at the sleazy motels begin to look like little fellows you've seen before, like maybe they're door-to-door peddlers that have to rent rooms too."

The young man chuckled. "You might have something there."

They sat quietly for a moment, welded in silence. Night had full grip on the desert now. A mammoth gold moon and billions of stars cast a whitish glow from eons away.

The wind picked up. The sand shifted, found new places to lie down. The undulations of it, slow and easy, were reminiscent of the midnight sea. The young man, who had crossed the Atlantic by ship once, said as much.

"The sea?" the old man replied. "Yes, yes, exactly like that. I was thinking the same. That's part of the reason it bothers me. Part of why I was stirred up this afternoon. Wasn't just the heat doing it. There are memories of mine out here," he nodded at the desert, "and they're visiting me again."

The young man made a face. "I don't understand."

"You wouldn't. You shouldn't. You'd think I'm crazy."

"I already think you're crazy. So tell me."

The old man smiled. "All right, but don't you laugh."

"I won't."

A moment of silence moved in between them. Finally the old man said, "It's fish night, boy. Tonight's the full moon and this is the right part of the desert if memory serves me, and the feel is right— I mean, doesn't the night feel like it's made up of some soft fabric, that it's different from other nights, that it's like being inside a big, dark bag, the sides sprinkled with glitter, a spotlight at the top, at the open mouth, to serve as a moon?"

"You lost me."

The old man sighed. "But it feels different. Right? You can feel it too, can't you?"

"I suppose. Sort of thought it was just the desert air. I've never camped out in the desert before, and I guess it is different."

"Different, all right. You see, this is the road I got stranded on twenty years back. I didn't know it at first, least not consciously. But down deep in my gut I must have known all along I was taking this road, tempting fate, offering it, as the football people say, an instant replay."

"I still don't understand about fish night. What do you mean, you were here before?"

"Not this exact spot, somewhere along in here. This was even less of a road back then than it is now. The Navajos were about the only ones who traveled it. My car conked out, like this one today, and I started walking instead of waiting. As I walked the fish came out. Swimming along in the starlight pretty as you please. Lots of them. All the colors of the rainbow. Small ones, big ones, thick ones, thin ones. Swam right up to me . . . *right through me!* Fish just as far as you could see. High up and low down to the ground.

"Hold on, boy. Don't start looking at me like that. Listen: You're a college boy, you know something about these things. I mean, about what was here before we were, before we crawled out of the sea and changed enough to call ourselves men. Weren't we once just slimy things, brothers to the things that swim?"

"I guess, but—"

"Millions and millions of years ago this desert was a sea bottom. Maybe even the birthplace of man. Who knows? I read that in some science books. And I got to thinking this: If the ghosts of people who have lived can haunt houses, why can't the ghosts of creatures long dead haunt where they once lived, float about in a ghostly sea?"

"Fish with a soul?"

"Don't go small-mind on me, boy. Look here: Some of the Indians I've talked to up north tell me about a thing they call the manitou. That's a spirit. They believe everything has one. Rocks, trees, you name it. Even if the rock wears to dust or the tree gets cut to lumber, the manitou of it is still around."

"Then why can't you see these fish all the time?"

"Why can't we see ghosts all the time? Why do some of us never see them? Time's not right, that's why. It's a precious situation, and I figure it's like some fancy time lock—like the banks use. The lock clicks open at the bank, and there's the money. Here it ticks open and we get the fish of a world long gone."

"Well, it's something to think about," the young man managed.

The old man grinned at him. "I don't blame you for thinking what you're thinking. But this happened to me twenty years ago and I've never forgotten it. I saw those fish for a good hour before they disappeared. A Navajo came along in an old pickup right after and I bummed a ride into town with him. I told him what I'd seen. He just looked at me and grunted. But I could tell he knew what I was talking about. He'd seen it too, and probably not for the first time.

"I've heard that Navajos don't eat fish for some reason or another, and I bet it's the fish in the desert that keep them from it. Maybe they hold them sacred. And why not? It was like being in the presence of the Creator; like crawling back inside your mother and being unborn again, just kicking around in the liquids with no cares in the world."

"I don't know. That sounds sort of . . ."

"Fishy?" The old man laughed. "It does, it does. So this Navajo drove me to town. Next day I got my car fixed and went on. I've never taken that cutoff again—until today, and I think that was more than accident. My subconscious was driving me. That night scared me, boy, and I don't mind admitting it. But it was wonderful too, and I've never been able to get it out of my mind."

The young man didn't know what to say.

The old man looked at him and smiled. "I don't blame you," he said. "Not even a little bit. Maybe I am crazy."

They sat awhile longer with the desert night, and the old man took his false teeth out and poured some of the warm water on them to clean them of coffee and cigarette residue.

"I hope we don't need that water," the young man said.

"You're right. Stupid of me! We'll sleep awhile, start walking before daylight. It's not too far to the next town. Ten miles at best." He put his teeth back in. "We'll be just fine."

The young man nodded.

No fish came. They did not discuss it. They crawled inside the car, the young man in the front seat, the old man in the back. They used their spare clothes to bundle under, to pad out the cold fingers of the night.

Near midnight the old man came awake suddenly and lay with his hands behind his head and looked up and out the window opposite him, studied the crisp desert sky.

And a fish swam by.

Long and lean and speckled with all the colors of the world, flicking its tail as if in goodbye. Then it was gone.

The old man sat up. Outside, all about, were the fish—all sizes, colors, and shapes.

"Hey, boy, wake up!"

The younger man moaned.

"Wake up!"

The young man, who had been resting face down on his arms, rolled over. "What's the matter? Time to go?"

"The fish."

"Not again."

"Look!"

The young man sat up. His mouth fell open. His eyes bloated. Around and around the car, faster and faster in whirls of dark color, swam all manner of fish.

"Well, I'll be . . . *How?*"

"I told you, I told you."

The old man reached for the door handle, but before he could pull it a fish swam lazily through the back window glass, swirled about the car, once, twice, passed through the old man's chest, whipped up and went out through the roof.

The old man cackled, jerked open the door. He bounced around beside the road. Leaped up to swat his hands through the spectral fish. "Like soap bubbles," he said. "No. Like smoke!"

The young man, his mouth still agape, opened his door and got out. Even high up he could see the fish. Strange fish, like nothing he'd ever seen pictures of or imagined. They flitted and skirted about like flashes of light.

As he looked up, he saw, nearing the moon, a big dark cloud. The only cloud in the sky. That cloud tied him to reality suddenly, and he thanked the heavens for it. Normal things still happened. The whole world had not gone insane.

After a moment the old man quit hopping among the fish and came out to lean on the car and hold his hand to his fluttering chest.

"Feel it, boy? Feel the presence of the sea? Doesn't it feel like the beating of your own mother's heart while you float inside the womb?"

And the younger man had to admit that he felt it, that inner rolling rhythm that is the tide of life and the pulsating heart of the sea.

"How?" the young man said. "Why?"

"The time lock, boy. The locks clicked open and the fish are free. Fish from a time before man was man. Before civilization started weighing us down. I know it's true. The truth's been in me all the time. It's in us all."

"It's like time travel," the young man said. "From the past to the future, they've come all that way."

"Yes, yes, that's it . . . Why, if they can come to our world, why can't we go to theirs? Release that spirit inside of us, tune into their time?"

"Now, wait a minute . . ."

"My God, that's it! They're pure, boy, pure. Clean and free of civilization's trappings. That must be it! They're pure and we're not. We're weighted down with technology. These clothes. That car."

The old man started removing his clothes.

"Hey!" the young man said. "You'll freeze."

"If you're pure, if you're completely pure," the old man mumbled, "that's it . . . yeah, that's the key."

"You've gone crazy."

"I won't look at the car," the old man yelled, running across the sand, trailing the last of his clothes behind him. He bounced about the desert like a jackrabbit. "God, God, nothing is happening, nothing," he moaned. "This isn't my world. I'm of that world. I want to float free in the belly of the sea, away from can openers and cars and—"

The young man called the old man's name. The old man did not seem to hear.

"I want to leave here!" the old man yelled. Suddenly he was springing about again. "The teeth!" he yelled. "It's the teeth. Dentist, science, foo!" He punched a hand into his mouth, plucked the teeth free, tossed them over his shoulder.

Even as the teeth fell the old man rose. He began to stroke. To swim up and up and up, moving like a pale, pink seal among the fish.

In the light of the moon the young man could see the pooched jaws of the old man, holding the last of the future's air. Up went the old man, up, up, up, swimming strong in the long-lost waters of a time gone by.

The young man began to strip off his own clothes. Maybe he could nab him, pull him down, put the clothes on him. Something . . . God, something. . . . But, what if *he* couldn't come back? And there were the fillings in his teeth, the metal rod in his back from a motorcycle accident. No, unlike the old man, this was his world and he was tied to it. There was nothing he could do.

A great shadow weaved in front of the moon, made a wriggling slat of darkness that caused the young man to let go of his shirt buttons and look up.

A black rocket of a shape moved through the invisible sea: a shark, the granddaddy of all sharks, the seed for all of man's fears of the deeps.

And it caught the old man in its mouth, began swimming upward toward the golden light of the moon. The old man dangled from the creature's mouth like a ragged rat from a house cat's jaws. Blood blossomed out of him, coiled darkly in the invisible sea.

The young man trembled. "Oh God," he said once.

Then along came that thick dark cloud, rolling across the face of the moon.

Momentary darkness.

And when the cloud passed there was light once again, and an empty sky.

No fish.

No shark.

And no old man.

Just the night, the moon, and the stars.

This was brought about by seeing Gandhi on TV one day. It was a special on him, I think. He was grinning at the camera, and I thought, man, this guy has got some serious teeth problems. A dentist needs to get a hold of him.

I lay on the couch and fell asleep, this on my mind, and when I awoke, the whole story was there. I jumped up, wrote it quickly, sent it in to T. E. D. Klein at Twilight Zone *and he bought it.*

I loved the illustration that went with it.

And I was proud to be in that magazine.

I'm still proud to have been there.

Chompers

OLD MAUDE, WHO LIVED IN ALLEYS, COMBED
trash cans, and picked rags, found the false teeth in a puddle
of blood back of Denny's. Obvious thing was that there had been a
mugging, and some unfortunate who'd been wandering around out
back had gotten his or her brains beaten out, and then hauled off
somewhere for who knows what.

But the teeth, which had probably hopped from the victim's
mouth like some kind of frightened animal, still remained, and the
blood they lay in was testimony to the terrible event.

Maude picked them up, looked at them. Besides the blood there
were some pretty nasty coffee stains on the rear molars and what
looked to be a smidgen of cherry pie. One thing Maude could spot
and tell with an amazing degree of accuracy was a stain or a food
dollop. Cruise alleyways and dig in trash cans most of your life, and
you get skilled.

Now, Maude was a practical old girl, and, as she had about as
many teeth in her head as a pomegranate, she wiped the blood off
on her dress—high fashion circa 1920—and put those suckers right
square in her gummy little mouth. Somehow it seemed like the
proper thing to do. Perfect fit. Couldn't have been any better than
if they'd been made for her. She got the old, blackened lettuce head
out of her carpetbag—she'd found the lettuce with a half a tomato
back of Burger King—and gave that vegetable a chomp. Sounded

like the dropping of a guillotine as those teeth snapped into the lettuce and then ground it to smithereens.

Man that was good for a change, thought Maude, to be able to go at your food like a pig to trough. Gumming your vittles gets old.

The teeth seemed a little tighter in her mouth than awhile ago, but Maude felt certain that after a time she'd get used to them. It was sad about the poor soul that had lost them, but that person's bad luck was her fortune.

Maude started toward the doorway she called home, and by the time she'd gone a block she found that she was really hungry, which surprised her. Not an hour back she'd eaten half a hamburger out of a Burger King trash can, three greasy fries, and half an apple pie. But, boy howdy, did she want to chow down now. She felt like she could eat anything.

She got the tomato half out of her bag, along with everything else in there that looked edible, and began to eat.

More she ate, hungrier she got. Pretty soon she was out of goodies, and the sidewalk and the street started looking to her like the bottom of a dinner plate that ought to be filled. God, but her belly burned. It was as if she'd never eaten and had suddenly become aware of the need.

She ground her big teeth and walked on. Half a block later she spotted a big alleycat hanging head down over the lip of a trash can, pawing for something to eat, and ummm, ummm, ummm, but that cat looked tasty as a Dunkin' Donut.

Chased that rascal for three blocks, but didn't catch it. It pulled a fade-out on her in a dark alley.

Disgusted, but still very, very hungry, Maude left the alley thinking: Chow, need me some chow.

Beat cop O'Hara was twirling his nightstick when he saw her nibbling the paint off a rusty old streetlamp. It was an old woman with a prune face, and when he came up she stopped nibbling and looked at him. She had the biggest, shiniest pair of choppers he had ever seen. They stuck out from between her lips like a gator's teeth, and in the light of the streetlamp, even as he watched, he thought for a moment that he had seen them grow. And, by golly, they looked pointed now.

O'Hara had walked his beat for twenty years, and he was used to eccentrics and weird getups, but there was something particularly weird about this one.

The old woman *smiled* at him.

Man, there were a lot of teeth there. (More than awhile ago?) O'Hara thought: Now that's a crazy thing to think.

He was about six feet from her when she jumped him, teeth gnashing, clicking together like a hundred cold Eskimo knees. They caught his shirt sleeve and ripped it off; the cloth disappeared between those teeth fast as a waiter's tip.

O'Hara struck at her with his nightstick, but she caught that in her mouth, and those teeth of hers began to rattle and snap like a pound full of rabid dogs. Wasn't nothing left of that stick but toothpicks.

He pulled his revolver, but she ate that too. Then she ate O'Hara, didn't even leave a shoe.

Little later on she ate a kid on a bicycle—the bicycle too—and hit up a black hooker for dessert. But that didn't satisfy her. She was still hungry, and, worse yet, the pickings had gotten lean.

Long about midnight, this part of the city went dead except for a bum or two, and she ate them. She kept thinking that if she could get across town to Forty-second Street, she could have her fill of hookers, kids, pimps, and heroin addicts. It'd be a regular buffet-style dinner.

But that was such a long ways off and she was *sooooo hungry.* And those damn teeth were so big now she felt as if she needed a neck brace just to hold her head up.

She started walking fast, and when she was about six blocks away from the smorgasbord of Forty-second, her mouth started watering like Niagara Falls.

Suddenly she had an attack. She had to eat NOW—as in "awhile ago." *Immediately.*

Halfway up her arm, she tried to stop. But my, was that tasty. Those teeth went to work, a-chomping and a-rending, and pretty soon they were as big as a bear trap, snapping flesh like it was chewing gum.

Wasn't nothing left of Maude but a puddle of blood by the time the teeth fell to the sidewalk, rapidly shrinking back to normal size.

Harry, high on life and high on wine, wobbled down the sidewalk, dangling left, dangling right. It was a wonder he didn't fall down.

He saw the teeth lying in a puddle of blood, and having no choppers of his own—the tooth fairy had them all—he decided, what the hell, what can it hurt? Besides, he felt driven.

Picking up the teeth, wiping them off, he placed them in his mouth.

Perfect fit. Like they were made for him.

He wobbled off, thinking: Man, but I'm hungry; gracious, but I sure could eat.

I don't remember a damn thing about this one. All I can say is it's obviously a Bradbury influenced story and it takes place in my fictional town of Mud Creek. And, I like it. I suspect, but can't verify, popcorn had something to do with it.

The Fat Man

*T*HE FAT MAN SAT ON HIS PORCH IN HIS SQUEAK-
ing swing and looked out at late October. Leaves coasted
from the trees that grew on either side of the walk, coasted down
and scraped the concrete with a dry, husking sound.

He sat there in his swing, pushing one small foot against the
porch, making the swing go back and forth; sat there in his faded
khaki pants, barefoot, shirtless, his belly hanging way out over his
belt, drooping toward his knees.

And just below his belly button, off-center right, was the tattoo.
A half-moon, lying on its back, the ends pointing up. A blue tattoo.
An obscene tattoo, made obscene by the sagging flesh on which it
was sculptured. Flesh that made the Fat Man look like a hippo, if a
hippo could stand on its hind legs or sit in a swing pushing itself
back and forth.

The Fat Man.

Late October.

Cool wind.

Falling leaves.

The Fat Man with the half-moon tattoo off-center beneath his
navel.

The Fat Man. Swinging.

Everyone wondered about the Fat Man. He had lived in the

little house at the end of Crowler Street for a long time. Forever it seemed. As long as that house had been there (circa 1920), he had been there. No one knew anything else about him. He did not go to town. He did not venture any farther than his front porch, as if his house were an oddball ship adrift forever on an endless sea. He had a phone, but no electric lights. He did not use gas and he had no car.

And everyone wondered about the Fat Man.

Did he pay taxes?

Where did he get the money that bought the countless boxes of chicken, pizza, egg foo yung, and hamburgers he ordered by phone; the countless grease-stained boxes that filled the garbage cans he set off the edge of his porch each Tuesday and Thursday for the sanitation men to pick up and empty?

Why didn't he use electric lights?

Why didn't he go to town?

Why did he sit on his porch in his swing looking out at the world smiling dumbly, going in the house only when night came?

And what did he do at night behind those closed doors? Why did he wear neither shirt nor shoes, summer or dead of winter?

And where in the world—and why—did he get that ugly half-moon tattooed on his stomach?

Whys and whats. Lots of them about the Fat Man. Questions aplenty, answers none.

Everyone wondered about the Fat Man.

But no one wondered as much as Harold and Joe, two boys who filled their days with comics, creek beds, climbing apple trees, going to school . . . and wondering about the Fat Man.

So one cool night, late October, they crept up to the Fat Man's house, crawling on hands and knees through the not-yet-dead weeds in the empty lot next to the Fat Man's house, and finally through the equally high weeds in the Fat Man's yard.

They lay in the cool, wind-rustled weeds beneath one of the Fat Man's windows and whispered to each other.

"Let's forget it," Harold said.

"Can't. We come this far, and we swore on a dead cat."

"A dead cat don't care."

"A dead cat's sacred, you know that."

"We made that up."

"And because we did that makes it true. A dead cat's sacred."

Harold could not find it in his heart to refute this. They found the dead cat on the street next to the curb the day before, and Joe had said right off that it was sacred. And Harold, without contesting, had agreed.

And how could he disagree? The looks of the cat were hypnotizing. Its little gray body was worm-worked. Its teeth exposed. Its lips were drawn back, black and stiff. All the stuff to draw the eye. All the stuff that made it sacred.

They took the cat over the creek, through the woods and out to the old "Indian" graveyard and placed it on the ground where Joe said an old Caddo Chief was buried. They took the cat and poked its stiff legs into the soft dirt so that it appeared to be running through quicksand.

Joe said, "I pronounce you a sacred cat with powers as long as there's hair on your body and you don't fall over, whichever comes first."

They made an oath on the sacred cat, and the oath was like this: They were going to sneak over to the Fat Man's house when their parents were asleep, and find out just what in hell and heaven the Fat Man did. Maybe see him eat so they could find out how quickly he went through those boxes and cartons of chicken, pizza, egg foo yung, hamburgers, and the like.

Above them candlelight flickered through the thin curtains and window. Joe raised up cautiously for a peek.

Inside he saw the candle residing in a broken dish on an end table next to the telephone. And that was it for the Fat Man's furniture. The rest of the room was filled with food boxes and cartons, and wading knee-deep in their midst was the Fat Man.

The Fat Man had two large trash cans next to him, and he was bending quite nimbly for a man his size (and as he bent the fat about his middle made three thick anaconda coils, one of which was spotted with the blue half-moon tattoo), picking up the boxes and tossing them in the cans.

Harold raised up for a look. Soon the cans were stuffed and overflowing and the Fat Man had cleared a space on the floor. With the handle of a can in either hand, the Fat Man swung the cans toward the door, outside and off the edge of the porch.

The Fat Man came back, closed the door, kicked his way through the containers until he reached the clearing he had made.

He said in a voice that seemed somewhat distant, and originating at the pit of his stomach, "Tip, tap, tip tap." Then his voice turned musical and he began to sing, "Tip, tap, tip tap."

His bare feet flashed out on the hardwood floor with a sound not unlike tap shoes or wood clicking against wood, and the Fat Man kept repeating the line, dancing around and around, moving light as a ninety-pound ballerina, the obscene belly swinging left and right to the rhythm of his song and his fast-moving feet.

"Tip, tap, tip tap."

There was a knock at the door.

The Fat Man stopped dancing, started kicking the boxes aside, making his way to answer the knock.

Joe dropped from the window and edged around the corner of the house and looked at the porch.

A delivery boy stood there with five boxes of pizza stacked neatly on one palm. It was that weird guy from Cab's Pizza. The one with all the personality of a puppet. Or at least that was the way he was these days. Once he had been sort of a joker, but the repetition of pizza to go had choked out and hardened any fun that might have been in him.

The Fat Man's hand came out and took the pizzas. No money was exchanged. The delivery boy went down the steps, clicked down the walk, got in the Volkswagen with Cab's Pizza written on the side, and drove off.

Joe crept back to the window, raised up next to Harold. The Fat Man put the pizza boxes on the end table by the phone, opened the top one and took out the pizza, held it balanced on his palm like a droopy painter's palette.

"Tip, tap, tip tap," he sang from somewhere down in his abdomen, then he turned, his back to the window. With a sudden movement, he slammed the pizza into his stomach.

"Ahhh," said the Fat Man, and little odd muscles like toy trucks drove up and down his back. His khaki-covered butt perked up and he began to rock on his toes. Fragments of pizza, gooey cheese, sticky sauce, and rounds of pepperoni dripped to the floor.

The Fat Man's hand floated out, clutched another box and ripped it open. Out came a pizza, wham, into the stomach, "Ah," went the Fat Man, and down dripped more pizza ingredients, and out went the Fat Man's hand once again.

Three pizzas in the stomach.

Now four.

"I don't think I understand all I know about this," Joe whispered.

Five pizzas, and a big "ahhhhhh," this time.

The Fat Man leaped, high and pretty, hands extended for a dive, and without a sound he disappeared into the food-stained cartons.

Joe blinked.

Harold blinked.

The Fat Man surfaced. His back humped up first like a rising porpoise, then disappeared. Loops of back popped through the boxes at regular intervals until he reached the far wall.

The Fat Man stood up, bursting cartons around him like scales. He touched the wall with his palm. The wall swung open. Joe and Harold could see light in there and the top of a stairway.

The Fat Man stepped on the stairway, went down. The door closed.

Joe and Harold looked at each other.

"That wall ain't even a foot thick," Harold said. "He can't do that."

"He did," Joe said. "He went right into that wall and down, and you know it because you saw him."

"I think I'll go home now," Harold said.

"You kidding?"

"No, I ain't kidding."

The far wall opened again and out popped the Fat Man, belly greased and stained with pizza.

Joe and Harold watched attentively as he leaped into the boxes, and swam for the clearing. Then, once there, he rose and put a thumb to the candle and put out the light.

He kicked his way through boxes and cartons this time, and his shadowy shape disappeared from the room and into another.

"I'm going to see how he went through the wall," Joe said.

Joe put his hands on the window and pushed. It wasn't locked. It slid up a few inches.

"Don't," Harold whispered, putting his hand on Joe's arm.

"I swore on the dead cat I was going to find out about the Fat Man, and that's what I'm going to do."

Joe shrugged Harold's arm off, pushed the window up higher and climbed through.

Harold swore, but followed.

They went as quietly as they could through the boxes and cartons until they reached the clearing where the pizza glop lay pooled and heaped on the floor. Then they entered the bigger stack of boxes, waded toward the wall. And though they went silently as possible, the cartons still crackled and popped, as if they were trying to call for their master, the Fat Man.

Joe touched the wall with his palm the way the Fat Man had. The wall opened. Joe and Harold crowded against each other and looked down the stairway. It led to a well-lit room below.

Joe went down.

Harold started to say something, knew it was useless. Instead he followed down the stairs.

At the bottom they stood awestruck. It was a workshop of sorts. Tubes and dials stuck out of the walls. Rods of glass were filled with pulsating colored lights. Cables hung on pegs. And there was something else hanging on pegs.

Huge marionettes.

And though they were featureless, hairless and sexless, they looked in form as real as living, breathing people. In fact, put clothes and a face on them and you wouldn't know the difference. Provided they could move and talk, of course.

Harold took hold of the leg of one of the bodies. It felt like wood, but it bent easily. He tied the leg in a knot.

Joe found a table with something heaped on it and covered with black cloth. He whipped off the cloth and said, "Good gracious."

Harold looked.

It was a row of jars, and in the jars, drooping over upright rods, were masks. Masks of people they knew.

Why there was Alice Dunn, the Avon Lady. They'd know that wart on her nose anywhere. It fit the grump personality she had these days.

Jerry James the constable. And my, didn't the eyes in his mask look just like his eyes? The way he always looked at them like he was ready to pull his gun and put them under arrest.

May Bloom, the town librarian, who had grown so foul in her old age. No longer willing to help the boys find new versions of King Arthur or order the rest of Edgar Rice Burroughs's Mars series.

And there was the face of the weird guy from Cab's Pizza, Jake was his name.

"Now wait a minute," Joe said. "All these people have got something in common. What is it?"

"They're grumps," Harold said.

"Uh huh. What else?"

"I don't know."

"They weren't always grumpy."

"Well, yeah," Harold said.

And Harold thought of how Jake used to kid with him at the pizza place. How the constable had helped him get his kite down from a tree. How Mrs. Bloom had introduced him to Edgar Rice Burroughs, Max Brand, and King Arthur. How Alice Dunn used to make her rounds, and come back special with a gift for him when he was sick.

"There's another thing," Joe said. "Alice Dunn, the Avon Lady. She always goes door to door, right? So she had to come to the Fat Man's door sometime. And the constable, I bet he came too, on account of all the weird rumors about the Fat Man. Jake, the delivery boy. Mrs. Bloom, who sometimes drives the bookmobile . . ."

"What are you saying?"

"I'm saying, that that little liquid in the bottom of each of these jars looks like blood. I think the Fat Man skinned them, and . . ." Joe looked toward the puppets on the wall, "replaced them with handmade versions."

"Puppets come to life?" Harold said.

"Like Pinocchio," Joe said.

Harold looked at the masks in the jars and suddenly they didn't look so much like masks. He looked at the puppets on the wall and thought he recognized the form of one of them; tall and slightly pudgy with a finger missing on the left hand.

"God, Dad," he said.

"He works for Ma Bell," Joe said. "Repairs lines. And if the Fat Man has phone trouble, and they call out a repairman . . ."

"Don't say it," Harold said.

Joe didn't, but he looked at the row of empty jars behind the row of filled ones.

"What worries me," Joe said, "are the empty jars, and," he turned and pointed to the puppets on the wall, "those two small puppets on the far wall. They look to be about mine and your sizes."

"Oh, they are," said the Fat Man.

Harold shrieked, turned. There at the foot of the stairs stood the Fat Man. And the half-moon tattoo was not a half-moon at all, it was a mouth, and it was speaking to them in the gut-level voice they had heard the Fat Man use to sing.

Joe grabbed up the jar holding Miss Bloom's face and tossed it at the Fat Man. The Fat Man swept the jar aside and it crashed to the floor; the mask (face) went skidding along on slivers of broken glass.

"Now that's not nice," said the half-moon tattoo, and this time it opened so wide the boys thought they saw something moving in there. "That's my collection."

Joe grabbed another jar, Jerry James this time, tossed it at the Fat Man as he moved lightly and quickly toward them.

Again the Fat Man swatted it aside, and now he was chasing them. Around the table they went, around and around like little Black Sambo being pursued by the tiger.

Harold bolted for the stairs, hit the bottom step, started taking them two at the time.

Joe hit the bottom step.

And the Fat Man grabbed him by the collar.

"Boys, boys," said the mouth in the Fat Man's stomach. "Here now, boys, let's have a little fun."

"Run," yelled Joe. "Get help. He's got me good."

The Fat Man took Joe by the head and stuffed the head into his stomach. The mouth slobbered around Joe's neck.

Harold stood at the top of the stairs dumbfounded. In went Joe, inch by inch. Now only his legs were kicking.

Harold turned, slapped his palm along the wall.

Nothing happened.

Up the stairs came the Fat Man.

Harold glanced back. Only one leg stuck out of the belly now, and it was thrashing. The tennis shoe flew off and slapped against the stairs. Harold could hear a loud gurgling sound coming from the Fat Man's stomach, and a voice saying, "Ahhhh, ahhhh."

Halfway up the steps came the Fat Man.

Harold palmed the wall, inch by inch.

Nothing happened.

He jerked a glance back again.

There was a burping sound, and the Fat Man's mouth opened wide and out flopped Joe's face, skinned, mask-looking. Harold could also see two large cables inside the Fat Man's mouth. The cable rolled. The mouth closed. Taloned, skinny hands stuck out of the blue tattoo and the fingers wriggled. "Come to Papa," said the voice in the Fat Man's stomach.

Harold turned, slapped his palm on the wall time and time again, left and right.

He could hear the Fat Man's tread on the steps right behind, taking it torturously slow and easy.

The wall opened.

Harold dove into the boxes and cartons and disappeared beneath them.

The Fat Man leaped high, his dive perfect, his toes wriggling like stubby, greedy fingers.

Poof, into the boxes.

Harold came up running, kicking boxes aside.

The Fat Man's back, like the fin of a shark, popped the boxes up. Then he was gone again.

Harold made the clearing in the floor. The house seemed to be rocking. He turned left toward the door and jerked it open.

Stepping out on the front porch he froze.

The Fat Man's swing dangled like an empty canary perch, and the night . . . was different. Thick as chocolate pudding. And the weeds didn't look the same. They looked like a foamy green sea—putrid sherbet—and the house bobbed as if it were a cork on the ocean.

Behind Harold the screen door opened. "There you are, you bad boy, you," said the voice in the belly.

Harold ran and leaped off the porch into the thick, high weeds, made his way on hands and knees, going almost as fast as a running dog that way. The ground beneath him bucked and rolled.

Behind him he heard something hit the weeds but he did not look back. He kept running on hands and knees for a distance, then he rose to his feet, elbows flying, strides deepening, parting the waist-level foliage like a knife through spoiled cream cheese.

And the grass in front of him opened up. A white face floated into view at belt-level.

The Fat Man. On his knees.

The Fat Man smiled. Skinny, taloned hands stuck out of the blue tattoo and the fingers wiggled.

"Pee-pie," said the Fat Man's belly.

Harold wheeled to the left, tore through the tall weeds yelling. He could see the moon floating in the sky and it looked pale and sick, like a yolkless egg. The houses outlined across the street were in the right place, but they looked off-key, only vaguely reminiscent of how he remembered them. He thought he saw something large and shadowy peek over the top of one of them, but in a blinking of an eye it was gone.

Suddenly the Fat Man was in front of him again.

Harold skidded to a halt.

"You swore on a dead cat," the voice in the belly said, and a little wizened, oily head with bugged-out eyes poked out of the belly and looked up at Harold and smiled with lots and lots of teeth.

"You swore on a dead cat," the voice repeated, only this time it was a perfect mockery of Joe.

Then, with a motion so quick Harold did not see it, the Fat Man grabbed him.

This was one I wrote for Twilight Zone, *but T. E. D. Klein thought it too dark. I sent it to* The Horror Show, *edited by David Silva, and he liked it, and bought it, with some reservations for the same reason.*

Considering other things I've written, I was a little surprised at this concern. And, we were talking horror. It has just a bit of social commentary in it, and that was what was making them nervous. They said so. Maybe you'll see it. I think it was necessary to give the story the impact it deserved.

It's not a well-known story of mine, or doesn't seem to be. I don't hear it mentioned much. But it's actually been reprinted quite a bit.

In a strange way, this is a forerunner for a better and very well-known story of mine called "Night They Missed the Horror Show."

That may not be readily apparent, but there is a connection.

On a Dark October

*T*HE OCTOBER NIGHT WAS DARK AND COOL. THE rain was thick. The moon was hidden behind dark clouds that occasionally flashed with lightning, and the sky rumbled as if it were a big belly that was hungry and needed filling.

A white Chrysler New Yorker came down the street and pulled up next to the curb. The driver killed the engine and the lights, turned to look at the building that sat on the block, an ugly tin thing with a weak light bulb shielded by a tin-hat shade over a fading sign that read BOB'S GARAGE. For a moment the driver sat unmoving, then he reached over, picked up the newspaper-wrapped package on the seat and put it in his lap. He opened it slowly. Inside was a shiny, oily, black-handled, ball peen hammer.

He lifted the hammer, touched the head of it to his free palm. It left a small smudge of grease there. He closed his hand, opened it, rubbed his fingers together. It felt just like . . . but he didn't want to think of that. It would all happen soon enough.

He put the hammer back in the papers, rewrapped it, wiped his fingers on the outside of the package. He pulled a raincoat from the back seat and put it across his lap. Then, with hands resting idly on the wheel, he sat silently.

A late model blue Ford pulled in front of him, left a space at the garage's drive, and parked. No one got out. The man in the Chrysler did not move.

Five minutes passed and another car, a late model Chevy, parked directly behind the Chrysler. Shortly thereafter three more cars arrived, all of them were late models. None of them blocked the drive. No one got out.

Another five minutes skulked by before a white van with MERTZ'S MEATS AND BUTCHER SHOP written on the side pulled around the Chrysler, then backed up the drive, almost to the garage door. A man wearing a hooded raincoat and carrying a package got out of the van, walked to the back and opened it.

The blue Ford's door opened, and a man dressed similarly, carrying a package under his arm, got out and went up the driveway. The two men nodded at one another. The man who had gotten out of the Ford unlocked the garage and slid the door back.

Car doors opened. Men dressed in raincoats, carrying packages, got out and walked to the back of the van. A couple of them had flashlights and they flashed them in the back of the vehicle, gave the others a good view of what was there—a burlap-wrapped, rope-bound bundle that wiggled and groaned.

The man who had been driving the van said, "Get it out."

Two of the men handed their packages to their comrades and climbed inside, picked up the squirming bundle, carried it into the garage. The others followed. The man from the Ford closed the door.

Except for the beams of the two flashlights, they stood close together in the darkness, like strands of flesh that had suddenly been pulled into a knot. The two with the bundle broke away from the others, and with their comrades directing their path with the beams of their flashlights, they carried the bundle to the grease rack and placed it between two wheel ramps. When that was finished, the two who had carried the bundle returned to join the others, to reform that tight knot of flesh.

Outside the rain was pounding the roof like tossed lug bolts. Lightning danced through the half-dozen small, barred windows. Wind shook the tin garage with a sound like a rattlesnake tail quivering for the strike, then passed on.

No one spoke for a while. They just looked at the bundle. The bundle thrashed about and the moaning from it was louder than ever.

"All right," the man from the van said.

They removed their clothes, hung them on pegs on the wall, pulled their raincoats on.

The man who had been driving the blue Ford—after looking

carefully into the darkness—went to the grease rack. There was a paper bag on one of the ramps. Earlier in the day he had placed it there himself. He opened it and took out a handful of candles and a book of matches. Using a match to guide him, he placed the candles down the length of the ramps, lighting them as he went. When he was finished, the garage glowed with a soft amber light. Except for the rear of the building. It was dark there.

The man with the candles stopped suddenly, a match flame wavering between his fingertips. The hackles on the back of his neck stood up. He could hear movement from the dark part of the garage. He shook the match out quickly and joined the others. Together, the group unwrapped their packages and gripped the contents firmly in their hands—hammers, brake-over handles, crowbars, heavy wrenches. Then all of them stood looking toward the back of the garage, where something heavy and sluggish moved.

The sound of the garage clock—a huge thing with DRINK COCA-COLA emblazoned on its face—was like the ticking of a time bomb. It was one minute to midnight.

Beneath the clock, visible from time to time when the glow of the candles was whipped that way by the draft, was a calendar. It read OCTOBER and had a picture of a smiling boy wearing overalls, standing amidst a field of pumpkins. The 31st was circled in red.

Eyes drifted to the bundle between the ramps now. It had stopped squirming. The sound it was making was not quite a moan. The man from the van nodded at one of the men, the one who had driven the Chrysler. The Chrysler man went to the bundle and worked the ropes loose, folded back the burlap. A frightened black youth, bound by leather straps and gagged with a sock and a bandana, looked up at him wide-eyed. The man from the Chrysler avoided looking back. The youth started squirming, grunting, and thrashing. Blood beaded around his wrists where the leather was tied, boiled out from around the loop fastened to his neck; when he kicked, it boiled faster because the strand had been drawn around his neck, behind his back and tied off at his ankles.

There came a sound from the rear of the garage again, louder than before. It was followed by a sudden sigh that might have been the wind working its way between the rafters.

The van driver stepped forward, spoke loudly to the back of the garage. "We got something for you, hear me? Just like always we're doing our part. You do yours. I guess that's all I got to say. Things will be the same come next October. In your name, I reckon."

For a moment—just a moment—there was a glimmer of a shape

when the candles caught a draft and wafted their bright heads in that direction. The man from the van stepped back quickly. "In your name," he repeated. He turned to the men. "Like always, now. Don't get the head until the very end. Make it last."

The faces of the men took on an expression of grimness, as if they were all playing a part in a theatric production and had been told to look that way. They hoisted their tools and moved toward the youth.

What they did took a long time.

When they finished, the thing that had been the young black man looked like a gigantic hunk of raw liver that had been chewed up and spat out. The raincoats of the men were covered in a spray of blood and brains. They were panting.

"Okay," said the man from the van.

They took off their raincoats, tossed them in a metal bin near the grease rack, wiped the blood from their hands, faces, ankles, and feet with shop rags, tossed those in the bin and put on their clothes.

The van driver yelled to the back of the garage. "All yours. Keep the years good, huh?"

They went out of there and the man from the Ford locked the garage door. Tomorrow he would come to work as always. There would be no corpse to worry about, and a quick dose of gasoline and a match would take care of the contents in the bin. Rain ran down his back and made him shiver.

Each of the men went out to their cars without speaking. Tonight they would all go home to their young, attractive wives and tomorrow they would all go to their prosperous businesses and they would not think of this night again. Until next October.

They drove away. Lightning flashed. The wind howled. The rain beat the garage like a cat-o'-nine-tails. And inside there were loud sucking sounds punctuated by grunts of joy.

Another story inspired by The Nightrunners.

In the book there's a scene where one of my characters sees the house where he is soon to live for the first time, and I gave a sort of over-the-top description of it that I thought worked quite well in context, but there was something in that description that spurred me to consider the house from another angle, a less grim one. What came out was this short story. It's a gonzo hoot with an echo of Bradbury and a lot of tongue in cheek.

My title was "Something Lumber This Way Comes," which my friend Bill Nolan, to put it mildly, hated. He suggested this title. Since I used the other title on a variation of this story which became a children's book, I agreed.

The Shaggy House

*T*HE OLD FORD MOVED SILENTLY THROUGH THE night, cruised down the street slowly. The driver, an elderly white-haired man, had his window down and he was paying more attention to looking out of it, studying the houses, than he was to his driving. The car bumped the curb. The old man cursed softly, whipped it back into the dark, silent street.

Beaumont Street came to a dead end. The old man turned around, drove back up. This was his third trip tonight, up and down the short street, and for the third time he was certain. The houses on Beaumont Street were dying, turning gray, growing ugly, looking dreadfully sick, and it all seemed to have happened overnight.

His own house was the sickest looking among them. The paint was peeling—he'd just had it painted last year!—the window panes looked like the bottom of a lover's leap for flies—yet there were no fly bodies—and there was a general sagginess about the place, as if it were old like himself and the spirit had gone out of its lumber bones.

The other houses on the block were not much better. A certain degree of that was to be expected. The houses were old, and the inhabitants of the houses, in many cases, were older. The entire block consisted of retired couples and singles, the youngest of which was a man in his late sixties. But still, the block had always taken pride in their houses, managed somehow to mow the lawns and get the painting done, and then one day it all goes to rot.

And it had happened the moment that creepy house had appeared in the neighborhood, had literally sprung up overnight on the vacant lot across from his house. A Gothic-hideous house, as brown and dead looking as the late fall grass.

Craziest thing, however, was the fact that no one had seen or heard it being built. Just one day the block had gone to bed and the next morning they had awakened to find the nasty old thing sitting over there, crouched like a big, hungry toad, the two upper story windows looking like cold, calculating eyes.

Who the hell ever heard of putting up a house overnight? For that matter, who ever heard of prefab, weathered Gothics? And last, but not least, why had they not seen anyone come out of or go into the house? It had been there a week, and so far no one had moved in, and there were no rent ads in the paper for it. He had checked.

Of course, a certain amount of the mystery might be explained if his wife were correct.

"Why you old fool, they moved that house in there. And for that matter, Harry, they just might have moved it in while we were sitting on the front porch watching. We're so old we don't notice what goes on anymore."

Harry gnashed his false teeth together so hard he ground powder out of the bicuspids. "Well," he said to the interior of the car, "you may be old, Edith, but I'm not."

No, he wasn't so old that he hadn't noticed the change in the neighborhood, the way the houses seemed to be infected with that old ruin's disease. And he knew that old house was somehow responsible for the damage, and he intended to get to the bottom of it.

A shape loomed in the headlights. Harry slammed his foot on the brakes and screeched the tires sharply.

An elderly, balding man ambled around to Harry's side of the car and stuck his face through the open window.

"Lem!" Harry said. "You trying to commit suicide?"

"No, I was fixing to go over there and burn that damned house down."

"You too, Lem?"

"Me too. Saw you cruising around looking. Figured you'd figured what I'd figured."

Harry looked at Lem cautiously. "And what have we figured?"

"That damned old house isn't up to any good, and that something's got to be done about it before the whole neighborhood turns to ruins."

"You've noticed how the houses look?"

"Any fool with eyes in his head and a pair of glasses can see what's going on."

"But why?"

"Who gives a damn why, let's just do something. I got some matches here, and a can of lighter fluid in my coat pocket—"

"Lem, we can't just commit arson. Look, get in. I don't like sitting here in the street."

Lem turned to look at the house. They were almost even with it. "Neither do I. That thing gives me the creeps."

Lem went around and got in. Harry drove up the block, parked at the far end where the street intersected another. Lem got out his pipe and packed it, filled the Ford with the smell of cinnamon.

"You're gonna get cancer yet," Harry said.

"Being as I'm ninety, it'll have to work fast."

Harry gnashed his bicuspids again. There was a certain logic in that, and just a month ago Edith had talked him into giving up his cigars for health reasons.

After a moment Lem produced a flask from his coat pocket, unscrewed the lid and removed the pipe from his mouth. "Cheers."

Harry sniffed. "Is that whiskey?"

"Prune juice." Lem smiled slyly.

"I bet."

Lem tossed a shot down his throat. "Wheee," he said, lifting the bottle away from his face. "That'll put lead in your pencil!"

"Let me have a snort of that."

Harry drank, gave the flask back to Lem who capped it, returned it to his pocket and put his pipe back into his face.

Unconsciously, they had both turned in their seats to look out the back window of the Ford, so they could see the house. Harry thought that the high-peaked roof looked a lot like a witch's hat there in the moonlight.

"Bright night," Lem said. "Holy Christ, Harry."

"I see it, I see it."

The old house trembled, moved.

It turned its head. No other image could possibly come to mind. The house was flexible, and now its two upstairs windows were no longer facing across the street, they were looking down the street, toward Harry and Lem. Then the head turned again, looked in the other direction, like a cautious pedestrian about to step out into a traffic zone. The turning of its head sounded like the creaking of an old tree in a high wind.

"God," Harry said.

The house stood, revealed thick, peasant girl legs and feet beneath its firm, wooden skirt, and then it stepped from the lot and began crossing the street. As it went, a window on either side of the house went up, and two spindly arms appeared as if suddenly poked through short shirt sleeves. The arms and hands were not as thick as the legs and feet; the hands were nearly flat, the fingers like gnarled oak branches.

"It's heading for my house," Harry said.

"Shut up!" Lem said. "You're talking too loud."

"Edith!"

"Edith's all right," Lem said. "Betcha a dog to a doughnut it's the house it wants. Watch!"

The house's rubbery front porch lips curled back and the front door opened to reveal rows of long, hollow, wood-screw teeth. With a creak it bent to nestle its mouth against the apex of Harry's roof, to latch its teeth there like a leech attaching itself to a swimmer's leg. And then came the low, soft sucking sounds, like gentle winds moaning against your roof at night; a sound you hear in your dreams and you almost wake, but from the back of your head comes a little hypnotic voice saying: "Sleep. It's only the wind crying, touching your roof, passing on," and so you sleep.

A shingle fell from Harry's house, caught a breeze and glided into the street. The front porch sagged ever so slightly. There was the soft sound of snapping wood from somewhere deep within. The windows grew darker and the glass rattled frightened in its frames.

After what seemed an eternity, but could only have been moments, the thing lifted its grotesque head and something dark and fluid dripped from its mouth, dribbled down the roof of Harry's house and splashed in the yard. Then there was a sound from the Gothic beast, a sound like a rattlesnake clacking, a sort of contented laughter from deep in its chest.

The house turned on its silly feet, crept and creaked, arms swinging, back across the street, turned to face Harry's house, then like a tired man home from work, it settled sighing into its place once more. The two upper story windows grew dark, as if thick lids had closed over them. The front porch lips smacked once, then there was silence and no movement.

Harry turned to Lem, who had replaced the pipe with the whiskey flask. The whiskey gurgled loudly in the cool fall night.

"Did you see. . . ?"

"Of course I did," Lem said, lowering the flask, wiping a sleeve across his mouth.

"Can't be."

"Somehow it is."

"But how?"

Lem shook his head. "Maybe it's like those science fiction books I read, like something out of them, an alien, or worse yet, something that has always been among us but has gone undetected for the most part.

"Say it's some kind of great space beast that landed here on Earth, a kind of chameleon that can camouflage itself by looking like a house. Perhaps it's some kind of vampire. Only it isn't blood it wants, but the energy out of houses." Lem tipped up his flask again.

"Houses haven't got energy."

Lem lowered the flask. "They've got their own special kind of energy. Listen: houses are built for the most part—least these houses were—by people who love them, people who wanted good solid homes. They were built before those soulless glass and plastic turd mounds that dot the skyline, before contractors were throwing dirt into the foundation instead of gravel, before they were pocketing the money that should have gone on good studs, two-by-fours and two-by-sixes. And these houses, the ones built with hope and love, absorbed these sensations, and what is hope and love but a kind of energy? You with me, Harry?"

"I guess, but . . . oh, rave on."

"So the walls of these houses took in that love and held it, and maybe that love, that energy, became the pulse, the heartbeat of the house. See what I'm getting at, Harry?

"Who appreciates and loves their homes more than folks our age, people who were alive when folks cared about what they built, people, who in their old age, find themselves more home-ridden, more dependent upon those four walls, more grateful of anything that keeps out the craziness of this newer world, keeps out the wind and the rain and the sun and those who would do us harm?

"This thing, maybe it can smell out, sense the houses that hold the most energy, and along it comes in the dead of night and it settles in and starts to draw the life out of them, like a vampire sucking out a victim's blood, and where the vampire's victims get weak and sag and grow pale, our houses do much the same. Because, you see, Harry, they have become living things. Not living in the way we normally think of it, but in a sort of silent, watchful way."

Harry blinked several times. "But why did it take the form of a Gothic-type house, why not a simple frame?"

"Maybe the last houses it was among looked a lot like that, and when it finished it came here. And to it these houses look basically the same as all the others. You see, Harry, it's not impersonating *our* houses, it's impersonating *a* house."

"That's wild, Lem."

"And the more I drink from this flask, the wilder I'll get. Take this for instance: it could look like anything. Consider all the ghettos in the world, the slums, the places that no amount of Federal Aid, money, and repair seem to fix. Perhaps these chameleons, or whatever you want to call them, live there as well—because despair fills walls as much as love—and they become the top floors of run-down tenement houses, the shanties alongside other shanties on Louisiana rivers—"

"And they feed on this love or despair, this energy?"

"Exactly, and when it's sucked out, the houses die and the creatures move on."

"What are we going to do about it?"

Lem turned up the flask and swigged. When he lowered it, he said, "*Something*, that's for sure."

They left the car, cat-pawed across the street, crept through backyards toward the sleeping house. When they were almost to the lot where the house squatted, they stopped beneath a sycamore tree and wore its shadow. They passed the flask back and forth.

Way out beyond the suburbs, in the brain of the city, they could hear traffic sounds. And much closer, from the ship channel, came the forlorn hoot of a plodding tug.

"Now what?" Harry asked.

"We sneak up on it from the rear, around by the back door—"

"Back door! If the front door is its mouth, Lem, the back door must be its—"

"We're not going inside, we're going to snoop, stupid, then we're going to do something."

"Like what?"

"We'll cross that blazing tightwire when we get to it. Now move!"

They moved, came to the back door. Lem reached out to touch the doorknob. "How about this?" he whispered. "No knob, just a black spot that looks like one. From a distance—hell, up close—you couldn't tell it was a fake without touching. Come on, let's look in the windows."

"Windows?" Harry said, but Lem had already moved around the edge of the house, and when Harry caught up with him, he was stooping at one of the windows, looking in.

"This is crazy," Lem said. "There's a stairway and furniture and cobwebs even . . . No, wait a minute. Feel!"

Harry crept up beside him, reluctantly touched the window. It was most certainly not glass, and it was not transparent either. It was cold and hard like the scale of a fish.

"It's just an illusion, like the doorknob," Harry said.

"Only a more complicated type of illusion, something it does with its mind probably. There's no furniture, no stairs, no nothing inside there but some kind of guts, I guess, the juice of our houses."

The house shivered, sent vibrations up Harry's palm. Harry remembered those long arms that had come out of the side windows earlier. He envisioned one popping out now, plucking him up.

The house burped, loudly.

Suddenly Lem was wearing Harry for a hat.

"Get down off me," Lem said, "or you're going to wake up with a tube up your nose."

Harry climbed down. "It's too much for us, Lem. In the movies they'd bring in the army, use nukes."

Lem took the can of lighter fluid out of his coat pocket. It was the large economy size.

"Sssshhhh," Lem said. He brought out his pocket knife and a book of matches.

"You're going to blow us up!"

Lem tore the lining out of one of his coat pockets, squirted lighter fluid on it, poked one end of the lining into the fluid can with the point of his knife. He put the rag-stuffed can on the ground, the matches beside it. Then he took his knife, stuck it quickly into the house's side, ripped down.

Something black and odorous oozed out. The house trembled.

"That's like a mosquito bite to this thing," Lem said. "Give me that can and matches."

"I don't like this," Harry said, but he handed the can and matches to Lem. Lem stuck the can halfway into the wound, let the rag dangle.

"Now run like hell," Lem said, and struck a match.

Harry started running toward the street as fast as his arthritic legs would carry him.

Lem lit the pocket lining. The fluid-soaked cloth jumped to bright life.

Lem turned to run. He hadn't gone three steps when the can blew. The heat slapped his back and the explosion thundered inside his head. He reached the street, looked back.

The house opened its front door and howled like a sixty-mile-an-hour tornado. The upstairs front window shades went up, eyes glinted savagely in the moonlight. A spear of flame spurted out of the house's side.

Harry was crossing the street, running for his house when he looked back. The creature howled again. Arms came out of its sides. All around windows went up and wings sprouted out of them.

"Jesus," Harry said, and he turned away from his house so as not to lead it to Edith. He started up the street toward his car.

Lem came up behind him laughing. "Ha! Ha! Flame on!"

Harry glanced back.

The explosion had ignited internal gases and the thing was howling flames now. Its tongue flapped out and slapped the street. Its wings fluttered and it rose up into the sky.

Doors opened all down the block. Windows went up.

Edith's head poked out of one of the windows. "Harry?"

"Be back, be back, be back," Harry said, and ran on.

Behind him Lem said, "Pacemaker, don't fail me now."

They reached the car wheezing.

"There . . . she . . . goes," Lem panted. "After it!" A bright, orange-red mass darted shrieking across the night sky, moved toward the ship channel, losing altitude.

The Ford coughed to life, hit the street. They went left, driving fast. Lem hung out of the window, pointing up, saying, "There it goes! Turn left. No, now over there. Turn right!"

"The ship channel!" Harry yelled. "It's almost to the ship channel."

"Falling, falling," Lem said.

It was.

They drove up the ship channel bridge. The house-thing blazed above them, moaned loud enough to shake the windows in the Ford. The sky was full of smoke.

Harry pulled over to the bridge railing, parked, jumped out with Lem. Other cars had pulled over. Women, men, and children burst out of them, ran to the railing, looked and pointed up.

The great flaming beast howled once more, loudly, then fell, hit the water with a thunderous splash.

"Ah, ha!" Harry yelled. "Dammit, Lem, we've done it, the block is free. Tomorrow we break out the paint, buy new windows, get some shingles . . ."

The last of the thing slipped under the waves with a hiss. A black cloud hung over the water for a moment, thinned to gray. There was a brief glow beneath the expanding ripples, then darkness.

Lem lifted his flask in toast. "Ha! Ha! Flame out!"

This was written for Twilight Zone, *but, alas, it wasn't picked up. I sent it to* The Horror Show, *and they grabbed it. It's an obvious Ray Bradbury influenced story. It's light, but I like it.*

The Man Who Dreamed

THE OLD MAN DROVE A RED PICKUP THAT looked ready to fall apart. He went up one street of Mud Creek and down another, driving slowly, looking out the window, sweating inside the pickup, cooking in the summer sunshine like a turkey in the oven.

Finally he found what he was looking for. A small, white frame house with a freshly mown lawn that you could smell from three blocks away. There was a low, decorative white fence that encased the yard and the old man parked in front of the curb next to that, got out on his rickety legs, went through the gate and up the walk.

A tricycle lay overturned near the front steps. The old man picked it up and set it right. He went up the steps and knocked on the door.

A young woman with her blonde hair tied back in a ponytail answered his knock. She had a white apron tied over her jeans and sweatshirt. She was barefoot. And very pretty. She smelled faintly of fried chicken.

"Yes?" she asked the old man.

The old man wore a sweaty cowboy hat and he took that off with a wave of his hand and held it in front of his stomach in a manner reminiscent of one clutching a wound. His face certainly seemed to show some sort of hurt—something deep and sour and unrelenting.

"Ma'am, my name is Homer Wall and I'm from Tulsa, Oklahoma—"

"Tulsa? I've got relatives there, the Mayners. This hasn't got anything to do with them, does it? They're okay?"

"I guess so. I don't know them. I'm not here about your relatives."

Her eyes housed some suspicion now. "Then you're selling something?"

"No ma'am, I'm not. I've come to tell you something very important. You see, Mrs. James—"

"How'd you know my name?"

"I'll explain that. I've got this gift, you see, and—"

"For me?"

"No ma'am. I mean, yes ma'am, in a way. But not the sort of gift you're thinking of . . . let me explain."

"Mr. Wall, I don't give to religious organizations, and I really have some work to do."

He shook his head. "No ma'am, I'm not a religious organization."

"Well now," she said, smiling, "I didn't think you were the whole thing."

The old man produced a pocket watch from his pants pocket and looked at the time. He felt the mainspring of his heart wind a little tighter. "We haven't got much time, Mrs. James. If you'll just give me a moment."

"Much time? What on Earth are—"

"Please. It takes some explaining to make it so you'll understand it right. My gift is special. I got struck by lightning three years ago. Just one of those things. I was working in my garden. Didn't hurt me at all. But it cured my bad hearing, made my hair grow back—"

"You are selling something! My husband has a full head of hair—"

"No ma'am, I'm not selling anything. Please listen. The lightning, it caused me to start having dreams. Dreams that come true. Like I dreamed my wife was going to die three weeks before she did. Happened just like I dreamed it. Her heart quit. You see, I dreamed my way right into her chest, saw her heart stop pumping, and three weeks later she died. Just like I'd seen it.

"After that it got worse. The dreams would come and grow more terrible each night; and then, finally it would stop, and three weeks after it stopped it would happen."

"What would happen?"

"The dream would come true. I dreamed about this air crash, and each night the dream showed me more. I even dreamed the headlines that would be written long before they were put into print, before the words were even thought up. It was terrible, the bodies in the water, the horror . . . always bad dreams. Never good ones. I dreamed about this little baby and the well down at my granddad's old place. I'd played there when I was a kid. And I dreamed this baby fell in, and I knew that child, and I talked to the parents and they listened, and it didn't happen. You see, they were thinking about buying that land, and there wasn't any way I could have known.

"So I put it together, that this lightning hadn't been any accident, that I was special and I was supposed to go out and try and stop these things. And sometimes, when folks listened, I found that I could—"

"Now, Mr. Wall—"

"Listen, three weeks ago to this day my dreams about you, this house, your husband, and your little boys, they stopped—"

"How'd you know I have little boys? What are you—"

"For God's sake, listen. I'm telling you. I dreamed it. And I could see them and you, and your husband, burning—"

She tried to close the door on him, but he moved fast, put his foot in the doorway. She pressed but made no progress. He didn't remove his foot.

"—dreamed this signpost that said: Mud Creek, and I dreamed the newspaper headlines off your local paper. I just kept dreaming enough things that I put it together, figured out the town's location. And when I saw your house, I knew it was the one in the dream. The one that was burning."

"Mr. Wall, my husband'll be home any minute."

"Yes, I know. And at five-thirty, while you're eating dinner—I know the time because I dreamed the clock over your kitchen sink and it showed five-thirty—there's going to be—"

"There's my husband. You best go."

The old man did not turn around. He heard a car pull up to the curb. "Listen to me, please. There will be a storm." A car door slammed. "Lightning will strike this house and you'll all die, horribly." The gate creaked open. "I tried to get here earlier, to warn you in plenty of time, but the truck broke down and I had to take some odd jobs to buy the parts it needed, and by the time I got that done and found you, well, it was the day, nearly the time—" A hand clamped the old man's bony shoulder.

"Get your foot out of the door."

The old man turned to look the other in the face. He was a young, handsome man in a blue business suit. "Mr. James, you've got to listen."

"Oh Robert, he's telling some awful thing about how he dreamed we were all going to die in a fire, that lightning is going to strike the house at five-thirty, that he's here to warn us—"

"I am here to warn you," the old man said. "I dreamed this place. Your names will be in tomorrow's paper, they'll call it a freak accident."

"Tomorrow's paper!" Mr. James said. "You are some kind of kook. Take your witchcraft stuff somewhere else."

"Mr. James." The old man's hand clutched at the man's lapel like a claw.

"I mean it."

"You've got to—"

Robert snatched the old man's hand free, pushed him back.

The old man stumbled over the tricycle and fell onto the grass.

"Robert! He's just a crazy old man. You'll hurt him."

"I didn't mean to do that," Robert said. "I didn't know I pushed that hard. I didn't mean for you to fall, but if you don't go, now, I'm going to call the police."

"Lightning will strike this house," the old man said, getting up, recovering his hat and placing it on his head. "And you'll all die. You've got to get out of this house."

"Get out of here," Robert said. "I mean it. Hon, call the police."

The old man sighed, nodded. "Very well, I tried."

"You tried something," Robert said.

The old man got in his truck. He looked longingly out the window at them for a moment, finally started the motor and drove away, heading north.

"Oh Robert, such a strange old man."

"A kook."

"Could . . . I mean—?"

"Of course not. That's hocus pocus nonsense. Besides, there's not a cloud in the sky. It's sunny and blue. He's just a nut, well meaning maybe, but still a nut."

"Poor man."

"Forget it. What's for dinner? Are the boys home?"

"Fried chicken and mashed potatoes. And yes, they're home and hungry and ready to see their daddy." He put his arm around her and kissed her on the cheek and they went inside.

The old man stopped just outside of Mud Creek and looked at his pocket watch. Five-twenty.

He shook his head sadly, a tear ran down his cheek. He put the truck in gear and drove on northward. Above him, blowing fast, a dark mass of clouds moved south.

I always wanted to be published in Ellery Queen *or* Alfred Hitchcock's Mystery Magazine. *I gave it a lot of shots, but never made it. Finally, the magazine changed so much it didn't interest me. It became a sort of simplistic don't strain and don't hurt your feelings kind of fiction designed to kill time between subway stops.*

But I still wanted to be published there. Now and again I would try and write a story I thought fit that mold, but I had changed so much, I just couldn't fit it.

Then one day I had this idea. It struck me as the perfect Alfred Hitchcock *magazine story. Entertaining enough, but forgettable. I know that sounds cold, but this sort of thing has its place too. This also applies to movies. Comics. Music. Etc.*

Anyway, I wrote this and sent it off.

They didn't buy it either.

So much for trying to write to market. I've always found that for me this is a bad idea.

But, I do think it did what I intended. I do think it should have fit in Alfred Hitchcock *or* Ellery Queen.

Walks

*M*Y SON WORRIES ME. HE ONLY LEAVES HIS room for long walks and he treats me like the hired help. I ought to throw him out, but I cannot. He is my son and I love him and I share his pain, though I am uncertain what that pain is.

Even as a little boy he was strange. Always strange. After his mama died he only got stranger. He was eighteen then, and of course it was a bad thing for him, but I thought he would have coped better at that age. It was not as if he were ten.

He certainly misses his mama.

He goes into the attic and digs through the trunk that holds her keepsakes. Perhaps I should have destroyed the trunk long ago, but it never occurred to me. I am one of those people who hangs onto everything.

These days he sits in his room at his desk and cuts things out of the newspaper. He does not think I've seen him, but I have. I walk quietly. I learned that when I was a boy. You did not walk quietly, my old man would fly off the handle. He hated a heavy walk. Me and my sisters got a lot of beltings because of the way we walked. My old man taught me to walk softly. When he was not drinking he would take me hunting and he would teach me how to walk like an Indian. When he was drinking, that was the way he wanted us to walk around the house. He never taught my sisters how to walk, he just expected it. He used to say girls ought to walk like girls, not water buffalo. My old man was a horrible, cruel drunk, and I am thankful that I managed to be a better father to my son.

But now the boy has pushed me out, will not let me in. I wish he respected me. I never did to him what my father did to me. I never made him walk quietly. I even let him come back home and take his old room when he lost his job.

When he was a child we used to talk about everything. Even the weird things he was interested in like horror movies and comic books and pyramid power. I did not like any of it, but I talked to him just the same, tried to understand his interests.

After his mother's death, he became quieter, more withdrawn. He will not accept she stepped out in front of a car and was killed and will not be back. I think he keeps expecting to look up and see her walk through the door.

I am sorry for him, even if his mother and I never got along. It happens that way sometimes.

And these clippings of his, they worry me. Why is he cutting them out and saving them? That makes me very nervous. He thinks I do not know about them. Thinks I have not seen him cutting them out and pondering them, gluing them in his scrapbook, putting them in the bottom desk drawer under the family photo album.

And these long walks. Where does he go and what does he do? I wonder all the time, then feel guilty for wondering. He's a grown man and can take walks if he wants to. He probably walks and worries about not having a job, though he has not yet pushed hard enough to find one if you ask me. But I am sure it worries him. The walks probably help him get his mind off things. Then he comes back here and collects his clippings as a sort of hobby.

I hope that's it. Hope that explains his fascination with the clippings. I hate it when I think there is more to it than that.

One time, when he went on one of his walks, I snuck in and opened the desk drawer and got his scrapbook and looked to see what he was cutting out.

It was articles about the Choker murders snipped from a dozen newspapers. Local papers, out-of-state papers. Just about everything the newsstand sells in the way of papers. He cut out the pictures of the whores who had been strangled and glued them all in a row and underlined their names in red.

That worries me. And he has a scrapbook full of articles about the Choker from a half dozen different papers.

And the way he acts around me. Strange. Nervous. Sullen.

Today I asked him if he wanted some soup and he glared at me and would not answer. He turned his back and stared at the window and watched the rain gather on the glass, then he got up and got his raincoat and umbrella and went for a walk.

It was like when he was a little boy and he got mad about something and started being obstinate for no real reason, or sometimes because you disappointed him.

That is always the worst thing, disappointing your son. Him knowing you are not the man you want him to be.

After he was gone, I went to the window to see which way he was going, then I went to the desk drawer and took out the scrapbook and looked at them.

He had a lot more clippings. He had his mother's picture in the scrapbook. The photo used to have me in it too, but he had cut me out.

Guilt or not. Grown man or not. I had to know where he went on those walks.

I put on my raincoat and pulled up the hood and went in the direction he took. I am getting old, but I am not getting slow or weak. In fact, I am probably in better condition than my boy. I do exercises. I can still walk fast and I can still walk quietly. My old man's legacy, walking quietly.

After a short time I saw him way ahead of me, walking over toward The District, where the poorer people live. It is a very bad place.

It was very dark because of the rain and it was getting darker because it was closer to nightfall.

He went into a bar and I crossed the street and stood under an old hotel awning and looked across the street at the bar and watched him through the glass. He ordered a drink and sat and took his time with it. I started to feel cold.

I waited, though, and after a bit he had yet another drink, then another.

Now I know where the money I give him goes.

I was about to give up waiting when out he came and started up the street, not wobbling or anything. He can hold his liquor, I guess, though where he got a taste for drink I'll never know. I do not allow it around the house.

I followed him and he walked deeper into the bad part of town, where the Choker murders take place.

It grew dark and the sun went down and the neon came out

and so did the hookers. They called to me from the protection of doorways, but I ignored them.

I thought of my son. They had to be calling to him too, and up ahead I saw him stop and go to a doorway, and though I could not see the girl, I knew she was there and that he was talking to her.

I felt very nervous suddenly. It hurt to know that my son was frequenting the bad parts of town, the way his mother had. Perhaps he knew about her. Perhaps he was trying to understand what she saw in places like this. And perhaps he was very much like her. God forbid.

I stopped and leaned against a building and waited, pulled the hood tight around my face to keep out the rain.

Then I saw my son go into the doorway and out of sight.

So now I knew where he went when he took his walks. He liked this part of town like his mother liked this part of town. Maybe, if he had a job, less to worry about, he would not need it anymore. I hoped that was it. Whores and whiskey were a sad way for a man to live.

A girl called to me from across the way. Something about "old man do you want to feel younger." It bothered me she could tell I was old from that far away. I had a raincoat and hood on, for Christ sake.

Guess it is the way I hold myself, even though I try to keep my back straight and try to walk like a younger man.

But I guess there is no hiding it. Even though I am strong and healthy, I have always looked old, even when I was young. My wife used to say I was born fifty years old. She used to tell me in bed that I acted eighty.

I do not miss her at all. If she were alive, I wonder what she would think if she knew her son was seeing whores. Would she feel proud he liked this part of town the way she had? Or would she feel ashamed?

No, I doubt she would feel ashamed. She loved the boy, but she was a bad influence. When I thought of her I always thought of her coming home with whiskey on her breath, her skin smelling of some man's cologne.

I crossed the street and the girl smiled at me and talked about what she could do for me. She reminded me of my wife standing there. They all do.

I smiled at her. I thought of my son and what he was doing and I felt so sad. I thought of his mother again, and how she had been, and I was glad I had done what I did. A woman like her did not deserve to live. Just a little push at a dark intersection at the right moment and it was all over. It was not as good as getting my hands on her throat, which is what I would have liked to do, but it was easier to explain. More efficient. The police believed it was an accident.

And now, when I am with the others, I pretend each of them is her and that it is her throat I am squeezing.

But my boy, does he know what I do? Is that why he collects my press? Maybe he takes his walks not only for the whiskey and the whores, but because he suspects me and does not want to be around me, thinks what I do is wrong.

I hope that is not it.

God, I hope he does not get a disease from that slut. Can he not find a nice girl?

I smiled at the whore again, got under the doorway with her, peeked out and looked both ways.

No one was coming.

I grabbed her and it only took a moment before I let her fall. I am old, but I am strong.

God, I hope my son does not get a disease.

As I went away, walking my quick but quiet walk, I told myself I would talk to him when he came in. Try to decide what he knows without giving myself away. Maybe he does not know it is me. He might collect the articles because he likes what he reads. Sympathizes with the Choker.

If so, if he would talk to me and try to understand, I think we could have the relationship I have always wanted. One like we had when he was little and we talked about the weird things that interested him, anything and everything under the sun.

I certainly hope it can be that way.

I do not want to have to choke him too.

Another old one that's hung around in my files forever. This one was written under the influence of what I call Bradbury's middle period. This was when he had consciously moved away from horror and more and more into fantasy. I'm not as fond of that period, but I do like it.

This was my attempt to write a Bradburyesque type of fantasy story.

It ain't bad. Kind of charming, actually.

Last of the Hopeful

*H*IGH UP, ON THE EDGE OF THE CLIFF, GREEN wings strained, gathered the wind and held it. But the breeze-bloated device did not lift the girl who wore it aloft. Two men, one old, one young, stood on either side of her, held her, served as an anchor for her lithe, brown body. They were her father and brother.

"Will I fly like a bird, father?" the young girl asked. Her voice was weak with fear. The wind seemed to clutch the words from her mouth and toss them out over the glistening green land of Oahu.

"No," her father said, "you will not fly like a bird and you must not try. Do not flap the wings. Let the wind rule and take you where it wants you to go. Glide. Do you understand?"

"Yes father," she said, "I understand."

"Good. Now tell me one more time what you know."

"I know all the songs of our people. I know all the hulas. I know where we lived and how it was when we lived our own way and were not controlled by others. I know all of this. I know of all the things before the coming of Kamehameha."

"You are the last of us, daughter. You are the last of our hope. I have long expected this day, dreamed once that we would be driven here and forced over the side, down to death on the rocks. But in the dream we did not scream, and we will not scream this day."

"And the bird, father," the young boy said.

"Yes, and there was a great bird in the sky, green and brown, and I came to understand what it meant. This day could not be avoided but there was still hope for our people. That is why I built the wings and taught you all these things, some are things that women have never been taught before."

"But maybe," the young girl said, "it was only a bird in your dream—a real bird."

The old man shook his head. "No."

"Perhaps it was my brother?"

"No. You are the lightest, you are our hope. If the wings bear anyone, it is you, the daughter of the king."

"Maybe we will win this day and there will be no need."

The old man smiled grimly. "Then you will not fly and things will be as they were, but I do not expect that. The time of our people has come to an end, but you will carry our thoughts, our dreams, our hopes with you."

The young girl's long black hair whipped in the wind. "Oh father, let me die with you. I do not want to be the only one left, the only one of us still alive."

"While you live," her brother said softly, "while you hold all the old songs and stories to your heart, we all live and we will never die. Some how, some way, you must pass these things on."

"But there are none left to pass them to," the young girl said.

"The war will end this day," her father said. "You must make a boat in the manner I have taught you, sail to one of the other islands and wait until the hate and fear have died. Then return. You will find a young man among them, one too young to know their hate, and he will give you children and you will teach them the ways of our people. Not so that these things will rule again, for that time is passed, but so that the memory of us will not die."

"Hold me," she said.

Brother and father pulled closer.

Down below, moving up toward the cliff, came the sound of battle, the cries of men, the smashing of clubs against clubs and clubs against flesh.

"These wings," the old man said, "they will make you a goddess in the sun. You will soar over the valley and turn with the wind toward the sea, and down there, far from them, you can hide."

"Yes father." The wind strained at the wings, tried to lift the girl up.

"Lift the wings," her father said.

She did as he asked.

The sound of yelling warriors was very close.

From where they stood, the trio could see a fine line of brown warriors falling back, being forced toward the edge of the cliff.

"Soon," the old man said, "we go over the cliff with the others."

"But not before we fight," said the boy. He looked into the face of his sister. "You are the last of the hopeful. Carry our hope far and wide."

Tears were in her eyes. "I will."

The warriors were very close now. You could smell the sweat of battle, feel the heat of hate and anger.

"Ride the wind," the old man said.

She turned to look out over the beautiful green valley. She spread the wings. The wind billowed them.

"You must go now," her brother said.

"Our hopes go with you," her father said.

And they released her into the wind.

It was a powerful wind. It caught the great green wings and pulled her up and out over the valley. For a moment her father and brother watched, then, picking up their war clubs, they turned to join the last of the battle.

A moment later, along with the rest of the warriors, the old man, who was known to his people as King Kalanikupule, went over the cliff and down into the green valley without a scream.

And moving out over the valley, slave to the wind, went his daughter.

Kamehameha, the sweat and blood of war coating his body, watched her soar.

Clubs were tossed at her, but all fell short.

The wind whipped her up high again, and then seemed to let go.

She plummeted like a stone.

But only for a moment, an updraft caught her, took her up again, and even as the victorious forces of Kamehameha stood on the cliff's edge and watched in awe, the slim brown girl glided down and over the tree tops, around their edge toward the shore line, shining in the sun like a great, green and brown bird before coasting behind tall trees and out of sight.

On the wind, for a brief instant, there floated the sound of her sweet, hopeful laughter.

This story came to me because I often meet male hunters who somehow think hunting defines them as a man.

I grew up on hunting. I've hunted. My father once told me if you get so you like to do it just to do it, and not for the satisfaction of food, maybe you shouldn't do it. He also told me, and I think rightfully, it is not a sport.

The idea of shooting something to put an animal's head on the wall, or even a fish's body, struck him as stupid and wasteful.

Me too.

Anyway, I probably came across one of these hunters, heard their line about how it made them one with the universe or something, and I thought, no, I don't think so.

I bet it was something like that.

Anyway, at some point, that kind of thinking inspired this.

Duck Hunt

*T*HERE WERE THREE HUNTERS AND THREE DOGS. The hunters had shiny shotguns, warm clothes, and plenty of ammo. The dogs were each covered in big, blue spots and were sleek and glossy and ready to run. No duck was safe.

The hunters were Clyde Barrow, James Clover, and little Freddie Clover, who was only fifteen and very excited to be asked along. However, Freddie did not really want to see a duck, let alone shoot one. He had never killed anything but a sparrow with his BB gun and that had made him sick. But he was nine then. Now he was ready to be a man. His father told him so.

With this hunt he felt he had become part of a secret organization. One that smelled of tobacco smoke and whiskey breath; sounded of swear words, talk about how good certain women were, the range and velocity of rifles and shotguns, the edges of hunting knives, the best caps and earflaps for winter hunting.

In Mud Creek the hunt made the man.

Since Freddie was nine he had watched with more than casual interest, how when a boy turned fifteen in Mud Creek, he would be invited to The Hunting Club for a talk with the men. Next step was a hunt, and when the boy returned he was a boy no longer. He talked deep, walked sure, had whiskers bristling on his chin, and could take up with the assurance of not being laughed at, cussing, smoking, and watching women's butts as a matter of course.

Freddie wanted to be a man too. He had pimples, no pubic hair to speak of (he always showered quickly at school to escape derisive remarks about the size of his equipment and the thickness of his foliage), scrawny legs, and little, gray, watery eyes that looked like ugly planets spinning in white space.

And truth was, Freddie preferred a book to a gun.

But came the day when Freddie turned fifteen and his father came home from the Club, smoke and whiskey smell clinging to him like a hungry tick, his face slightly dark with beard and tired-looking from all-night poker.

He came into Freddie's room, marched over to the bed where Freddie was reading THOR, clutched the comic from his son's hands, sent it fluttering across the room with a rainbow of comic panels.

"Nose out of a book," his father said. "Time to join the Club."

Freddie went to the Club, heard the men talk ducks, guns, the way the smoke and blood smelled on cool morning breezes. They told him the kill was the measure of a man. They showed him heads on the wall. They told him to go home with his father and come back tomorrow bright and early, ready for his first hunt.

His father took Freddie downtown and bought him a flannel shirt (black and red), a thick jacket (fleece lined), a cap (with ear-flaps), and boots (waterproof). He took Freddie home and took a shotgun down from the rack, gave him a box of ammo, walked him out back to the firing range, and made him practice while he told his son about hunts and the war and about how men and ducks died much the same.

Next morning before the sun was up, Freddie and his father had breakfast. Freddie's mother did not eat with them. Freddie did not ask why. They met Clyde over at the Club and rode in his jeep down dirt roads, clay roads and trails, through brush and briars until they came to a mass of reeds and cattails that grew thick and tall as Japanese bamboo.

They got out and walked. As they walked, pushing aside the reeds and cattails, the ground beneath their feet turned marshy. The dogs ran ahead.

When the sun was two hours up, they came to a bit of a clearing in the reeds, and beyond them Freddie could see the break-your-heart blue of a shiny lake. Above the lake, coasting down, he saw a duck. He watched it sail out of sight.

"Well boy?" Freddie's father said.

"It's beautiful," Freddie said.

"Beautiful, hell, are you ready?"

"Yes, sir."

On they walked, the dogs way ahead now, and finally they stood within ten feet of the lake. Freddie was about to squat down into hiding as he had heard of others doing, when a flock of ducks burst up from a mass of reeds in the lake and Freddie, fighting off the sinking feeling in his stomach, tracked them with the barrel of the shotgun, knowing what he must do to be a man.

His father's hand clamped over the barrel and pushed it down. "Not yet," he said.

"Huh?" said Freddie.

"It's not the ducks that do it," Clyde said.

Freddie watched as Clyde and his father turned their heads to the right, to where the dogs were pointing noses, forward, paws upraised—to a thatch of underbrush. Clyde and his father made quick commands to the dogs to stay, then they led Freddie into the brush, through a twisting maze of briars and out into a clearing where all the members of The Hunting Club were waiting.

In the center of the clearing was a gigantic duck decoy. It looked ancient and there were symbols carved all over it. Freddie could not tell if it were made of clay, iron, or wood. The back of it was scooped out, gravy bowl-like, and there was a pole in the center of the indention; tied to the pole was a skinny man. His head had been caked over with red mud and there were duck feathers sticking in it, making it look like some kind of funny cap. There was a ridiculous, wooden duck bill held to his head by thick elastic straps. Stuck to his butt was a duster of duck feathers. There was a sign around his neck that read DUCK.

The man's eyes were wide with fright and he was trying to say or scream something, but the bill had been fastened in such a way he couldn't make any more than a mumble.

Freddie felt his father's hand on his shoulder. "Do it," he said. "He ain't nobody to anybody we know. Be a man."

"Do it! Do it! Do it!" came the cry from The Hunting Club.

Freddie felt the cold air turn into a hard ball in his throat. His scrawny legs shook. He looked at his father and The Hunting Club. They all looked tough, hard, and masculine.

"Want to be a titty baby all your life?" his father said.

That put steel in Freddie's bones. He cleared his eyes with the back of his sleeve and steadied the barrel on the derelict's duck's head.

"Do it!" came the cry. "Do it! Do it! Do it!"

At that instant he pulled the trigger. A cheer went up from The Hunting Club, and out of the clear, cold sky, a dark blue norther blew in and with it came a flock of ducks. The ducks lit on the great idol and on the derelict. Some of them dipped their bills in the derelict's wetness.

When the decoy and the derelict were covered in ducks, all of The Hunting Club lifted their guns and began to fire.

The air became full of smoke, pellets, blood, and floating feathers.

When the gunfire died down and the ducks died out, The Hunting Club went forward and bent over the decoy, did what they had to do. Their smiles were red when they lifted their heads. They wiped their mouths gruffly on the backs of their sleeves and gathered ducks into hunting bags until they bulged. There were still many carcasses lying about.

Fred's father gave him a cigarette. Clyde lit it.

"Good shooting, son," Fred's father said and clapped him manfully on the back.

"Yeah," said Fred, scratching his crotch, "got that sonofabitch right between the eyes, pretty as a picture."

They all laughed.

The sky went lighter, and the blue norther that was rustling the reeds and whipping feathers about blew up and out and away in an instant. As the men walked away from there, talking deep, walking sure, whiskers bristling on all their chins, they promised that tonight they would get Fred a woman.

I came up with this before we had kids, or I would say quarreling kids gave me the idea.

I don't really know where this one came from.

No memory of it really.

But I think it may have come from the fact that sometimes, no matter how much you know better, no matter how many books you may have read on relationships or how many Doctor Phil shows you've watched, and no matter how hard you try to avoid pitfalls and fight in a manner that's correct, sometimes, well, you just screw up and get into something nasty with a friend, spouse, brother, sister, child, what have you. And when it's over, you think, how did that happen? Where did it come from? And now that I think about it, was really silly.

And man, the stuff I said.

I think that was its inspiration.

Like many of the stories I was writing at this time, it came quickly.

I sent it to Twilight Zone *sensing a sure sale.*

T. E. D. Klein passed.

I was shocked. I thought it was one of the best pieces of its type that I had shown him. I felt it fit snugly beside other tales I had written for him. And, was in fact, better than a couple of the others.

Hell, I liked it a lot.

He still passed.

It ended up in Masques, *an interesting anthology from Maclay & Associates (John Maclay is also a writer, and an underrated one, I might add), and the book was edited by J. N. Williamson. There have been several others in this series, but the first one was the best. The best story in it was "Nightcrawlers" by Robert McCammon. It made a great* Amazing Stories.

I think this story would have been fun there.

Few special effects.

Odd.

Creepy.

Down by the Sea Near the Great Big Rock

OWN BY THE SEA NEAR THE GREAT BIG ROCK, they made their camp and toasted marshmallows over a small, fine fire. The night was pleasantly chill and the sea spray cold. Laughing, talking, eating the gooey marshmallows, they had one swell time; just them, the sand, the sea and the sky, and the great big rock.

The night before they had driven down to the beach, to the camping area; and on their way, perhaps a mile from their destination, they had seen a meteor shower, or something of that nature. Bright lights in the heavens, glowing momentarily, seeming to burn red blisters across the ebony sky.

Then it was dark again, no meteoric light, just the natural glow of the heavens—the stars, the dime-size moon.

They drove on and found an area of beach on which to camp, a stretch dominated by pale sands and big waves, and the great big rock.

Toni and Murray watched the children eat their marshmallows and play their games, jumping and falling over the great big rock, rolling in the cool sand. About midnight, when the kids were crashed out, they walked along the beach like fresh-found lovers, arm in arm, shoulder to shoulder, listening to the sea, watching the sky, speaking words of tenderness.

"I love you so much," Murray told Toni, and she repeated the words and added, "and our family too."

They walked in silence now, the feelings between them words enough. Sometimes Murray worried that they did not talk as all the marriage manuals suggested, that so much of what he had to say on the world and his work fell on the ears of others, and that she had so little to truly say to him. Then he would think: What the hell? I know how I feel. Different messages, unseen, unheard, pass between us all the time, and they communicate in a fashion words cannot. He said some catch phrase, some pet thing between them, and Toni laughed and pulled him down on the sand. Out there beneath that shiny-dime moon, they stripped and loved on the beach like young sweethearts, experiencing their first night together after long expectation.

It was nearly two A.M. when they returned to the camper, checked the children and found them sleeping comfortably as kittens full of milk.

They went back outside for a while, sat on the rock and smoked and said hardly a word. Perhaps a coo or a purr passed between them, but little more.

Finally they climbed inside the camper, zipped themselves into their sleeping bags and nuzzled together on the camper floor.

Outside the wind picked up, the sea waved in and out, and a slight rain began to fall.

Not long after, Murray awoke and looked at his wife in the crook of his arm. She lay there with her face a grimace, her mouth opening and closing like a guppy, making an "uhhh, uhh" sound.

A nightmare perhaps. He stroked the hair from her face, ran his fingers lightly down her cheek and touched the hollow of her throat and thought: What a nice place to carve out some fine, white meat. . . .

What in the hell is wrong with me? Murray thought, and he rolled away from her, out of the bag. He dressed, went outside and sat on the rock. With shaking hands on his knees, buttocks resting on the warmth of the stone, he brooded. Finally he dismissed the possibility that such a thought had actually crossed his mind, smoked a cigarette and went back to bed.

He did not know that an hour later Toni awoke and bent over him and looked at his face as if it were something to squash. But finally she shook it off and slept.

The children tossed and turned. Little Roy squeezed his hands open, closed, open, closed. His eyelids fluttered rapidly.

Robyn dreamed of striking matches.

Morning came and Murray found that all he could say was, "I had the oddest dream."

Toni looked at him, said, "Me, too," and that was all. Placing lawn chairs on the beach, they put their feet on the rock and watched the kids splash and play in the waves; watched as Roy mocked the sound of the *Jaws* music and made fins with his hands and chased Robyn through the water as she scuttled backwards and screamed with false fear.

Finally they called the children from the water, ate a light lunch, and, leaving the kids to their own devices, went in for a swim.

The ocean stroked them like a mink-gloved hand, tossed them, caught them, massaged them gently. They washed together, laughing, kissing—

Then tore their lips from one another as up on the beach they heard a scream.

Roy had his fingers gripped about Robyn's throat, held her bent back over the rock and was putting a knee in her chest. There seemed no play about it. Robyn was turning blue.

Toni and Murray waded for shore, and the ocean no longer felt kind. It grappled with them, held them, tripped them with wet, foamy fingers. It seemed an eternity before they reached the shore, yelling at Roy.

Roy didn't stop. Robyn flopped like a dying fish. Murray grabbed the boy by the hair and pulled him back, and for a moment, as the child turned, he looked at his father with odd eyes that did not seem his, but looked instead as cold and firm as the great big rock.

Murray slapped him, slapped him so hard Roy spun and went down, stayed there on hands and knees, panting.

Murray went to Robyn, who was already in Toni's arms, and on the child's throat were blue-black bands like thin, ugly snakes.

"Baby, baby, are you okay?" Toni asked over and over. Murray wheeled, strode back to the boy, and Toni was now yelling at him, crying, "Murray, Murray, easy now. They were just playing and it got out of hand."

Roy was on his feet, and Murray, gritting his teeth, so angry he could not believe it, slapped the child down.

"MURRAY," Toni yelled, and she let go of the sobbing Robyn and went to stay his arm, for he was already raising it for another strike. "That's no way to teach him not to hit, not to fight."

Murray turned to her, almost snarling, but then his face relaxed and he lowered his hand. Turning to the boy, feeling very criminal, Murray reached down to lift Roy by the shoulder. But Roy pulled away, darted for the camper.

"Roy," he yelled, and started after him. Toni grabbed his arm. "Let him be," she said. "He got carried away and he knows it. Let him mope it over. He'll be all right." Then softly: "I've never known you to get that mad."

"I've never been so mad before," he said honestly.

They walked back to Robyn, who was smiling now. They all sat on the rock, and about fifteen minutes later Robyn got up to see about Roy. "I'm going to tell him it's okay," she said. "He didn't mean it." She went inside the camper.

"She's sweet," Toni said.

"Yeah," Murray said, looking at the back of Toni's neck as she watched Robyn move away. He was thinking that he was supposed to cook dinner today, make hamburgers, slice onions; big onions cut thin with a freshly sharpened knife. He decided to go get it.

"I'll start dinner," he said flatly, and stalked away.

As he went, Toni noticed how soft the back of his skull looked, so much like an overripe melon.

She followed him inside the camper.

Next morning, after the authorities had carried off the bodies, taken the four of them out of the bloodstained, fire-gutted camper, one detective said to another:

"Why does it happen? Why would someone kill a nice family like this? And in such horrible ways . . . set fire to it afterwards?"

The other detective sat on the huge rock and looked at his partner, said tonelessly, "Kicks maybe."

That night, when the moon was high and bright, gleaming down like a big spotlight, the big rock, satiated, slowly spread its flippers out, scuttled across the sand, into the waves, and began to swim toward the open sea. The fish that swam near it began to fight.

There are people who like pain and inflict in on themselves, and I am not one of those who believe it is lifestyle or a valid choice.

People like this have, to put it mildly, problems.

Maybe not as severe as the problems my two characters have in this story, but problems.

You don't hurt yourself as a normal course of events. It goes against solid survival instincts. I'm not talking about piercing your ear, and I'm not talking about learning to deal with pain because you box, do martial arts, or any sport or self defense system.

I'm talking about pain for pain itself.

And if you like to give pain for pain itself, that's another problem, in reverse.

That's fucked up. Either end of it.

Take my word for it.

Or don't.

I no longer remember what inspired this story. Maybe the fact that this sort of thinking struck me as so amazing. We're not talking about people who are mentally ill, we're talking about people who make these choices because they get a kick out of it.

Ouch. Times ten.

I Tell You It's Love

THE BEAUTIFUL WOMAN HAD NO EYES, JUST sparklers of light where they should have been—or so it seemed in the candlelight. Her lips, so warm and inviting, so wickedly wild and suggestive of strange pleasures, held yet a hint of disaster, as if they might be fat, red things skillfully molded from dried blood.

"Hit me," she said.

That is my earliest memory of her; a doll for my beating, a doll for my love.

I laid it on her with that black silk whip, slapping it across her shoulders and back, listening to the whisper of it as it rode down, delighting in the flat, pretty sound of it striking her flesh.

She did not bleed, which was a disappointment. The whip was too soft, too flexible, too difficult to strike hard with.

"Hurt me," she said softly. I went to where she knelt. Her arms were outstretched, crucifixion style, and bound to the walls on either side with strong silk cord the color and texture of the whip in my hand.

I slapped her. "Like it?" I asked. She nodded and I slapped her again . . . and again. A one-two rhythm, slow and melodic, time and again.

"Like it?" I repeated, and she moaned. "Yeah, oh yeah."

Later, after she was untied and had tidied up the blood from her lips and nose, we made brutal love; me with my thumbs bending the flesh of her throat, she with her nails entrenched in my back. She said to me when we were finished, "Let's do someone."

That's how we got started. Thinking back now, once again I say I'm glad for fate; glad for Gloria; glad for the memory of the crying sounds, the dripping blood, and the long, sharp knives that murmured through flesh like a lover's whisper cutting the dark.

Yeah, I like to think back to when I walked hands in pockets down the dark wharves in search of that special place where there were said to be special women with special pleasures for a special man like me.

I walked on until I met a sailor leaning against a wall smoking a cigarette, and he says when I ask about the place, "Oh, yeah, I like that sort of pleasure myself. Two blocks down, turn right, there between the warehouses, down the far end. You'll see the light." And he points and I walk on, faster.

Finding it, paying for it, meeting Gloria was the goal of my dreams. I was more than a customer to that sassy, dark mamma with the sparkler eyes. I was the link to fit her link. We made two strong, solid bonds in a strange, cosmic chain. You could feel the energy flowing through us; feel the iron of our wills. Ours was a mating made happily in hell.

So time went by and I hated the days and lived for the nights when I whipped her, slapped her, scratched her, and she did the same to me. Then one night she said, "It's not enough. Just not enough anymore. Your blood is sweet and your pain is fine, but I want to see death like you see a movie, taste it like licorice, smell it like flowers, touch it like cold, hard stone."

I laughed, saying, "I draw the line at dying for you." I took her by the throat, fastened my grip until her breathing was a whistle, and her eyes protruded like bloated corpse bellies.

"That's not what I mean," she managed. And then came the statement that brings us back to what started it all. "Let's do someone."

I laughed and let her go.

"You know what I mean?" she said. "You know what I'm saying."

"I know what you said. I know what you mean." I smiled. "I know very well."

"You've done it before, haven't you?"

"Once," I said, "in a shipyard, not that long ago."

"Tell me about it. God, tell me about it."

"It was dark and I had come off ship after six months out, a long six months with the men, the ship, and the sea. So I'm walking down this dark alley, enjoying the night like I do, looking for a place with the dark ways, our kind of ways, baby, and I came upon this old wino lying in a doorway, cuddling a bottle to his face as if it were a lady's loving hand."

"What did you do?"

"I kicked him," I said, and Gloria's smile was a beauty to behold.

"Go on," she said.

"God, how I kicked him. Kicked him in the face until there was no nose, no lips, no eyes. Only red mush dangling from shrapneled bone; looked like a melon that had been dropped from on high, down into a mass of broken white pottery chips. I touched his face and tasted it with my tongue and my lips."

"Ohh," she signed, and her eyes half closed. "Did he scream?"

"Once. Only once. I kicked him too hard, too fast, too soon. I hammered his head with the toes of my shoes, hammered until my cuffs were wet and sticking to my ankles."

"Oh, God," she said, clinging to me. "Let's do it, let's do it."

We did. First time was a drizzly night and we caught an old woman out. She was a lot of fun until we got the knives out and then she went quick. There was that crippled kid next, lured him from the theater downtown, and how we did that was a stroke of genius. You'll find his wheelchair not far from where you found the van and the other stuff.

But no matter. You know what we did, about the kinds of tools we had, about how we hung that crippled kid on that meat hook in my van until the flies clustered around the doors thick as grapes.

And of course there was the little girl. It was a brilliant idea of Gloria's to get the kid's tricycle into the act. The things she did with those spokes. Ah, but that woman was a connoisseur of pain.

There were two others, each quite fine, but not as nice as the last. Then came the night Gloria looked at me and said, "It's not enough. Just won't do."

I smiled. "No way, baby. I still won't die for you."

"No," she gasped, and took my arm. "You miss my drift. It's the pain I need, not just the watching. I can't live through them, can't feel it in me. Don't you see, it would be the ultimate."

I looked at her, wondering did I have it right.

"Do you love me?"

"I do," I said.

"To know that I would spend the last of my life with you, that my last memories would be the pleasure on your face, the feelings of pain, the excitement, the thrill, the terror."

Then I understood, and understood good. Right there in the car I grabbed her, took her by the throat and cracked her head against the windshield, pressed her back, choked, released, choked, made it linger. By this time I was quite a pro. She coughed, choked, smiled. Her eyes swung from fear to love. God it was wonderful and beautiful and the finest experience we had ever shared.

When she finally lay still there in the seat, I was trembling, happier than I had ever been. Gloria looked fine, her eyes rolled up, her lips stretched in a rictus smile.

I kept her like that at my place for days, kept her in my bed until the neighbors started to complain about the smell.

I've been talking to this guy and he's got some ideas. Says he thinks I'm one of the future generation, and the fact of that scares him all to hell. A social mutation, he says. Man's primitive nature at the height of the primal scream.

Dog shit, we're all the same, so don't look at me like I'm some kind of freak. What does he do come Monday night? He's watching the football game, or the races or boxing matches, waiting for a car to overturn or for some guy to be carried out of the ring with nothing but mush left for brains. Oh, yeah, he and I are similar, quite alike. You see, it's in us all. A low pitch melody not often heard, but there just the same. In me it peaks and thuds, like drums and brass and strings. Don't fear it. Let it go. Give in to the beat and amplify. I tell you it's love of the finest kind.

So I've said my piece and I'll just add this: when they fasten my arms and ankles down and tighten the cap, I hope I feel the pain and delight in it before my brain sizzles to bacon, and may I smell the frying of my very own flesh. . . .

Dan Lowry came up with this story, talked about it forever, but he couldn't seem to get around to writing it. I listened to him tell me about it, and how he wanted to do it, and one day, at my house, I cornered him. I said, write it, man.

He didn't.

I said, want to write it together?

He liked the idea.

We worked on it together at my kitchen table, then he went home and worked on it on his own, and I did the same, and we took the best of what we were doing and made a story. I did a draft, gave it to Dan for the same. Then I did a polish.

Sent it to Twilight Zone.

I knew it was a sure sale.

It wasn't. But T. E. D. Klein, the editor at TZ, thought it would make a great movie.

We sent it out a few more places, but, no dice.

I put it in a drawer and pretty much forgot about it until one day Ed Gorman asked if I had anything for a book he was putting together called Stalkers.

I knew this was perfect for that book, but, my hopes weren't high. So far, no one had really shown any interest. Our best response was from Klein, about how it would make a neat movie.

Ed liked it, bought it, and it appeared in Stalkers. *Since that time it's been on audio, been reprinted a bit, and there's been a great comic book adaptation, and a new adaptation is in the works.*

There was even a bit of film interest, but, alas, it collapsed.

I believe T. E. D. Klein, or Ted, as most everyone knows him, was right.

It would make a neat film.

Bottom line. It's a tribute to the pulps and was written during the height of the CB craze, which is why there's so much CB lingo.

Pilots

with Dan Lowry

*M*ICKY WAS AT IT AGAIN. HIS SCREAMS ECHOED up the fuselage, blended with the wind roaring past the top gunner port. The Pilot released Sparks from his radio duty long enough to send him back to take care of and comfort Micky.

The day had passed slowly and they had passed it in the hanger, listening to the radios, taking turns at watch from the tower, making battle plans. Just after sundown they got into their gear and took off, waited high up in cover over the well-traveled trade lanes. Waited for prey.

Tonight they intended to go after a big convoy. Get as many kills as they could, then hit the smaller trade lanes later on, search out and destroy. With luck their craft would be covered with a horde of red kill marks before daybreak. At the thought of that, the Pilot formed the thing he used as a mouth into a smile. He was the one who painted the red slashes on the sides of their machine (war paint), and it was a joy to see them grow. It was his hope that some-day they would turn the craft from black to red.

Finally the Pilot saw the convoy. He called to Sparks.

In the rear, Micky had settled down to sobs and moans, had pushed the pain in the stumps of his legs aside, tightened his will to the mission at hand.

As Sparks came forward at a stoop, he reached down and patted Ted, the turret gunner, on the flight jacket, then settled back in with the radio.

"It's going to be a good night for hunting," Sparks said to the Pilot. "I've been intercepting enemy communiqués. There must be a hundred in our operational area. There are twelve in the present enemy convoy, sir. Most of the state escorts are to the north, around the scene of last night's sortie."

The Pilot nodded, painfully formed the words that came out of his fire-gutted throat. "It'll be a good night, Sparks. I can feel it."

"Death to the enemy," Sparks said. And the words were repeated as one by the crew.

So they sat high up, on the overpass, waiting for the convoy of trucks to pass below.

"This is the Tulsa Tramp. You got the Tulsa Tramp. Have I got a copy there? Come back."

"That's a big 10-4, Tramp. You got the L. A. Flash here."

"What's your 20, L. A.?"

"East bound and pounded down on this I-20, coming up on that 450 marker. How 'bout yourself, Tramp?"

"West bound for Dallas town with a truck load of cakes. What's the Smokey situation? Come back?"

"Got one at the Garland exit. Big ole bear. How's it look over your shoulder?"

"Got it clear, L. A., clear back to that Hallsville town. You got a couple County Mounties up there at the Owentown exit. Where's all the super troopers?"

"Haven't you heard, Tramp?"

"Heard what, L. A.? Come back."

"Up around I-30, that Mount Pleasant town. Didn't you know about Banana Peel?"

"Don't know Banana Peel. Come back with it."

"Black Bird got him."

"Black Bird?"

"You have been out of it."

"Been up New York way for a while, just pulled down and loaded up at Birmingham, heading out to the West Coast."

"Some psycho's knocking off truckers. Banana Peel was the last one. Someone's been nailing us right and left. Banana Peel's cab was shot to pieces, just like the rest. Someone claims he saw the car that got Banana Peel. A black Thunderbird, all cut down and rigged special. Over-long looking. Truckers have got to calling it the Black Bird. There's even rumor it's a ghost. Watch out for it."

"Ghosts don't chop down and rerig Thunderbirds. But I'll sure watch for it."

"10-4 on that. All we need is some nut case messing with us. Business is hard enough as it is."

"A big 10-4 there. Starting to fade, catch you on the flip-flop."

"10-4."

"10-4. Puttin' the pedal to the metal and gone."

The Tramp, driving a White Freight Liner equipped with shrunken head dangling from the cigarette lighter knob and a men's magazine fold-out taped to the cab ceiling, popped a Ronny Milsap tape into the deck, sang along with three songs and drowned Milsap out.

It was dead out there on the highway. Not a truck or car in sight. No stars above. Just a thick, black cloud cover with a moon hidden behind it.

Milsap wasn't cutting it. Tramp pulled out the tape and turned on the stereo, found a snappy little tune he could whistle along with. For some reason he felt like whistling, like making noise. He wondered if it had something to do with the business L. A. had told him about. The Black Bird.

Or perhaps it was just the night. Certainly it was unusual for the Interstate to be this desolate, this dead. It was as if his were the only vehicle left in the world. . . .

He saw something. It seemed to have appeared out of nowhere, had flicked beneath the orangish glow of the upcoming underpass lights. It looked like a car running fast without lights.

Tramp blinked. Had he imagined it? It had been so quick. Certainly only a madman would be crazy enough to drive that fast on the Interstate without lights.

A feeling washed over him that was akin to pulling out of a dive; like when he was in Nam and he flew down close to the foliage to deliver flaming death, then at the last moment he would lift his chopper skyward and leave the earth behind him in a burst of red-yellow flame. Then, cruising the Vietnamese skies, he could only feel relief that his hands had responded and he had not been peppered and salted all over Nam.

Tramp turned off the stereo and considered. A bead of sweat balled on his upper lip. *Perhaps he had just seen the Black Bird.*

". . . ought to be safe in a convoy this size . . ." the words filtered out of Tramp's C.B. He had been so lost in thought, he had missed the first part of the transmission. He turned it up. The chatter was furious. It was a convoy and its members were exchanging thoughts, stories, and good time rattle like a bunch of kids swapping baseball cards.

The twangy, scratchy voices were suddenly very comfortable; forced memories of Nam back deep in his head, kept that black memory-bat from fluttering.

He thought again of what he might have seen. But now he had passed beneath the underpass and there was nothing. No car. No shape in the night. Nothing.

Imagination, he told himself. He drove on, listening to the C.B.

The bead of sweat rolled cold across his lips and down his chin.

Tramp wasn't the only one who had seen something in the shadows, something like a car without lights. Sloppy Joe, the convoy's back door, had glimpsed an odd shape in his sideview mirror, something coming out of the glare of the overpass lights, something as sleek and deadly looking as a hungry barracuda.

"Breaker 1-9, this is Sloppy Joe, your back door."

"Ah, come ahead, back door, this is Pistol Pete, your front door. Join the conversation."

"Think I might have something here. Not sure. Thought I saw something in the sideview, passing under those overpass lights."

Moment of silence.

"You say, think you saw? Come back."

"Not sure. If I did, it was running without lights."

"Smokey?" another trucker asked.

"Don't think so . . . Now wait a minute. I see something now. A pair of dim, red lights."

"Uh oh, cop cherries," a new trucker's voice added.

"No. Not like that."

Another moment of silence.

Sloppy Joe again: "Looks a little like a truck using nothing but its running lights . . . but they're hung too far down for that . . . and they're shaped like eyes."

"Eyes! This is Pistol Pete, come back."

"Infrared lights, Pistol Pete, that's what I'm seeing."

"Have . . . have we got the Black Bird here?"

Tramp, listening to the C.B., felt that pulling-out-of-a-dive sensation again. He started to reach for his mike, tell them he was their back door, but he clenched the wheel harder instead. No. He was going to stay clear of this. What could a lone car—if in fact it was a car—do to a convoy of big trucks anyway?

The C.B. chattered.

"This is Sloppy Joe. Those lights are moving up fast."

"The Black Bird?" asked Pistol Pete.

"Believe we got a big positive on that."

"What can he do to a convoy of trucks anyway," said another trucker.

My sentiments exactly, thought Tramp.

"Pick you off one by one," came a voice made of smoke and hot gravel.

"What, back door?"

"Not me, Pistol Pete."

"Who? Bear Britches? Slipped Disk? Merry—"

"None of them. It's me, the Black Bird."

"This is Sloppy Joe. It's the Black Bird, all right. Closing on my tail, pulling alongside"

"Watchyerself!"

"I can see it now . . . running alongside . . . I can make out some slash marks—"

"Confirmed kills," said the Pilot. *"If I were an artist, I'd paint little trucks."*

"Back door, back door! This is Pistol Pete. Come in."

"Sloppy Joe here . . . There's a man with a gun in the sunroof."

"Run him off the road, Sloppy Joe! Ram him!"

Tramp, his window down, cool breeze blowing against his face, heard three quick, flat snaps. Over the whine of the wind and the roar of the engine, they sounded not unlike the rifle fire he had heard over the wind and the rotor blades of his copter in Nam. And he thought he had seen the muzzle blast of at least one of those shots. Certainly he had seen something light up the night.

"I'm hit! Hit!" Sloppy Joe said.

"What's happening? Come back, Sloppy Joe. This is Pistol Pete. What's happening?"

"Hit . . . can't keep on the road."

"Shut down!"

Tramp saw an arc of flame fly high and wide from the dark T-bird—which looked like little more than an elongated shadow racing along the highway—and strike Sloppy Joe's truck. The fire boomed suddenly, licked the length of the truck, blossomed in the wind. A Molotov, thought Tramp.

Tramp pulled over, tried to gear down. Cold sweat popped on his face like measles, his hands shook on the wheel.

Sloppy Joe's Mack had become a quivering, red flower of flame. It whipped its tail, jackknifed and flipped, rolled like a toy truck across the concrete highway divider. When it stopped rolling, it was wrapped in fire and black smoke, had transformed from glass and metal to heat and wreckage.

The Bird moved on, slicing through the smoke, avoiding debris, blending with the night like a dark ghost.

As Tramp passed the wrecked truck he glimpsed something moving in the cab, a blackened, writhing thing that had once been human. But it moved only for an instant and was still.

Almost in a whisper, came: "This is Bear Britches. I'm the back door now. Sloppy Joe's in flames . . . Gone . . ."

Those flames, that burnt-to-a-crisp body, sent Tramp back in time, back to Davy Cluey that hot-as-hell afternoon in Nam. Back to when God gave Tramp his personal demon.

They had been returning from a routine support mission, staying high enough to avoid small arms fire. Their rockets and most of their M-60 ammo were used up. The two choppers were scurrying back to base when they picked up the urgent call. The battered remains of a platoon were pinned down on a small hill off Highway One. If the stragglers didn't get a dust-off in a hurry, the Cong were going to dust them off for good.

He and Davy had turned back to aid the platoon, and soon they were twisting and turning in the air like great dragonflies performing a sky ballet. The Cong's fire buzzed around them.

Davy sat down first and the stranded Marines rushed the copter. That's when the Cong hit.

Why they hadn't waited until he too was on the ground he'd never know. Perhaps the sight of all those Marines—far too many to cram into the already heavily manned copter—was just too tempting for patience. The Cong sent a stream of liquid fire rolling lazily out of the jungle, and it had entered Davy's whirling rotors. When it hit the blades it suddenly transformed into a spinning parasol of flames.

That was his last sight of the copter and Davy. He had lifted upward and flown away. To this day, the image of that machine being showered by flames came back to him in vivid detail. Sometimes it seemed he was no longer driving on the highway, but flying in Nam, the rhythmic beat of the tires rolling over tar strips in the highway would pick up tempo until they became the twisting chopper blades, and soon, out beyond the windshield, the highway would fade and the cement would become the lush jungles of Nam.

Sometimes, the feeling was so intense he'd have to pull over until it passed.

A C.B. voice tossed Nam out of Tramp's head.

"This is Bear Britches. The Bird is moving in on me."

"Pistol Pete here. Get away, get away."

"He's alongside me now. Can't shake him. Something sticking out of a hole in the trunk—a rifle barrel!"

A shot could be heard clearly over the open airwaves, then the communications button was released and there was silence. Ahead of him Tramp could see the convoy and he could see the eighteen wheeler that was its back door. The truck suddenly swerved, as if to ram the Black Bird, but Tramp saw a red burst leap from the Bird's trunk, and instantly the eighteen wheeler was swerving back, losing control. It crossed the meridian, whipping its rear end like a crocodile's tail, plowed through a barbwire fence and smacked a row of pine trees with a sound like a thunderclap. The cab smashed up flat as a pancake. Tramp knew no one could have lived through that.

And now ahead of him, Tramp saw another Molotov flipping through the air, and in an instant, another truck was out of commission, wearing flames and flipping in a frenzy along the side of the road. Tramp's last memory of the blazing truck was its tires, burning brightly, spinning wildly around and around like little inflamed Ferris wheels.

"Closing on me," came a trucker's voice. "The sonofabitch is closing on me. Help me! God, someone help me here."

Tramp remembered a similar communication from Davy that day in Nam; the day he had lifted up to the sky and flown his bird away and left Davy there beneath that parasol of fire.

Excited chatter sounded over the airwaves as the truckers tried to summon up the highway boys, tried to call for help.

Tramp saw a sign for a farm road exit, half a mile away. The stones settled in his gut again, his hands filmed with sweat. It was like that day in Nam, when he had the choice to turn back and help or run like hell.

No trucks took the exit. Perhaps their speed was up too much to attempt it. But he was well back of them and the Bird. What reason did he have to close in on the Bird? What could he do? As it was, the Bird could see his lights now and they might pop a shot at him any second.

Tramp swallowed. It was him or them.

He slowed, took the exit at fifty, which was almost too fast, and the relief that first washed over him turned sour less than a second later. He felt just like he had that day in Nam when he had lifted up and away, saved himself from Death at the expense of Davy.

"Report!" said the Pilot.

Through the headphones came Micky's guttural whine. "Tail gunner reporting, sir. Three of the enemy rubbed out, sir."

"Confirmed," came the voice of the turret gunner. "I have visual confirmation on tail gunner's report. Enemy formation affecting evasive maneuvers. Have sighted two more sets of enemy lights approaching on the port quarter. Request permission to break off engagement with forward enemy formation and execute strafing attack on approaching formation."

"Permission granted," said the Pilot. "Sparks! Report State Escort whereabouts."

"Catching signals of approaching State Escorts, sir. ETA three minutes."

"Number of Escorts?"

"Large squadron, sir."

"Pilot to flight crew. Change in orders. Strafe forward formation, to prepare to peel off at next exit."

The Bird swooped down on the forward truck, the turret gun slamming blast after blast into the semi's tires. The truck was suddenly riding on the rims. Steel hit concrete and sparks popped skyward like overheated fireflies.

The Bird moved around the truck just as it lost control and went through a low guardrail fence and down into a deep ditch.

Black smoke boiled up from the Black Bird's tires, mixed with the night. A moment later the sleek car was running alongside another truck. The turret gunner's weapon barked like a nervous dog, kept barking as it sped past the trucks and made its way to the lead semi. The turret gunner barked a few more shots as they whipped in front of the truck, and the tail gunner put twenty fast rounds through the windshield. Even as the driver slumped over the semi's wheel and the truck went barreling driverless down the highway, the Bird lost sight of it and took a right exit, and like a missile, was gone.

Black against black, the Bird soared, and inside the death machine the Pilot, with the internal vision of his brain, turned the concrete before him into a memory:

Once he had been whole, a tall, young man with a firm body and a head full of Technicolor dreams. The same had been true of his comrades. There had been a time when these dreams had been guiding lights. They had wanted to fly, had been like birds in the nest longing for the time when they would try their wings; thinking of that time, living for that time when they would soar in silver arrows against a fine blue sky, or climb high up to the face of the moon.

Each of them had been in the Civil Air Patrol. Each of them had hours of air time, and each of them had plans for the Air Force. And these plans had carried them through many a day and through many a hard exam and they had talked these plans until they felt they were merely reciting facts from a future they had visited.

But then there was the semi and that very dark night.

The four of them had been returning from Barksdale Air Force Base. They had made a deal with the recruiter to keep them together throughout training, and their spirits were high.

And the driver who came out of the darkness, away from the honky-tonk row known as Hell's Half Mile, had been full of spirits too.

There had been no lights, just a sudden looming darkness that turned into a White Freight Liner crossing the middle of the highway; a stupid, metallic whale slapdash in the center of their path.

The night screamed with an explosion of flesh, metal, glass, and chrome. Black tire smoke boiled to the heavens and down from the heavens came a rain of sharp, hot things that engulfed the four; and he, the one now called the Pilot, awoke to whiteness. White everywhere, and it did not remind him of cleanliness, this whiteness. No. It was empty, this whiteness, empty like the ever-hungry belly of time; and people floated by him in white, not angel-white, but wraith-white; and the pain came to live with him and it called his body home.

When enough of the pain had passed and he was fully aware, he found a monster one morning in the mirror. A one-legged thing with a face and body like melted plastic. But the eyes. Those sharp hawk eyes, that had anticipated seeing the world from the clouds, were as fine as ever; little green gems that gleamed from an over-cooked meat rind.

And the others:

Sparks had lost his left arm and half his head was metal. He had been castrated by jagged steel. Made sad jokes about being the only man who could keep his balls in a plastic bag beside his bed.

Ted had metal clamps on his legs and a metal jaw. His scalp had been peeled back like an orange. Skin grafts hadn't worked. Too burned. From now on, across his head—like some sort of toothless mouth—would be a constantly open wound behind which a smooth, white skull would gleam.

Micky was the worst. Legs fried off. One eye cooked to boiled egg consistency—a six-minute egg. Face like an exploding sore. Throat and vocal cords nearly gone. His best sound was a high, piercing whine.

Alone they were fragments of humanity. Puzzle parts of a horrid whole.

Out of this vengeance grew.

They took an old abandoned silo on Spark's farm—inherited years back when his father had died—fixed it up to suit their needs; had the work done and used Spark's money.

They also pooled their accounts, and with the proper help, they had elevators built into the old gutted silo. Had telescopes installed. Radios. And later they bought maps and guns. Lots of guns. They bought explosives and made super Molotovs of fuel and plastic explosives. Bad business.

And the peculiar talents that had been theirs individually, became a singular thing that built gadgets and got things done. So before long, the Pilot, stomping around on his metallic leg, looking like a run-through-the-wringer Ahab, became their boss. They cut Micky's T-Bird down and rerigged it, rebuilt it as a war machine. And they began to kill. Trucks died on the highway, became skeletons, black charred frames. And the marks on the sides of the Black Bird grew and grew as they went about their stalks. . . .

Highway now. Thoughts tucked away. Cruising easily along the concrete sky. Pilot and crew.

Tramp felt safe, but he also felt low, real low. He kept wondering about Nam, about the trucks, about that turnoff he'd taken a few miles and long minutes back, but his considerations were cut short when fate took a hand.

To his left he saw eyes, red eyes, wheeling out of a dark connecting road, and the eyes went from dim to sudden-bright (fuck this sneaking around), and as Tramp passed that road, the eyes followed and in the next instant they were looking up his tailpipe, and Tramp knew damn good and well whose eyes they were, and he was scared.

Cursing providence, Tramp put the pedal to the metal and

glanced into his sideview mirror and saw the eyes were very close. Then he looked forward and saw that the grade was climbing. He could feel the truck losing momentum. The Bird was winging around on the left side.

The hill was in front of him now, and though he had the gas pedal to the floor, things were Slow-City, and the truck was chugging, and behind him, coming ass-over-tires was the Black Bird.

Tramp trembled, thought: *This is redemption.* The thought hung in his head like a shoe on a peg. It was another chance for him to deal the cards and deal them right.

Time started up for Tramp again, and he glanced into the sideview mirror at the Bird, whipped his truck hard left in a wild move that nearly sent the White Freight Liner side-over-side. He hit the Bird a solid bump and drove it off the road, almost into a line of trees. The Bird's tires spat dirt and grass in dark gouts. The Bird slowed, fell back.

Tramp cheered, tooted his horn like a mad man and made that hill; two toots at the top and he dipped over the rise and gave two toots at the bottom.

The Black Bird made the road again and the Pilot gave the car full throttle. In a moment the Bird found its spot on Tramp's ass.

Tramp's moment of triumph passed. That old Boogy Man sat down on his soul again. Sweat dripped down his face and hung on his nose like a dingleberry on an ass hair, finally fell with a plop on the plastic seat cover between Tramp's legs, and in the fearful silence of the cab the sound was like a boulder dropping on hard ground.

Tramp's left side window popped and became a close-weave net of cracks and clusters. A lead wasp jumped around the cab and died somewhere along the floorboard. It was a full five seconds before Tramp realized he'd been grazed across the neck, just under his right ear. The glass from the window began to fall out like slow, heavy rain.

Tramp glanced left and saw the Bird was on him again, and he tried to whip in that direction, tried to nail the bastard again. But the Bird wasn't having any. It moved forward and away, surged around in front of Tramp.

The Bird, now directly in front of him, farted a red burst from its trunk. The front window of the truck became a spiraling web and the collar of Tramp's shirt lifted as if plucked by an unseen hand. The bullet slammed into the seat and finally into the back wall of the truck.

The glass was impossible to see out of. Tramp bent forward and tried to look out of a small area of undamaged windshield. The Bird's gun farted again, and Tramp nearly lost control as fragments flew in on him like shattered moonlight. Something hot and sharp went to live in his right shoulder, down deep next to the bone. Tramp let out a scream and went momentarily black, nearly lost the truck.

Carving knives of wind cut through the windshield and woke him, watered his eyes and made the wound ache like a bad tooth. He thought: *The next pop that comes I won't hear, because that will be the one that takes my skull apart, and they say the one that gets you is the one you don't hear.*

But suddenly the two asslights of the bird fell away and dipped out of sight.

The road fell down suddenly into a dip, and though it was not enormous, he had not expected it and his speed was up full tilt. The truck cab lifted into the air and shot forward and dragged the whipping cargo trailer behind it. As the cab came down, Tramp fully expected the trailer to keep whipping and jackknife him off the road, but instead it came down and fell in line behind the cab and Tramp kept going.

Ahead a narrow bridge appeared, its suicide rails painted phosphorescent white. The bridge appeared just wide enough to keep the guardrail post from slicing the door handles off a big truck.

Tramp's hand flew to the gearshift. He shifted and gassed and thought: *This is it, the moment of truth, the big casino, die dog or eat the hatchet; my big shot to repay the big fuckup.* Tramp shifted again and gave the White Freight Liner all it had.

The White Freight Liner was breathing up the tailpipe of the Black Bird and the Pilot was amazed at how much speed the driver was getting out of that rig; a part of him appreciated the skill involved in that. No denying, that sonofabitch could drive.

Then the Pilot caught a scream in his ruptured throat. They were coming up on the bridge, and there were no lefts or rights to take them away from that. The bridge was narrow. Tight. Room for one, and the Pilot knew what the truck driver had in mind. The truck was hauling ass, pushing to pass, trying to run alongside the Bird, planning to push it through the rails and down twenty feet into a wet finale of fast-racing creek. The senseless bastard was going to try and get the Bird if he had to go with it.

The Pilot smiled. He could understand that. He smelled death, and it had the odor of gasoline fumes, burning rubber, and flying shit.

Behind the Bird, like a leviathan of the concrete seas, came the White Freight Liner. It bumped the Bird's rear and knocked the car to the right, and in that moment, the big truck, moving as easily as if it were a compact car, came around on the Bird's left.

The semi began to bear right, pushing at the Bird. The Pilot knew his machine was fated to kiss the guardrail post.

"Take the wheel!" the Pilot screamed to Sparks, and he rose up to poke his head through the sunroof, pull on through and crawl along top. He grabbed the semi's left sideview mirror and allowed the truck's momentum to pull him away from the car, keeping his good and his ruined leg high to keep from being pinched in half between the two machines.

Sparks leaped for the steering wheel, got a precious grip on it even as the Pilot was dangling on top of the car, reaching for the truck's mirror frame. But Sparks saw immediately that his grabbing the wheel meant nothing. He and the others were goners; he couldn't get the Bird ahead of the truck and there just wasn't room for two, they were scraping the guardrail post as it was, and now he felt the Bird going to the right and it hit the first post with a *kaplodata* sound, then the car gathered in three more posts, and just for an instant, Sparks thought he might be able to keep the Bird on the bridge, get ahead of the semi. But it was a fleeting fancy. The Bird's right wheels were out in the air with nothing to grab, and the Bird smashed two more posts, one of which went through the window, then hurtled off the bridge. In dim chorus the crew of the Bird screamed all the way down to where the car struck the water and went nose first into the creek bed. Then the car's rear end came down and the car settled under the water, except for a long strip of roof.

No one swam out.

The Pilot saw the car go over out of the corner of his eye, heard the screams, but so be it. He has tasted doom before. It is his job to kill trucks.

Tramp jerked his head to the right, saw the maimed face of the Pilot, and for one brief moment, he felt as if he were looking not at a face, but into the cold, dark depths of his very own soul.

The Pilot smashed the window with the hilt of a knife he pulled from a scabbard on his metal leg, and started scuttling through the window.

Tramp lifted his foot off the gas and kicked out at the door handle, and the door swung open and carried the Pilot with it. The Pilot and the door hit a guardrail post and sparks flew up from the Pilot's metal leg as it touched concrete.

The door swung back in, the Pilot still holding on, and Tramp kicked again, and out went the door, and another post hit the Pilot and carried him and the door away, down into the water below.

And in the same moment, having stretched too far to kick the door, and having pulled the wheel too far right, the White Freight Liner went over the bridge and smashed half in the water and half out.

Crawling through the glassless front of the truck, Tramp rolled out onto the hood and off, landed on the wet ground next to the creek.

Rising up on his knees and elbows, Tramp looked out at the creek and saw the Pilot shoot up like a porpoise, splash back down and thrash wildly in the water, thrashing in a way that let Tramp know that the Pilot's body was little more than shattered bones and ruptured muscles held together by skin and clothes.

The Pilot looked at him, and Tramp thought he saw the Pilot nod, though he could not be sure. And just before the Pilot went under as if diving, the tip of his metal leg winking up and then falling beneath the water, Tramp lifted his hand and shot the Pilot the finger.

"Jump up on that and spin around," Tramp said.

The Pilot did not come back up.

Tramp eased onto his back and felt the throbbing of the bullet wound and thought about the night and what he had done. In the distance, but distinct, he could hear the highway whine of truck tires on the Interstate.

Tramp smiled at that. Somehow it struck him as amusing. He closed his eyes, and just before he drifted into an exhausted sleep, he said aloud, "How about that, Davy? How about that?"

This is a kind of prose poem. Or, it's probably as close as I will ever come to a poem. I can't tell you the exact influence, but I think it had to do a bit with All Quiet on the Western Front, *which I had recently read.*

My situation is placed in the future, and bears little resemblance to the novel that inspired it. But like the classic novel, my little tale is about the ugliness of war; necessary or unnecessary, it's always ugly.

In the Cold, Dark Time

*I*T WAS THE TIME OF THE ICING, AND THE SNOW and razor-winds blew across the lands and before and behind them came the war and the war went across the lands worse than the ice, like a plague, and there were those who took in the plague and died by it, or were wounded deeply by it, and I was one of the wounded, and at first I wished I was one of the dead.

I lay in bed hour on hour in the poorly heated hospital and watched the night come, then the day, then the night, then the day, and no time of night or day seemed lost to me, for I could not sleep, but could only cough out wads of blood-tainted phlegm and saliva that rose from my injured lungs like blobby bubbly monsters to remind me of my rendering flesh. I lay there and prayed for death, for I knew all my life had been lost to me, and that my job in the war was no longer mine, and when the war was over, if it was ever over, I would never return to civilized life to continue the same necessary job I had pursued during wartime. The job with the children. The poor children. Millions of them. Parentless, homeless, forever being pushed onward by the ice and the war. It was a horror to see them. Little, frostbitten waifs without food or shelter or good coats and there was no food or shelter or good coats to give them. Nothing to offer them but the war and a cold, slow death.

There were more children than adults now, and the adults were about war and there were only a few like myself there to help them. One of the few that could be spared for the Army's Children Corp. And now I could help no one, not even myself.

In the bed beside me in the crumbling, bomb-shook hospital, was an old man with his arm blown off at the elbow and his face splotched with the familiar frostbite of a front-line man. He lay turned toward me, staring, but not speaking. And in the night, I would turn, and there would be his eyes, lit up by the night-lamp or by the moonlight, and that glow of theirs would strike me and I would imagine they contained the sparks of incendiary bombs for melting ice, or the red-hot destruction of rockets and bullets. In the daylight the sunlight toured the perimeters of his eyes like a fire-fight, but the night was the worst, for then they were the brightest and the strangest.

I thought I should say something to him, but could never bring myself to utter a word because I was too lost in my misery and waiting for the change of day to night, night to day, and I was thinking of the children. Or I tell myself that now. My thoughts were mostly on me and how sad it was that a man like me had been born into a time of war and that none of what was good in me and great about me could be given to the world.

The children crossed my mind, but I must admit I saw them less as my mission in life than as crosses I had borne on my back while climbing Christlike toward the front lines. Heavy crosses that had caused me to fall hard to the ground, driving the pain into my lungs, putting me here where I would die in inches far from home.

"Why do you fret for yourself?" the old man said one morning. I turned and looked at him and his eyes were as animal bright as ever and there was no expression on his crunched, little face.

"I fret for the children."

"Ah," he said. "The children. Your job in the Corp."

I said nothing in reply and he said not another word until the middle of the night when I drifted into sleep momentarily, for all my sleep was momentary, and opened my eyes to the lamplight and the cold hospital air. I pulled a Kleenex from the box beside my bed and coughed blood into it.

"You are getting better," he said.

"I'm dying," I said.

"No. You are getting better. You hardly cough at all. Your sleep is longer. You used to cough all night."

"You're a doctor, I suppose?"

"No, but I am a soldier. Or was. Now I am a useless old man with no arm."

"In the old days a man your age would have been retired or put behind a desk. Not out on the front lines."

"I suppose you're right. But this is not the old days. This is now, and I'm finished anyway because of the arm."

"And I'm finished because of my wound."

"The lungs heal faster than anything. You are only finished if you are too bitter to heal. To be old and bitter is all right. It greases the path to the other side. To be young and bitter is foolish."

"How do you know so much about me?"

"I listen to the nurses and I listen to you and I observe."

"Have you nothing else to do but meddle in my affairs?"

"No."

"Leave me be."

"I would if I could, but I'm an old man and will not live long anyway, wounded or not. I have the pains of old age and no family and nothing I would be able to do if I leave here. All I know is the life of a soldier. But you will recover if you believe you will recover. It is up to you now."

"So you are a doctor?"

"An old soldier has seen wounds and sickness, and he knows a man that can get well if he chooses to get well. A coward will die. Which are you?"

I didn't answer and he didn't repeat the question. I turned my back to him and went to sleep and later in the night I heard him calling.

"Young man."

I lay there and listened but did not move.

"I think you can hear me and this may be the last I have to say on the matter. You are getting better. You sleep better. You cough less. The wound is healing. It may not matter what your attitude is now, you may heal anyway, but let me tell you this, if you heal, you must heal with your soul intact. You must not lose your love for the children, no matter what you've seen. It isn't your wound that aches you, makes you want to die, it's the war. There are few who are willing to do your job, to care for the children. They need you. They run in hungry, naked packs, and all that is between them and suffering is the Children's Corp and people like you. The love of children, the need not to see them hungry and in pain, is a necessary human trait if we are to survive as a people. When, if, this war is over, it must not be a war that has poisoned our hopes for the future. Get well. Do your duty."

I lay there when he was finished and thought about all I had done for the children and thought about the war and all that had to be done afterwards, knew then that my love for the children, their needs, were the obsessions of my life. They were my reason to live, more than just living to exist. I knew then that I had to let their cause stay with me, had to let my hatred of the world and the war go, because there were the children.

The next day they came and took the old man away. He had pulled the bandage off of the nub of his arm during the night and chewed the cauterized wound open with the viciousness of a tiger and had bled to death. His sheets were the color of gunmetal rust when they came for him and pulled the stained sheet over his head and rolled him away.

They brought in a young, wounded pilot then, and his eyes were cold and hard and the color of grave dirt. I spoke to him and he wouldn't speak back, but I kept at it, and finally he yelled at me, and said he didn't want to live, that he had seen too much terror to want to go on, but I kept talking to him, and soon he was chattering like a machine gun and we had long conversations into the night about women and chess and the kind of beers we were missing back home. And he told me his hopes for after the war, and I told him mine. Told him how I would get out of my bed and go back to the front lines to help the refugee children, and after the war I would help those who remained.

A month later they let me out of the bed to wander.

I think often of the old man now, especially when the guns boom about the camp and I'm helping the children, and sometimes I think of the young man and that I may have helped do for him with a few well-placed words what the old man did for me, but mostly I think of the old one and what he said to me the night before he finished his life. It's a contradiction in a way, him giving me life and taking his own, but he knew that my life was important to the children. I wish I had turned and spoken to him, but that opportunity is long gone.

Each time they bring the sad, little children in to me, one at a time, and I feed them and hold them, I pray the war will end and there will be money for food and shelter instead of the care of soldiers and the making of bullets, but wishes are wishes, and what is, is.

And when I put the scarf around the children's necks and tighten it until I have eased their pain, I am overcome with an even simpler wish for spare bullets or drugs to make it quicker, and I have to mentally close my ears to the drumming of their little feet and shut my nose to the smell of their defecation, but I know that this is the best way, a warm meal, a moment of hope, a quick, dark surrender, the only mercy available to them, and when I take the scarf from their sad, little necks and lay them aside, I think again of the old man and the life he gave me back and the mercy he gives the children through me.

This is an old story I revised for a short story collection titled Fistful of Stories. *The book came out spelled* A Fist Full of Stories. *I thought that fit the idea I had in mind, but everyone just thought it was a misspelling.*

That is neither here nor there.

"Bar Talk" is just what it is.

A few minutes of story that I hope you'll enjoy.

Bar Talk

*H*EY, WHAT'S HAPPENING?
Not much, eh?

No, no, we haven't met. But I'm here to brighten your day. I got a story you aren't going to believe . . . No, no, I'm not looking for money, and I'm not drunk. This is my first beer. I just seen you come in, and I was sitting over there by my lonesome, and I says to myself, self, there's a guy that could use some company.

Sure you can. Everyone needs some company. And you look like a guy that likes to hear a first-class story, and that's just the kind of story I got: first class.

Naw, this isn't going to take too long. I'll keep it short.

You see, I'm a spy.

No, no, no. Not that kind of spy. No double-ought stuff. I'm not working for the CIA or the KGB. I work for Mudziplickt.

Yeah, I know you never heard of it. Few have.

Just us Martians.

Oh yeah, that's right. I said Martians. I'm from Mars.

No, I tell you, I'm not drunk.

Well, it doesn't matter what the scientists or the space probes say. I'm from Mars.

You see, we Martians have been monitoring this planet of yours for years, and now with you guys landing up there, saying there's no life and all, we figure things are getting too close for comfort, so we've decided to beat you to it and come down here. I'm what you might call part of the advance landing force. A spy, so to speak. You see, we Martians aren't visible to your satellite cameras. Has to do with light waves, and an ability we have to make ourselves blend with the landscape. Chameleon-like, you might say. And we'd just scare you anyway if you saw us. We'd look pretty strange to you Earthlings.

Oh this. This isn't the real me. Just a body I made up out of protoplasmic energy.

The way I talk? Oh, I know your culture well. I've studied it for years. I've even got a job.

Huh?

Oh. Well, I'm telling you all this for one simple reason. We Martians can adapt to almost everything on this world—even all this oxygen. But the food, that's a problem. We find alcohol agrees pretty well with us, but the food makes us sick. Sort of like you going down to Mexico and eating something off a street vendor's cart and getting ill . . . only it's a lot worse for us.

Blood is the ticket.

Yeah, human blood.

Find that funny, huh? Vampires from Mars? Yeah, does sound like a cheap science-fiction flick, doesn't it?

You see—ho, hold it. Almost fell off your stool there. No, I don't think the beer here is that strong. There, just put your head on the bar. Yeah, weak, I understand. I know why you're feeling that way. It's this little tube that comes out of my side, through the slit in my clothing. I stuck it in you when I sat down here. Doesn't hurt. Has a special coating on it, a natural anesthesia, you might say. That's why you didn't notice. Actually, if you could see me without this human shell, you'd find I'm covered with the things. Sort of like a big jellyfish, only cuter.

Just rest.

No use trying to call out. Nothing will work now. The muscles in your throat just won't have enough strength to make your voice work. They're paralyzed. The fluid that keeps the tube from hurting you also deadens the nerves and muscles in your body, while allowing me to draw your blood.

There's some folks looking over here right now, but they aren't thinking a thing about it. They can't see the tube from this angle; just me smiling, and you looking like a passed-out drunk. They think it's kind of funny, actually. They've seen drunks before.

Yeah, that's it. Just relax. Go with the flow, as you people say. Can't really do anything else but that anyway. Won't be a drop of blood left in you in a few seconds anyway. I'll have it all and I'll feel great. Only food here that really agrees with us. That and a spot of alcohol now and then.

But I've told you all that. There, I'm finished. I feel like a million dollars.

Don't know if you can still hear me or not, but I'm taking the tube out now. Thanks for the nourishment. Nothing personal. And don't worry about the beer you ordered. I'll pay for it on the way out. It's the least I can do.

Ever feel like no one's paying attention? That you're lost in the crowd? Everyone feels that way from time to time, but there are people who feel that way all the time.
Shy people.
Insecure people.
I've known them.
That knowledge inspired this story.

Listen

*T*HE PSYCHIATRIST WORE BLUE, THE COLOR OF Merguson's mood.

"Mr. . . . uh?" the psychiatrist asked.

"Merguson. Floyd Merguson."

"Sure, Mr. . . ."

"Merguson."

"Right. Come into the office."

It was a sleek office full of sleek black chairs the texture of a lizard's underbelly. The walls were decorated with paintings of explosive color; a metal-drip sculpture resided on the large walnut desk. And there was the couch, of course, just like in the movies. It was chocolate-brown with throw pillows at each end. It looked as if you could drift down into it and disappear in its softness.

They sat in chairs, however. The psychiatrist on his side of the desk, Merguson on the client's side.

The psychiatrist was a youngish man with a fine touch of premature white at the temples. He looked every inch the intelligent professional.

"Now," the psychiatrist said, "what exactly is your problem?"

Merguson fiddled his fingers, licked his lips, and looked away.

"Come on, now. You came here for help, so let's get started."

"Well," Merguson said cautiously. "No one takes me seriously."

"Tell me about it."

"No one listens to me. I can't take it anymore. Not another moment. I feel like I'm going to explode if I don't get help. Sometimes I just want to yell out, *Listen to me!*"

Merguson leaned forward and said confidentially, "Actually, I think it's a disease. Yeah, I know how that sounds, but I believe it is, and I believe I'm approaching the terminal stage of the illness.

"I got this theory that there are people others don't notice, that they're almost invisible. There's just something genetically wrong with them that causes them to go unnoticed. Like a little clock that ticks inside them, and the closer it gets to the hour hand the more unnoticed these people become.

"I've always had the problem of being shy and introverted—and that's the first sign of the disease. You either shake it early or you don't. If you don't, it just grows like cancer and consumes you. With me the problem gets worse every year, and lately by the moment.

"My wife, she used to tell me it's all in my head, but lately she doesn't bother. But let me start at the first, when I finally decided I was ill, that the illness was getting worse and that it wasn't just in my head, not some sort of complex.

"Just last week I went to the butcher, the butcher I've been going to for ten years. We were never chummy, no one has ever been chummy to me but my wife, and she married me for my money. I was at least visible then; I mean you had to go to at least some effort to ignore me, but God, it's gotten worse . . .

"I'm off the track. I went to the butcher, asked him for some choice cuts of meat. Another man comes in while I'm talking to him and asks for a pound of hamburger. Talks right over me, mind you. What happens? You guessed it. The butcher starts shooting the breeze with the guy, wraps up a pound of hamburger and hands it over to him!

"I ask him about my order and he says, 'Oh, I forgot.' "

Merguson lit a cigarette and held it between unsteady fingers after a long, deep puff. "I tell you, he waited on three other people before he finally got to me, and then he got my order wrong, and I must have told him three times, at least.

"It's more than I can stand, Doc. Day after day people not noticing me, and it's getting worse all the time. Yesterday I went to a movie and I asked for a ticket and it happened. I mean I went out completely, went transparent, invisible. I mean completely. This was the first time. The guy just sits there behind the glass, like he's looking right through me. I asked him for a ticket again. Nothing.

"I was angry, I'll tell you. I just walked right on toward the door. Things had been getting me down bad enough without not being able to take off and go to a movie and relax. I thought I'd show him. Just walk right in. Then they'd sell me a ticket.

"No one tried to stop me. No one seemed to know I was there. I didn't bother with the concession stand. No one would have waited on me anyway.

"Well, that was the first time of the complete fadeouts. And I remember when I was leaving the movie, I got this funny idea. I went into the bathroom and looked in the mirror. I swear to you, Doc, on my mother's grave, there wasn't an image in the mirror. I gripped the sink to keep upright, and when I looked up again I was fading in, slowly. Well, I didn't stick around to see my face come into view. I left there and went straight home.

"That afternoon was the corker. My wife, Connie, I know she's been seeing another man. Why not? She can't see me. And when she can I don't have the presence of a one-watt bulb. I came home from the movie and she's all dressed up and talking on the phone.

"I say, 'Who are you talking to?' "

Merguson crushed his cigarette out in the ashtray on the psychiatrist's desk. "Doesn't say doodly squat, Doc. Not a word. I'm mad as hell. I go upstairs and listen on the extension. It's a man, and they're planning a date.

"I broke in over the line and started yelling at them. Guess what? The guy says, 'Do you hear a buzzing or something or other?' 'No,' she says. And they go right on with their plans.

"I was in a homicidal rage. I went downstairs and snatched the phone out of her hand and threw it across the room. I wrecked furniture and busted up some lamps and expensive pottery. Just made a general wreck out of the place.

"She screamed then, Doc. I tell you she screamed good. But then she says the thing that makes me come here. 'Oh God,' she says. 'Ghost! Ghost in this house!'

"That floored me, and I knew I was invisible again. I went upstairs and looked in the bathroom mirror. Sure enough. Nothing there. So I waited until I faded back and I called your secretary. It took me five tries before she finally wrote my name down, gave me an appointment. It was worse than when I tried to get the meat from the butcher. So I hurried right over. I had to get this out. I swear I'm not going crazy, it's a disease, and it's getting worse and worse and worse.

"So what can I do, Doc? How can I handle this? I know it's not in my head, and I've got to have some advice. Please, Doc. Say something. Tell me what to do. I've never been this desperate in my entire life. I might fade out again and not come back."

The psychiatrist took his hand from his chin where it had been resting. "Wha. . . ? Sorry. I must have dozed. What was it again, Mr. . . . uh?"

Merguson dove across the desk, clawing for the psychiatrist's throat.

Later when the law came and found the psychiatrist strangled and slumped across his desk, his secretary said "Funny, I don't remember anyone coming in or leaving. Couldn't have come in while I was here. He had an appointment with a Mr. . . . uh." She looked at the appointment book. "A Mr. Merguson. But he never showed."

This one came to me in a flash, and like many stories of this period, it was written in a flash. And, like most stories of this period, it pretty much came out of the typewriter finished, and went into an envelope and was gone, leaving me with a faded carbon copy only.

"The Dump" was a story that I sent in without even having a copy. I just wrote it and sent it. I had trained myself to come up with "clever" ideas and to write them out almost as fast as I could think of them. It was the only way to sell enough short stories to make any kind of money or draw any attention to my name.

Fortunately, I had the knack for it and the bulk of these stories turned out well.

They were a great training ground for writing longer, more ambitious stories later, and of course, novels. I wrote chapters for my early books almost as if I were writing short stories, trying to pull the reader in, make them want to read more, get to that next short story like chapter.

My intro is getting as long as this story, so, it's time to move on.

Personality Problem

*Y*EAH, I KNOW, DOC. I LOOK TERRIBLE AND don't smell any better. But you would, too, if you stayed on the go like I do, had a peg sticking out of either side of your neck and this crazy scar across the forehead. You'd think they might have told me to use cocoa butter on the place, after they took the stitches out, but naw, no way. They didn't care if I had a face like a train track. No meat off *their* nose.

And how about this getup? Nice, huh? Early wino or late drug addict. You ought to walk down the street wearing this mess, you really get the stares. Coat's too small, pants too short. And these boots, now they get the blue ribbon. You know, I'm only six-five, but with these on I'm nearly seven feet! That's some heels, Doc.

But listen, how can I do any better? I can't even afford to buy myself a tie at Goodwill, let alone get myself a new suit of clothes. And have you ever tried to fit someone my size? This shoulder is higher than the other one. The arms don't quite match, and—well, you see the problem. I tell you, Doc, it's no bed of roses.

Worst part of it is how people are always running from me, and throwing things, and trying to set me on fire. Oh, that's the classic one. I mean, I've been frozen for a while, covered in mud, you name it, but the old favorite is the torch. And I *hate* fire . . . Which reminds me, think you could refrain from smoking, Doc? Sort of makes me nervous.

See, I was saying about the fire. They've trapped me in wind-mills, castles, and labs. All sorts of places. Some guy out there in the crowd always gets the wise idea about the fire, and there we go again —Barbecue City. Let me tell you, Doc, I've been lucky. Spell that L-U-C-K-Y. We're talking a big lucky here. I mean, that's one reason I look as bad as I do. These holes in this already ragged suit . . . Yeah, that's right, bend over. Right there, see? This patch of hide was burned right off my head, Doc—and it didn't feel like no sunburn either. I mean it hurt.

And I've got no childhood. Just a big dumb boy all my life. No dates. No friends. Nothing. Just this personality complex, and this feeling that everybody hates me on sight.

If I ever get my hands on that Victor, or Igor, oh boy, gonna have to snap 'em, Doc. And I can do it, believe me. That's where they crapped in the mess kit, Doc. They made me strong. Real strong.

Give me a dime. Yeah, thanks.

Now watch this. Between thumb and finger . . . *Uhhhh.* How about that? Flat as a pancake.

Yeah, you're right, I'm getting a little excited. I'll lay back and take it easy . . . Say, do you smell smoke? Doc?

Doc?

Doc, damn you, put out that fire! Not you, too? Hey, I'm not a bad guy, really. Come back here, Doc! Don't leave me in here. Don't lock that door. . . .

I wrote this one for Twilight Zone, *but T. E. D. Klein didn't like it. I didn't either. It sort of fizzled out. I showed it to my wife, and she thought she saw what was wrong with it, gave me an ending and corrected some interior lines and dialogue. I revised it to her suggestions, made her co-author, sent it in, and she was right.*

Klein thought we had it now.

He bought it.

My wife's inspiration was simple.

We needed the money. She has written a few articles, couple of stories, has co-edited with me, and without her inspiration, and confidence, and ability to put up with the oddness of a freelance writer's life, and perhaps my own personal oddness, I'd probably be making chairs in an aluminum chair plant factory.

When I see this story all I think about is how lucky a man I am to have met the woman I'm married to.

Thirty years and counting as of 2003, friends. Thirty years and counting.

A Change of Lifestyle
with Karen Lansdale

*G*OT UP THIS MORNING AND COULDN'T TAKE IT anymore. I'd had all the cutesy words and hugs I could take from the old bag, and I'd also had it with my food. She thought that just because I liked something once, I couldn't wait to have it every day.

'Course, it beat hell out of that McWhipple burger I got out of the next-door neighbor's trash can. I saw him toss it out, and as I recall, he was looking mighty green and holding his stomach. Didn't bother me none, though; I'd eaten out of his trash can before. (He even took a shot at me one night on account of it.) But this McWhipple burger would have made a vulture choke! Must've been kangaroo meat or something. Or maybe the burger had just been lying on the assembly line too long. In any case, it sure made me sick, and up until then I could eat anything short of strychnine.

See, that's part of the problem. Suddenly I couldn't stand the way I'd been living. Just came over me, you know? One day I was fine and happy as a tick in an armpit, and the next day things were no longer hokay-by-me. I wanted a change of lifestyle.

It was all so goofy . . . the way I was feeling in the head, I thought maybe I'd got some medical problems, you know? So first thing I thought of was to go see the doc. Figured I ought to do that before I made any drastic changes—changes like getting the old lady out of my life, finding a new place to live, that sort of thing. I just wanted to make sure I wasn't having a spell of some sort, one of them metabolistic shake-ups.

So the doc was the ticket. I mean, he'd always been nice to me. A few pills and needles, but that's to be expected, right?

Next problem was getting out of the house without making a scene. Old gal treated me like some sort of prisoner, and that didn't make it easy.

The window over the sink was open, though, and that's how I plotted my escape. It was hard for me to get my body up and through the opening, but I managed. Made the six-foot drop without so much as a sprained ankle.

I got my thoughts together, charted out the doc's office, and set out. On the way, I noticed something weird: not only was I having this change in attitude, I seemed to be having some physical problems, too. I could feel stuff shifting around inside me, the way you feel the wind when it changes.

When I finally reached the doc's, man, was I bushed. Caught this lady coming out with a white cat under her arm, and she looked at me like I was the strange one. I mean, here she was with a cat under her arm, things hanging off her ears and wrists and wearing as much war paint as an Indian in a TV western, and she looks at me like I'm wearing a propeller beanie or something.

I slid in before she closed the door, and I looked around. People were sitting all over the place, and they had their pets with them. Dogs, cats, even a pet monkey.

I suddenly felt mighty sick, but I figured the best thing to do was to hang tough and not think about my problem. I decided to get a magazine down from the rack, but I couldn't get one down. Couldn't seem to hold onto it.

People were staring.

So were their pets.

I decided the heck with this and went right over to the receptionist. Standing on my hind legs, I leaned against the desk and said, "Listen, sweetheart, I've got to see the doc, and pronto."

"Oh, my God!" she screamed. "A talking Siberian husky!" Then she bounced her appointment book off one of my pointy ears.

Was this any way to run a veterinarian's office?

Man, did that place clear out fast. Nothing but a few hairs—dog, cat, and blue rinse—floating to the floor.

The doc obviously wasn't the ticket. I cleared out of there myself and ran three blocks on my hind legs before I realized it. I felt good, too. Problem was, it tended to stop traffic.

I got down on all fours again, and though it hurt my back, I walked like that until I got to the park. As soon as I reached it, I stood up on my hind legs and stretched my back. I tell you, that felt some better.

There was a bum sitting on a park bench tipping a bottle, and when he lamped me coming toward him, he jumped up, screamed, and ran away, smashing his bottle on a tree as he went.

Sighing, I took his place on the bench, crossed my legs, and noticed that a fleshy pink knee was poking up through a rip in my fur. Man, what next?

There was a newspaper lying beside me, and having nothing better to do, I picked it up. Didn't have a lick of trouble holding it. My toes had lengthened now, and my dew claw could fold and grasp. The hair on the back of my paws had begun to fall off.

The paper was the morning edition. The first article that caught my eye was about this guy over on Winchester—and why not? That was right next door to where I'd been living with the old hag. It was the fellow who'd tossed out the hamburger.

Seems he went weird. Woke up in the middle of the night and started baying at the moon through his bedroom window. Later on he got to scratching behind his ears with his feet, even though he was still wearing slippers. Next he got out of the house somehow and started chasing cars. Lady finally had to beat him with a newspaper to make him stop—at which point he raised his legs and peed on her, then chased the neighbor's cat up a tree.

That's when the old lady called the nut-box people.

By the time they got there the guy'd gotten a case of hairy knees, a wet nose, and a taste for the family dog's Gravy Train. In fact, the man and the dog got into a fight over it, and the man bit the rat terrier's ear off.

Yeeecccchhh—fighting over Gravy Train! They can have the stuff. Give me steak and 'taters.

Lady said she didn't know what had gone wrong. Said he'd gone to bed with a stomachache and feeling a bit under the weather. And why not?—he'd got hold of a week-old hamburger from McWhipple's that she'd set on top of the refrigerator and forgotten about. Seems this guy was a real chow hound and went for it. Ate a couple of big bites before his taste buds had time to work and he realized he was chomping sewer fodder.

Ouch and flea bites! That must have been the same green meat I got a bite of.

I tossed the paper aside and patted my chest for a cigarette. No pockets, of course.

Just then, my tail fell off. It went through the slats in the park bench and landed on the ground. I looked down and saw it turn to dust, hair and all, till a little wind came along and whipped it away.

Man, some days the things that happen to you shouldn't happen to a dog.

This is a collaboration with my children.

Here's what we did before we wrote anything. We kicked our idea around until we understood the framework. We talked out the scenes, the character, the locale, and the kind of mood we wanted to establish. We wanted an old-fashioned scary campfire story. Something that once read could be told and retold; and if not told exactly right, would still succeed, if kept within the original framework.

Next, we outlined the story on paper. Dad sat at the machine, and Keith and Kasey sat next to him as we got started. We revised sentences, suggested sentences, and talked out scenes. After each scene was written, we read it aloud and discussed it, wrote and rewrote until we had it the way we wanted.

When it was finished, copies were made, and we each looked them over and made notes. Then we wrote a final draft.

Was it fun?

Most of the time.

There was a bit of unpleasantness. Sibling rivalry and a nervous dad, but in the end we made it.

Out of it came "The Companion."

We liked doing it enough, if the opportunity arose, we would do it again.

The Companion

with Keith Lansdale and Kasey Jo Lansdale

*T*HEY WEREN'T BITING.

Harold sat on the bank with his fishing pole and watched the clear creek water turn dark as the sunlight faded. He knew he should pack up and go. This wonderful fishing spot he'd heard about was a dud, but the idea of going home without at least one fish for supper was not a happy one. He had spent a large part of the day before bragging to his friends about what a fisherman he was. He could hear them now, laughing and joking as he talked about the big one that got away.

And worse yet, he was out of bait.

He had used his little camp shovel to dig around the edge of the bank for worms. But he hadn't turned up so much as a grub or a doodlebug.

The best course of action, other than pack his gear on his bike and ride home, was to cross the bank. It was less wooded over there, and the ground might be softer. On the other side of the creek, through a thinning row of trees, he could see an old farm field. There were dried stalks of broken-down corn and tall dried weeds the plain brown color of a cardboard box.

Harold looked at his watch. He decided he had just enough time to find some bait and maybe catch one fish. He picked up his camp shovel and found a narrow place in the creek to leap across.

After walking through the trees and out into the huge field, he noticed a large and odd-looking scarecrow on a post. Beyond the scarecrow, some stretch away, surrounded by saplings and weeds, he saw what had once been a fine two-story farmhouse. Now it was not much more than an abandoned shell of broken glass and aging lumber.

As Harold approached the scarecrow, he was even more taken with its unusual appearance. It was dressed in a stovepipe hat that was crunched and moth-eaten and leaned to one side. The body was constructed of hay, sticks, and vines, and the face was made of some sort of cloth, perhaps an old towsack. It was dressed in a once expensive evening jacket and pants. Its arms were outstretched on a pole, and poking out of its sleeves were fingers made of sticks.

From a distance, the eyes looked like empty sockets in a skull. When Harold stood close to the scarecrow, he was even more surprised to discover it had teeth. They were animal teeth, still in the jawbone, and someone had fitted them into the cloth face, giving the scarecrow a wolflike countenance. Dark feathers had somehow gotten caught between the teeth.

But the most peculiar thing of all was found at the center of the scarecrow. Its black jacket hung open, its chest was torn apart, and Harold could see inside. He was startled to discover that there was a rib cage, and fastened to it by a cord was a large faded valentine heart. A long, thick stick was rammed directly through that heart.

The dirt beneath the scarecrow was soft, and Harold took his shovel and began to dig. As he did, he had a sensation of being watched. Then he saw a shadow, as if the scarecrow were nodding its head.

Harold glanced up and saw that the shadow was made by a large crow flying high overhead. The early rising moon had caught its shape and cast it on the ground. This gave Harold a sense of relief, but he realized that any plans to continue fishing were wasted. It was too late.

A grunting noise behind him caused him to jump up, leaving his camp shovel in the dirt. He grabbed at the first weapon he saw— the stick jammed through the scarecrow. He jerked it free and saw the source of the noise—a wild East Texas boar. A dangerous animal indeed.

It was a big one. Black and angry-looking, with eyes that caught the moonlight and burned back at him like coals. The beast's tusks shone like wet knives, and Harold knew those tusks could tear him apart as easily as he might rip wet construction paper with his hands.

The boar turned its head from side to side and snorted, taking in the boy's smell. Harold tried to maintain his ground. But then the moonlight shifted in the boar's eyes and made them seem even brighter than before. Harold panicked and began running toward the farmhouse.

He heard the boar running behind him. It sounded strange as it came, as if it were chasing him on padded feet. Harold reached the front door of the farmhouse and grabbed the door handle. In one swift motion, he swung inside and pushed it shut. The boar rammed the door, and the house rattled like dry bones.

The door had a bar lock, and Harold pushed it into place. He leaped back, holding the stick to use as a spear. The ramming continued for a moment, then everything went quiet.

Harold eased to a window and looked out. The boar was standing at the edge of the woods near where he had first seen it. The scarecrow was gone, and in its place there was only the post that had held it.

Harold was confused. How had the boar chased him to the house and returned to its original position so quickly? And what had happened to the scarecrow? Had the boar, thinking the scarecrow was a person, torn it from the post with its tusks?

The boar turned and disappeared into the woods. Harold decided to give the animal time to get far away. He checked his watch, then waited a few minutes. While he waited, he looked around.

The house was a wreck. There were overturned chairs, a table, and books. Near the fireplace, a hatchet was stuck in a large log. Everything was coated in dust and spider webs, and the stairs that twisted up to the second landing were shaky and rotten.

Harold was about to return to his fishing gear and head for the bike when he heard a scraping noise. He wheeled around for a look. The wind was moving a clutch of weeds, causing them to scrape against the window. Harold felt like a fool. Everything was scaring him.

Then the weeds moved from view and he discovered they weren't weeds at all. In fact, they looked like sticks . . . or fingers.

Hadn't the scarecrow had sticks for fingers?

That was ridiculous. Scarecrows didn't move on their own.

Then again, Harold thought as he looked out the window at the scarecrow's post, where was it?

The doorknob turned slowly. The door moved slightly, but the bar lock held. Harold could feel the hair on the back of his neck bristling. Goose bumps moved along his neck and shoulders.

The knob turned again.

Then something pushed hard against the door. Harder.

Harold dropped the stick and wrenched the hatchet from the log.

At the bottom of the door was a space about an inch wide, and the moonlight shining through the windows made it possible for him to see something scuttling there—sticks, long and flexible.

They poked through the crack at the bottom of the door, tapped loudly on the floor, and stretched, stretched, stretched farther into the room. A flat hand made of hay, vines, and sticks appeared. It began to ascend on the end of a knotty vine of an arm, wiggling its fingers as it rose. It climbed along the door, and Harold realized, to his horror and astonishment, that it was trying to reach the bar lock.

Harold stood frozen, watching the fingers push and free the latch.

Harold came unfrozen long enough to leap forward and chop down on the knotty elbow, striking it in two. The hand flopped to the floor and clutched so hard at the floorboards that it scratched large strips of wood from them. Then it was still.

But Harold had moved too late. The doorknob was turning again. Harold darted for the stairway, bolted up the staircase. Behind him came a scuttling sound. He was almost to the top of the stairs when the step beneath him gave way and his foot went through with a screech of nails and a crash of rotten lumber.

Harold let out a scream as something grabbed hold of the back of his coat collar. He jerked loose, tearing his jacket and losing the hatchet in the process. He tugged his foot free and crawled rapidly on hands and knees to the top of the stairs.

He struggled to his feet and raced down the corridor. Moonlight shone through a hall window and projected his shadow and that of his capering pursuer onto the wall. Then the creature sprang onto Harold's back, sending both of them tumbling to the floor.

They rolled and twisted down the hallway. Harold howled and clutched at the strong arm wrapped around his throat. As he turned over onto his back, he heard the crunching of sticks beneath him. The arm loosened its grip, and Harold was able to free himself. He scuttled along the floor like a cockroach, regained his footing, then darted through an open door and slammed it.

Out in the hall he heard it moving. Sticks crackled. Hay swished. The thing was coming after him.

Harold checked over his shoulder, trying to find something to jam against the door, or some place to hide. He saw another

doorway and sprinted for that. It led to another hall, and down its
length were a series of doors. Harold quickly entered the room at
the far end and closed the door quietly. He fumbled for a lock, but
there was none. He saw a bed and rolled under it, sliding up against
the wall where it was darkest.

The moon was rising, and its light was inching under the bed.
Dust particles swam in the moonlight. The ancient bed smelled
musty and wet. Outside in the hall, Harold could hear the thing
scooting along as if it were sweeping the floor. Scooting closer.

A door opened. Closed.

A little later another door opened and closed.

Then another.

Moments later he could hear it in the room next to his. He knew
he should try to escape, but to where? He was trapped. If he tried to
rush out the door, he was certain to run right into it. Shivering like
a frightened kitten, he pushed himself farther up against the wall, as
close as possible.

The bedroom door creaked open. The scarecrow shuffled into
the room. Harold could hear it moving from one side to the other,
pulling things from shelves, tossing them onto the floor, smashing
glass, trying to find his hiding place.

Please, please, thought Harold, *don't look under the bed.*

Harold heard it brushing toward the door, then he heard
the door open. *It's going to leave,* thought Harold. *It's going to
leave!*

But it stopped. Then slowly turned and walked to the bed.
Harold could see the scarecrow's straw-filled pants legs, its shapeless
straw feet. Bits of hay floated down from the scarecrow, coasted
under the bed and lay in the moonlight, just inches away.

Slowly the scarecrow bent down for a look. The shadow of its hat
poked beneath the bed before its actual face. Harold couldn't stand
to look. He felt as if he might scream. The beating of his heart
seemed as loud as thunder.

It looked under the bed.

Harold, eyes closed, waited for it to grab him.

Seconds ticked by and nothing happened.

Harold snapped his eyes open to the sound of the door slamming.

It hadn't seen him.

The thick shadows closest to the wall had protected him. If it
had been a few minutes later, the rising moonlight would have
expanded under the bed and revealed him.

Harold lay there, trying to decide what to do. Strangely enough, he felt sleepy. He couldn't imagine how that could be, but finally he decided that a mind could only take so much terror before it needed relief—even if it was false relief. He closed his eyes and fell into a deep sleep.

When he awoke, he realized by the light in the room that it was near sunrise. He had slept for hours. He wondered if the scarecrow was still in the house, searching.

Building his nerve, Harold crawled from under the bed. He stretched his back and turned to look around the room. He was startled to see a skeleton dressed in rotting clothes and sitting in a chair at a desk.

Last night he had rolled beneath the bed so quickly that he hadn't even seen the skeleton. Harold noticed a bundle of yellow papers lying on the desk in front of it.

He picked up the papers, carried them to the window, and held them to the dawn's growing light. It was a kind of journal. Harold scanned the contents and was amazed.

The skeleton had been a man named John Benner. When Benner had died, he was sixty-five years old. At one time he had been a successful farmer. But when his wife died, he grew lonely—so lonely that he decided to create a companion.

Benner built it of cloth and hay and sticks. Made the mouth from the jawbone of a wolf. The rib cage he unearthed in one of his fields. He couldn't tell if the bones were human or animal. He'd never seen anything like them. He decided it was just the thing for his companion.

He even decided to give it a heart—one of the old valentine hearts his beloved wife had made him. He fastened the heart to the rib cage, closed up the chest with hay and sticks, dressed the scarecrow in his old evening clothes, and pinned an old stovepipe hat to its head. He kept the scarecrow in the house, placed it in chairs, set a plate before it at meal times, even talked to it.

And then one night it moved.

At first Benner was amazed and frightened, but in time he was delighted. Something about the combination of ingredients, the strange bones from the field, the wolf's jaw, the valentine heart, perhaps his own desires, had given it life.

The scarecrow never ate or slept, but it kept him company. It listened while he talked or read aloud. It sat with him at the supper table.

But come daylight, it ceased to move. It would find a place in the shadows—a dark corner or the inside of a cedar chest. There it would wait until the day faded and the night came.

In time, Benner became afraid. The scarecrow was a creature of the night, and it lost interest in his company. Once, when he asked it to sit down and listen to him read, it slapped the book from his hand and tossed him against the kitchen wall, knocking him unconscious.

A thing made of straw and bones, cloth and paper, Benner realized, was never meant to live, because it had no soul.

One day, while the scarecrow hid from daylight, Benner dragged it from its hiding place and pulled it outside. It began to writhe and fight him, but the scarecrow was too weak to do him damage. The sunlight made it smoke and crackle with flame.

Benner hauled it to the center of the field, raised it on a post, and secured it there by ramming a long staff through its chest and paper heart.

It ceased to twitch, smoke, or burn. The thing he created was now at rest. It was nothing more than a scarecrow.

The pages told Harold that even with the scarecrow controlled, Benner found he could not sleep at night. He let the farm go to ruin, became sad and miserable, even thought of freeing the scarecrow so that once again he might have a companion. But he didn't, and in time, sitting right here at his desk, perhaps after writing his journal, he died. Maybe of fear, or loneliness.

Astonished, Harold dropped the pages on the floor. The scarecrow had been imprisoned on that post for no telling how long. From the condition of the farm, and Benner's body, Harold decided it had most likely been years. *Then I came along,* he thought, *and removed the staff from its heart and freed it.*

Daylight, thought Harold. In daylight the scarecrow would have to give up. It would have to hide. It would be weak then.

Harold glanced out the window. The thin rays of morning were growing longer and redder, and through the trees he could see the red ball of the sun lifting over the horizon.

Less than five minutes from now he would be safe. A sense of comfort flooded over him. He was going to beat this thing. He leaned against the glass, watching the sunrise.

A pane fell from the window and crashed onto the roof outside.

Uh-oh, thought Harold, looking toward the door.

He waited. Nothing happened. There were no sounds. The scarecrow had not heard. Harold sighed and turned to look out the window again.

Suddenly, the door burst open and slammed against the wall. As Harold wheeled around he saw a figure charging toward him, flapping its arms like the wings of a crow taking flight.

It pounced on him, smashed him against the window, breaking the remaining glass. Both went hurtling through the splintering window frame and fell onto the roof. They rolled together down the slope of the roof and onto the sandy ground.

It was a long drop—twelve feet or so. Harold fell on top of the scarecrow. It cushioned his fall, but he still landed hard enough to have the breath knocked out of him.

The scarecrow rolled him over, straddled him, pushed its hand tightly over Harold's face. The boy could smell the rotting hay and decaying sticks, feel the wooden fingers thrusting into his flesh. Its grip was growing tighter and tighter. He heard the scarecrow's wolf teeth snapping eagerly as it lowered its face to his.

Suddenly, there was a bone-chilling scream. At first Harold thought he was screaming, then he realized it was the scarecrow.

It leaped up and dashed away. Harold lifted his head for a look and saw a trail of smoke wisping around the corner of the house.

Harold found a heavy rock for a weapon, and forced himself to follow. The scarecrow was not in sight, but the side door of the house was partially open. Harold peeked through a window.

The scarecrow was violently flapping from one end of the room to the other, looking for shadows to hide in. But as the sun rose, its light melted the shadows away as fast as the scarecrow could find them.

Harold jerked the door open wide and let the sunlight in. He got a glimpse of the scarecrow as it snatched a thick curtain from a window, wrapped itself in it, and fell to the floor.

Harold spied a thick stick on the floor—it was the same one he had pulled from the scarecrow. He tossed aside the rock and picked up the stick. He used it to flip the curtain aside, exposing the thing to sunlight.

The scarecrow bellowed so loudly that Harold felt as if his bones and muscles would turn to jelly. It sprang from the floor, darted past him and out the door.

Feeling braver now that it was daylight and the scarecrow was weak, Harold chased after it. Ahead of him, the weeds in the field were parting and swishing like cards being shuffled. Floating above the weeds were thick twists of smoke.

Harold found the scarecrow on its knees, hugging its support post like a drowning man clinging to a floating log. Smoke coiled up from around the scarecrow's head and boiled out from under its coat sleeves and pant legs.

Harold poked the scarecrow with the stick. It fell on its back, and its arms flopped wide. Harold rammed the stick through its open chest, and through the valentine heart.

He lifted it from the ground easily with the stick. It weighed very little. He lifted it until its arms draped over the cross on the post. When it hung there, Harold made sure the stick was firmly through its chest and heart. Then he raced for his bike.

Sometimes even now, a year later, Harold thinks of his fishing gear and his camp shovel. But more often he thinks of the scarecrow. He wonders if it is still on its post. He wonders what would have happened if he had left it alone in the sunlight. Would that have been better? Would it have burned to ashes?

He wonders if another curious fisherman has been out there and removed the stick from its chest.

He hopes not.

He wonders if the scarecrow has a memory. It had tried to get Benner, but Benner had beat it, and Harold had beat it too. But what if someone else freed it and the scarecrow got him? Would it come after Harold too? Would it want to finish what it had started?

Was it possible, by some kind of supernatural instinct, for the scarecrow to track him down? Could it travel by night? Sleep in culverts and old barns and sheds, burying itself deep under dried leaves to hide from the sun?

Could it be coming closer to his home while he slept?

He often dreamed of it coming. In his dreams, Harold could see it gliding with the shadows, shuffling along, inching nearer and nearer.

And what about those sounds he'd heard earlier tonight, outside his bedroom window? Were they really what he had concluded — dogs in the trash cans?

Had that shape he'd glimpsed at his window been the fleeting shadow of a flying owl, or had it been—Harold rose from bed, checked all the locks on the doors and windows, listened to the wind blow around the house, and decided not to go outside for a look.

"Old Charlie" is a fishing story. Sort of.

I grew up in the woods and along the creeks of East Texas. I loved it. I fished a lot when I was a kid, and I still do it occasionally, though, to tell the truth, I don't really have the bug. And I prefer nothing fancy, no fly fishing, or clever casting. Just put the line in the water and hope.

I tried deep-sea fishing once, but then it occurred to me I might catch something I couldn't eat, and that bothered me. What would I do with a sailfish? I couldn't see any reason to kill one and I could care less about a dead fish mounted on the wall. That's always sort of seemed dumb to me.

Besides. I got seasick, didn't catch anything, and the only thing caught was a barracuda that thrashed about on the deck for a while until it got its head stove in by the captain. This was sold to a restaurant in St. Croix, probably as some fish other than barracuda, if I were to guess.

Anyway, I like the idea of fishing better than doing it, and that has little to nothing to do with this story.

Hope you enjoy it.

Old Charlie

*H*I THERE. CATCHING MUCH?

Well, they're in there. Just got to have the right bait and be patient. You don't mind if I sit down on the bank next to you, do you?

Good, good. Thanks.

Yeah, I like it fine. I never fish with anything but a cane pole. An old-fashioned way of doing things, I guess, but it suits me. I like to sharpen one end a bit, stick that baby in the ground, and wait it out. Maybe find someone like yourself to chat with for a while.

Whee, it's hot. Near sundown, too. You know, every time I'm out fishing in heat like this, I think of Old Charlie.

Huh? No, no. You couldn't really say he was a friend of mine. You see, I met him right on this bank, sort of like I'm meeting you, only he came down and sat beside me.

It was hot, just like today. So damned hot you'd think your nose was going to melt off your face and run down your chin. I was out here trying to catch a bite before sundown, because there's not much I like better than fish, when here comes this old codger with a fishing rig. It was just like he stepped out of nowhere.

Don't let my saying he was old get you to thinking about white hair and withered muscles. This old boy was stout looking, like maybe he'd done hard labor all his life. Looked, and was built, a whole lot like me, as a matter of fact.

He comes and sits down about where I am now and smiles at me. That was the first time I'd ever seen that kind of smile, sort of strange and satisfied. And it looked wavery, as if it was nothing more than a reflection in the water.

After he got settled, got his gear all worked out, and put his bait on, he cast his line and looked at me with that smile again. "Catching much?" he asked me.

"No," I say. "Nothing. Haven't had a bite all day."

He smiled that smile. "My name's Charlie. Some folks just call me Old Charlie."

"Ned," I say.

"I sure do love to fish," he says. "I drive out every afternoon, up and down this Sabine River bank, shopping for a fresh place to fish."

"You don't say," I says to him. "Well, ain't much here."

About that time, Old Charlie gets him a bite and pulls in a nice-sized bass. He puts it on a chain and stakes it out in the water.

Then Old Charlie rebaits his hook and tosses it again. A bass twice the size of the first hits it immediately and he adds it to his chain.

Wasn't five minutes later and he'd nabbed another.

Me, I hadn't caught doodlysquat. So I sort of forgot about the old boy and his odd smile and got to watching him haul them in. I bet he had nine fish on that chain when I finally said, "That rod and reel must be the way to go."

He looked at me and smiled again. "No, don't matter what you fish with, it's the bait that does it. Got the right bait, you can catch anything."

"What do you use?"

"I've tried many baits," he said smiling, "but there isn't a one that beats this one. Came by using it in an odd way, too. My wife gave me the idea. Course, that was a few years back. Not married now. You see, my wife was a young thing, about thirty-two years younger than me, and I married her when she was just a kid. Otherwise, she wouldn't have been fool enough to marry an old man like me. I knew I was robbing the cradle, impressing her with my worldly knowledge so I could have someone at home all the time, but I couldn't help myself.

"Her parents didn't mind much. They were river trash and were ready to get shed of her anyway. Just one more mouth to feed far as they were concerned. I guess that made it all the easier for me.

"Anyway, we got married. Things went right smart for the first few years. Then one day this Bible-thumper came by. He was something of a preacher and a Bible salesman, and I let him in to talk to us. Well, he talked a right nice sermon, and Amy, my wife, insisted that we invite him to dinner and buy one of his Bibles.

"I noticed right then and there that she and that Bible-thumper were exchanging looks, and not the sort to make you think of church and gospel reading.

"I was burned by it, but I'm a realistic old cuss, and I knew I was pretty old for Amy and that there wasn't any harm in her looking. Long as that was all she did. Guess by that time, she'd found out I wasn't nearly as worldly as she had thought. All I had to offer her was a hardscrabble farm and what I could catch off the river, and neither was exactly first-rate. Could hardly grow a cotton-pickin' thing on that place, the soil was so worked out, and I didn't have money for no store-bought fertilizer—and didn't have no animals to speak of that could supply me with any barnyard stuff, neither. Fishing had got plumb rotten. This was before the bait.

"Well, me not being about to catch much fish was hurtin' me the most. I didn't care much for plowing them old, hot fields. Never had. But fishing . . . now that was my pride and joy. That and Amy.

"So, we're scraping by like usual, and I start to notice this change in Amy. It started taking place the day after that Bible-thumper's visit. She still fixed meals, ironed and stuff, but she spent a lot of time looking out the windows, like she was expecting something. Half the time when I spoke to her, she didn't even hear me.

"And damned if that thumper didn't show up about a week later. We'd already bought a Bible, and since he didn't have no new product to sell us, he just preached at us. Told us about the Ten Commandments and about hellfire and damnation. But from the way he was looking at Amy, I figured there was at least one or two of them commandments he didn't take too serious, and I don't think he gave a hang about hellfire and damnation.

"I kept my temper, them being young and all. I figured the thumper would give it up pretty soon anyway, and when he was gone Amy would forget.

"But he didn't give it up. Got so he came around often, his suit all brushed up, his hair slicked back, and that Bible under his arm like it was some kind of key to any man's home. He even took to coming early in the day while I was working the fields, or in the barn sharpening my tools.

"He and Amy would sit on the front porch, and every once in a while I'd look up from my old mules and quit plowing and see them sitting there in the rocking chairs on the porch. Him with that Bible on his knee—closed—and her looking at him like he was the very one that hung the moon.

"They'd be there when I quit the fields and went down to the river in the cool of the afternoon, and though I didn't like the idea of them being alone like that, it never really occurred to me that anything would come of it—I mean, not really.

"Old men can be such fools.

"Well, I remember thinking that it had gone far enough. Even if they were young and all, I just couldn't go on with that open flirting right in front of my eyes. I figured they must have thought me pretty stupid, and maybe that bothered me even more.

"Anyway, I went down to the river that afternoon. Told myself that when I got back I'd have me a talk with Amy, or if that Bible-thumper was still there amoonin' on the porch, I'd pull him aside and tell him politely that if he came back again I was going to blow his head off.

"This day I'm down at the river there's not a thing biting. Not only do we need the food, but my pride is involved here. I'd been a fisherman all of my life, and it was getting so I couldn't seine a minnow out of a washtub. I just couldn't have imagined at that time how fine that bait was going to work . . . But I'm getting ahead of myself.

"Disgusted, I decided to come back from the creek early, and what do I see but this Bible fella's car still parked in our yard, and it getting along toward sundown, too. I'll tell you, I hadn't caught a thing and I wasn't in any kind of friendly mood, and it just went all over me like a bad dose of wood ticks. When I got to the front porch I was even madder, because the rockers were empty. The Bible that thumper always toted was lying on the seat of one of them, but they weren't anywhere to be seen.

"Guess I was thinking it right then, but I was hoping that I wasn't going to find what I thought I was going to find. Wanted to think they had just went in to have a drink of water or a bite to eat, but my mind wouldn't rightly settle on that.

"Creeping, almost, I walked up on the porch and slipped inside. The noises I heard from the bedroom didn't sound anything like water-drinking, eating, or gospel-talking.

"Just went nuts. Got the butcher knife off the cabinet, and . . . I don't half remember.

"Later, when the police came out there looking for the thumper, they didn't find a thing. Turned out he was a real blabbermouth. Everyone in town knew about him and Amy before I did—I mean, you know, in that way. So they believed me when I said I figured they'd run off together. I'm sure glad they didn't seine the river, or they'd have found his car where I run it off in the deep water.

"Guess that wouldn't have mattered much though. Even if they'd found the car, they wouldn't have had no bodies. And without the bodies, they can't do a thing to you. You see, I'd cut them up real good and lean and laid me out about twenty lines. Fish hit that bait like it was made for them. Took me maybe three days to use it up—which is about when the police showed up. But by then the bait was gone and I'd sold most of the fish and turned myself a nice dollar. Hell, rest of the mess I cooked up and ate. Matter-of-fact, them officers were there when I was eating the last of it.

"I was a changed man after that. Got to smiling all the time. Just couldn't help myself. Loved catchin' them fish. Fishing is just dear to my heart, even more so now. You might say I owed it all to Amy.

"Got so I started making up more of the bait—you know, other folks I'd find on the river, kind of out by themselves. It got so I was making a living off fishing alone."

That's Old Charlie's story, fella . . . Hey why are you looking at me like that?

Me, Old Charlie?

No sir, not me. This here on my right is Old Charlie.

What do you mean there's no one there? Sure there is . . .

Oh yeah, I forgot. No one else seems to see Old Charlie but me. Can't understand that. Old Charlie tells me it used to be no one could see *me*. Can you believe that? Townsfolks used to say Old Charlie had gone crazy over his wife running off and all. Said he'd taken to talking to himself, calling the other self Ned.

Ain't so. I'm Ned. I work for Old Charlie now. Odd thing is, I can't remember ever doing anything else. Old Charlie has got to where he can't bring himself to kill folks for the bait anymore. Says it upsets him. So he has me do it. I mean, we've got to go on living, don't we? Fishing is all we know. You're a fisherman. You understand, don't you?

You sure are looking at me odd, fella. Is it the smile? Yeah, guess it is. You see, I got it, too. Once . . . Wait a minute. What's that, Charlie? . . . Yes, yes, I'm hurrying. Just a minute.

You see, once you get used to hauling in them fish, using that sort of bait, it's the only kind you want to use from then on. Just keeps me and Charlie smiling all the time. So when we see someone like yourself sitting out here all alone, we just can't help ourselves. Just got to have the bait. That's another reason I keep the end of this cane pole so sharp.

There's not much I can say about this story that it doesn't say for itself. I don't really remember the source that well.

Now and again I'll see something that sticks in my mind but has no story with it, just a resonance. I think it's like songwriters who find one line, and then find the rest of the song months or years later.

It was resting in my head on the to-be-used shelf, gathering dust, when one day the idea popped into my awareness again, and I took it off the shelf, dusted it, and found the connection I had been looking for.

I like it.

I think it's fun.

It fits in with a kind of story I had been writing years earlier. Many of which appeared in Twilight Zone Magazine or certain anthologies of that nature.

Billie Sue

ABOUT A WEEK BEFORE THE HOUSE NEXT DOOR sold to the young couple, Billie Sue and I broke up. It was painful and my choice. Some stupid argument we'd had, but I tried to tell myself I had made the right decision.

And in the light of day it seemed I had. But come night when the darkness set in and the king size bed was like a great raft on which I floated, I missed Billie Sue. I missed her being next to me, holding her. The comfort she had afforded me had been greater than I imagined, and now that she was gone, I felt empty, as if I had been drained from head to toe and that my body was a husk and nothing more.

But the kids next door changed that. For a time.

I was off for the summer. I teach math during the high school term, and since Billie Sue and I had broken up, I had begun to wish that I had signed on to teach summer school. It would have been some kind of diversion. Something to fill my days with besides thinking of Billie Sue.

About the second day the kids moved in, the boy was out mowing their yard, and I watched him from the window for a while, then made up some lemonade and took it out on the patio and went over and stood by where he was mowing.

He stopped and killed the engine and smiled at me. He was a

nice looking kid, if a little bony. He had very blond hair and was shirtless and was just starting to get hair on his chest. It looked like down, and the thought of that made me feel ill at ease, because, bizarrely enough, the downlike hair made me think of Billie Sue, how soft she was, and that in turn made me think of the empty house and the empty bed and the nights that went on and on.

"Hey," the boy said. "You're our neighbor?"

"That's right. Kevin Pierce."

"Jim Howel. Glad to meet you." We shook hands. I judged him to be about twenty. Half my age.

"Come on and meet my wife," he said. "You married?"

"No," I said, but I felt strange saying it. It wasn't that Billie Sue and I were married, but it had seemed like it. The way I felt about her, a marriage license wasn't necessary. But now she was gone, and the fact that we had never officially been hitched meant nothing.

I walked with him to the front door, and about the time we got there, a young woman, his wife, of course, opened the screen and looked out. She wore a tight green halter top that exposed a beautiful brown belly and a belly button that looked as if it had been made for licking. She had on white shorts and thongs. Her black hair was tied back, and some of it had slipped out of the tie and was falling over her forehead and around her ears, and it looked soft and sensual. In fact, she was quite the looker.

It wasn't that her face was all that perfect, but it was soft and filled with big brown eyes, and she had those kind of lips that look as if they've been bruised and swollen. But not too much. Just enough to make you want to put your lips on them, to maybe soothe the pain.

"Oh, hi," she said.

"Hi," I said.

Jim introduced us. Her name was Sharon.

"I've got some lemonade next door, if you two would like to come over and share it," I said. "Just made it."

"Well, yeah," said Jim. "I'd like that. I'm hot as a pistol."

"I guess so," said the girl, and I saw Jim throw her a look. A sort of, hey, don't be rude kind of look. If she saw the look, she gave no sign of it.

As we walked over to my house, I said, "You folks been married long?"

"Not long," Jim said. "How long, honey?"

"Eighteen months."

"Well, congratulations," I said. "Newlyweds."

We sat out on the patio and drank the lemonade, and Jim did most of the talking. He wanted to be a lawyer, and Sharon was working at some cafe in town putting him through. He tried to talk like he was really complimenting her, and I think he was, but I could tell Sharon wasn't feeling complimented. There was something about her silence that said a lot. It said, Look what I've got myself into. Married this chatterbox who wants to be a lawyer and can't make a dollar 'cause he's got to study, so I've got to work, and law school isn't any hop, skip, and a jump. We're talking years of tips and pinches on the ass, and is this guy worth it anyhow?

She said all that and more without so much as opening her mouth. When we finished off the lemonade, Jim got up and said he had to finish the lawn.

"I'll sit here awhile," Sharon said. "You go on and mow."

Jim looked at her, then he looked at me and made a smile. "Sure," he said to her: "We'll eat some lunch after a while."

"I ate already," she said. "Get you a sandwich, something out of the box."

"Sure," he said, and went back to mow.

As he went, I noticed his back was red from the sun. I said, "You ought to tell him to get some lotion on. Look at his back."

She swiveled in her chair and looked, turned back to me, said, "He'll find out soon enough he ought to wear lotion. You got anything stronger than lemonade?"

I went in the house, got a couple of beers and a bottle of Jack Daniel's, and some glasses. We drank the beers out on the veranda, then, as it turned hotter, we came inside and sat on the couch and drank the whiskey. While Jim's mower droned on, we talked about this and that, but not really about anything. You know what I mean. Just small talk that's so small it's hardly talk.

After about an hour, I finally decided what we were really talking about, and I put my hand out and touched her hand on the couch and she didn't move it. "Maybe you ought to go on back."

"You want me to?"

"That's the problem, I don't want you to."

"I just met you."

"I know. That's another reason you ought to go back to your husband."

"He's a boring son of a bitch. You know that. I thought he was all right when we met. Good looking and all, but he's as dull as a cheap china plate, and twice as shallow. I'm nineteen years old. I don't want to work in any goddamn cafe for years while he gets a job where he can wear a suit and get people divorces. I want to get my divorce now."

She slid over and we kissed. She was soft and pliant, and there were things about her that were better than Billie Sue, and for a moment I didn't think of Billie at all. I kissed her for a long time and touched her, and finally the mower stopped.

"Goddamn it," she said. "That figures."

She touched me again, and in the right place. She got up and retied her halter top, which I had just managed to loosen.

"I'm sorry," I said. "I let this get out of hand."

"Hell, I'm the one sorry it didn't get completely out of hand. But it will. We're neighbors."

I tried to avoid Sharon after that, and managed to do so for a couple days. I even thought about trying to patch things up with Billie Sue, but just couldn't. My goddamn pride.

On the fourth night after they'd moved in, I woke up to the sound of dishes breaking. I got out of bed and went into the living room and looked out the window at my neighbor's house, the source of the noise. It was Sharon yelling and tossing things that had awakened me. The yelling went on for a time. I got a beer out of the box and sat down with a chair pulled up at the window and watched. There was a light on in their living room window, and now and then their shadows would go across the light, then move away.

Finally I heard the front door slam, and Jim went out, got in their car and drove away. He hadn't so much as departed when Sharon came out of the house and started across the yard toward my place.

I moved the chair back to its position and sat down on the couch and waited. She knocked on the door. Hard. I let her knock for a while, then I got up and answered the door. I was in my underwear when I answered, but of course, I didn't care. She was in a short black nightie, no shoes, and she didn't care either.

I let her in. She said, "We had a fight. I hope the son of a bitch doesn't come back."

She took hold of me then, and we kissed, and then we made our way to the bedroom, and it was sweet, the way she loved me, and finally, near morning, we fell asleep.

When I awoke it was to Jim's voice. In our haste, we had left the front door open, and I guess he'd seen the writing on the wall all along, and now he was in the house, standing over the bed yelling.

Sharon sat up in bed, and the sheet fell off her naked breasts and she yelled back. I sat up amazed, more than embarrassed. I had to learn to lock my doors, no matter what.

This yelling went on for a time, lots of cussing, then Jim grabbed her by the wrist and jerked her out of the bed and onto the floor.

I jumped up then and hit him, hit him hard enough to knock him down. He sat up and opened his mouth and a tooth fell out.

"Oh my God, Jim," Sharon said. She slid across the floor and took his head in her hands and kissed his cheek. "Oh, baby, are you all right?"

"Yeah, I'm all right," he said.

I couldn't believe it. "What the hell?" I said.

"You didn't have to hit him," Sharon said. "You're older, stronger. You hurt him."

I started to argue, but by that time Jim was up and Sharon had her arm around him. She said, "I'm sorry, baby, I'm so sorry. Let's go home."

Sharon pulled on her nightie, and away they went. I picked up the panties she'd left and put them over my head, trying to look as foolish as I felt. They smelled good though.

Dumb asshole, I said to myself. How many times have they done this? There are strange people in this world. Some get their kicks from wearing leather, being tied down and pissed on, you name it, but this pair has a simpler method of courtship. They fight with each other, break up, then Sharon flirts and sleeps around until Jim discovers her, then they yell at each other and he forgives her, and he's all excited to think she's been in bed with another man, and she's all excited to have been there, and they're both turned on and happy.

Whatever. I didn't want any part of it.

That night I decided to make up with Billie Sue. I got my shovel out of the garage and went out and dug her up from under the rose bushes. I got her out of there and brushed the dirt off and carried her inside. I washed her yellow body off in the sink. I fondled her bill and told her I was sorry. I was so sorry I began to cry. I just couldn't help myself. I told her I'd never bury her in the dirt again.

I filled the bathtub with water and put Billie Sue in there and watched her float. I turned her in the water so that she could watch me undress. I stripped off my clothes slowly and got in the tub with her. She floated and bobbed toward me, and I picked her up and squeezed her and dirt puffed from the noisemaker in her beak and the sound she made was not quite a squeak or a quack.

I laughed. I squeezed her hard, the way she likes it, the way she's always liked it since the first time my mother gave her to me when I was a child. I squeezed her many times. I floated her in the tub with me, moved her around my erection, which stuck up out of the water like a stick in a pond, and I knew then what I should have always known.

Billie Sue was the love of my life.

Perhaps we were not too unlike that silly couple next door. We fought too. We fought often. We had broken up before. I had buried her under the rose bushes before, though never for this long. But now, holding her, squeezing her hard, listening to her quack, I knew never again. I began to laugh and laugh and laugh at what she was saying. She could be like that when she wanted. So funny. So forgiving.

Oh, Billie Sue. Billie Sue. My little rubber duckie poo.

In 1983 I had the worst year of my life. Part of the reason was I started writing different types of stories: "The Pit" and "By Bizarre Hands" being examples, and none of it was selling. No one even knew what they were. Every anthology or magazine rejected them, or wanted me to put a twist in the end, which assured me they didn't have a clue what I was doing. I refused. So, I didn't sell. Things got worse. I decided to write a more traditional tale, but something that would contain the seeds of my frustration, and I suppose my reading a number of ill-written bestsellers added to that frustration, and this came out.

Bestsellers Guaranteed

*L*ARRY HAD A HEADACHE, AS HE OFTEN DID. IT was those all-night stints at the typewriter, along with his job and his boss, Fraggerty, yelling for him to fry the burgers faster, to dole them out lickity-split on mustard-covered sesame seed buns.

Burgers and fries, typing paper and typewriter ribbons—the ribbons as gray and faded as the thirty-six years of his life. There really didn't seem to be any reason to keep on living. Another twenty to thirty years of this would be foolish. Then again, that seemed the only alternative. He was too cowardly to take his own life.

Washing his face in the bathroom sink, Larry jerked a rough paper towel from the rack and dried off, looking at himself in the mirror. He was starting to look like all those hacks of writer mythology. The little guys who turned out the drek copy. The ones with the blue-veined, alcoholic noses and eyes like volcanic eruptions.

My God, he thought, *I look forty easy. Maybe even forty-five.*

"You gonna stay in the can all day?" a voice yelled through the door. It was Fraggerty, waiting to send him back to the grill and the burgers. The guy treated him like a bum.

A sly smile formed on Larry's face as he thought: *I am a bum. I've been through three marriages, sixteen jobs, eight typewriters, and all I've got to show for it are a dozen articles, all of them in obscure magazines that either paid in copies or pennies.* He wasn't even as good as the hack he looked like. The hack could at least point to a substantial body of work, drek or not.

And I've been at this . . . God, twelve years! An article a year. Some average. Not even enough to pay back his typing supplies.

He thought of his friend Mooney—or James T. Mooney, as he was known to his fans. Yearly, he wrote a bestseller. It was a bestseller before it hit the stands. And except for Mooney's first novel, *The Goodbye Reel*, a detective thriller, all of them had been dismal. In fact, dismal was too kind a word. But the public lapped them up.

What had gone wrong with his own career? He used to help Mooney with his plots; in fact, he had helped him work out his problems on *The Goodbye Reel*, back when they had both been scrounging their livings and existing out of a suitcase. Then Mooney had moved to Houston, and a year later *The Goodbye Reel* had hit the stands like an atomic bomb. Made record sales in hardback and paper, and gathered in a movie deal that boggled the imagination.

Being honest with himself, Larry felt certain that he could say he was a far better writer than Mooney. More commercial, even. So why had Mooney gathered the laurels while he bagged burgers and ended up in a dirty restroom contemplating the veins in his nose?

It was almost too much to bear. He would kill to have a bestseller. Just one. That's all he'd ask. Just one.

"Tear the damned crapper out of there and sit on it behind the grill!" Fraggerty called through the door. "But get out here. We got customers lined up down the block."

Larry doubted that, but he dried his hands, combed his hair and stepped outside.

Fraggerty was waiting for him. Fraggerty was a big fat man with bulldog jowls and perpetual blossoms of sweat beneath his meaty arms. Mid-summer, dead of winter—he had them.

"Hey," Fraggerty said, "you work here or what?"

"Not anymore," Larry said. "Pay me up."

"What?"

"You heard me, fat ass. Pay up!"

"Hey, don't get tough about it. All right. Glad to see you hike."

Five minutes later, Larry was leaving the burger joint, a fifty-dollar check in his pocket.

He said aloud: "Job number seventeen."

The brainstorm had struck him right when he came out of the restroom. He'd go see Mooney. He and Mooney had been great friends once, before all that money and a new way of living had carried Mooney back and forth to Houston and numerous jet spots around the country and overseas.

Maybe Mooney could give him a connection, an *in*, as it was called in the business. Before, he'd been too proud to ask, but now he didn't give a damn if he had to crawl and lick boots. He had to sell his books; had to let the world know he existed.

Without letting the landlord know, as he owed considerable back rent, he cleaned out his apartment.

Like his life, there was little there. A typewriter, copies of his twelve articles, a few clothes, and odds and ends. There weren't even any books. He'd had to sell them all to pay his rent three months back.

In less than twenty minutes, he snuck out without being seen, loaded the typewriter and his two suitcases in the trunk of his battered Chevy, and looked up at the window of his dingy apartment. He lifted his middle finger in salute, climbed in the car and drove away.

Mooney was easy to find. His estate looked just the part for the residence of a bestselling author. A front lawn the size of a polo field, a fountain of marble out front, and a house that looked like a small English castle. All this near downtown Houston.

James T. Mooney looked the part, too. He answered the door in a maroon smoking jacket with matching pajamas. He had on a pair of glossy leather bedroom slippers that he could have worn with a suit and tie. His hair was well groomed with just the right amount of gray at the temples. There was a bit of a strained look about his eyes, but other than that he was the picture of health and prosperity.

"Well, I'll be," Mooney said. "Larry Melford. Come in."

The interior of the house made the outside look like a barn. There were paintings and sculptures and shelves of first-edition books. On one wall, blown up to the size of movie posters and placed under glass and frame, were copies of the covers of his bestsellers. All twelve of them. A thirteenth glass and frame stood empty beside the others, waiting for the inevitable.

They chatted as they walked through the house, and Mooney said, "Let's drop off in the study. We can be comfortable there. I'll have the maid bring us some coffee or iced tea."

"I hope I'm not interrupting your writing," Larry said.

"No, not at all. I'm finished for the day. I usually just work a couple hours a day."

A couple hours a day? thought Larry. A serpent of envy crawled around in the pit of his stomach. For the last twelve years, he had worked a job all day and had written away most of the night, generally gathering no more than two to three hours' sleep a day. And here was Mooney writing these monstrous bestsellers and he only wrote a couple of hours in the mornings.

Mooney's study was about the size of Larry's abandoned apartment. And it looked a hell of a lot better. One side of the room was little more than a long desk covered with a word processor and a duplicating machine. The rest of the room was taken up by a leather couch and rows of bookshelves containing nothing but Mooney's work. Various editions of foreign publications, special collectors' editions, the leather-bound Christmas set, the paperbacks, the bound galleys of all the novels. Mooney was surrounded by his success.

"Sit down; take the couch," Mooney said, hauling around his desk chair. "Coffee or tea? I'll have the maid bring it."

"No, I'm fine."

"Well then, tell me about yourself."

Larry opened his mouth to start, and that's when it fell out. He just couldn't control himself. It was as if a dam had burst open and all the water of the world was flowing away. The anguish, the misery, the years of failure found expression.

When he had finished telling it all, his eyes were glistening. He was both relieved and embarrassed. "So you see, Mooney, I'm just about over the edge. I'm craving success like an addict craves a fix. I'd kill for a bestseller."

Mooney's face seemed to go lopsided. "Watch that kind of talk."

"I mean it. I'm feeling so small right now, I'd have to look up to see a snake's belly. I'd lie, cheat, steal, kill—anything to get published in a big way. I don't want to die and leave nothing of me behind."

"And you don't want to miss out on the good things either, right?"

"Damned right. You've got it."

"Look, Larry, worry less about the good things and just write your books. Ease up some, but do it your own way. You may never have a big bestseller, but you're a good writer, and eventually you'll crack and be able to make a decent living."

"Easy for you to say, Mooney."

"In time, with a little patience . . ."

"I'm running out of time and patience. I'm emotionally drained, whipped. What I need is an *in*, Mooney, an *in*. A name. Anything that can give me a break."

"Talent is the name of the game, Larry, not an *in*," Mooney said very softly.

"Don't give me that garbage. I've got talent and you know it. I used to help you with the plots of your short stories. And your first novel—remember the things I worked out for you there? I mean, come on, Mooney. You've read my writing. It's good. Damned good! I need help. An *in* can't hurt me. It may not help me much, but it's got to give me a damn sight better chance than I have now."

Larry looked at Mooney's face. Something seemed to be moving there behind the eyes and taut lips. He looked sad, and quite a bit older than his age. Well, okay. So he was offended by being asked right out to help a fellow writer.

That was too bad. Larry just didn't have the pride and patience anymore to beat around the bush.

"An *in*, huh?" Mooney finally said.

"That's right."

"You sure you wouldn't rather do it your way?"

"I've been doing it my way for twelve years. I want a break, Mooney."

Mooney nodded solemnly. He went over to his desk and opened a drawer. He took out a small, white business card and brought it over to Larry.

It read:

BESTSELLERS GUARANTEED
Offices in New York, Texas, California
and
Overseas

The left-hand corner of the card had a drawing of an open book, and the right-hand corner had three phone numbers. One of them was a Houston number.

"I met a lady when I first moved here," Mooney said, "a big name author in the romance field. I sort of got this thing going with her . . . finally asked her for . . . an *in*. And she gave me this card. We don't see each other anymore, Larry. We stopped seeing each other the day she gave it to me."

Larry wasn't listening. "This an editor?"

"No."

"An agent?"

"No."

"Publisher, book packager?"

"None of those things and a little of all, and a lot more."

"I'm not sure . . ."

"You wanted your *in*, so there it is. You just call that number. And Larry, do me a favor. Never come here again."

The first thing Larry did when he left Mooney's was find a telephone booth. He dialed the Houston number and a crisp female voice answered: "Bestsellers Guaranteed."

"Are you the one in charge?"

"No sir. Just hold on and I'll put you through to someone who can help you."

Larry tapped his finger on the phone shelf till a smooth-as-well-water male voice said: "B. G. here. May I be of assistance?"

"Uh . . . yes, a friend of mine . . . a Mr. James T. Mooney—"

"Of course, Mr. Mooney."

"He suggested . . . he gave me a card. Well, I'm a writer. My name is Larry Melford. To be honest, I'm not exactly sure what Mooney had in mind for me. He just suggested I call you."

"All we need to know is that you were recommended by Mr. Mooney. Where are you now?"

Larry gave the address of the 7-Eleven phone booth.

"Why don't you wait there . . . oh, say . . . twenty minutes and we'll send a car to pick you up? That suit you?"

"Sure, but . . ."

"I'll have an agent explain it to you when he gets there, okay?"

"Yes, yes, that'll be fine."

Larry hung up and stepped outside to lean on the hood of his car. By golly, he thought, that Mooney does have connections, and now after all these years, maybe, just maybe, I'm going to get connected, too.

He lit a cigarette and watched the August heat waves bounce around the 7-Eleven lot, and twenty minutes later, a tan, six-door limousine pulled up next to his Chevy.

The man driving the limo wore a chauffeur's hat and outfit. He got out of the car and walked around to the tinted, far back seat window and tapped gently on the glass. The window slid down with a short whoosh. A man dressed in black with black hair, a black mustache, and thick-rimmed black shades, looked out at Larry. He said, "Mr. Melford?"

"Yes," Larry said.

"Would you like to go around to the other side? Herman will open the door for you."

After Larry had slid onto the seat and Herman had closed the door behind him, his eyes were drawn to the plush interior of the car. Encased in the seat in front of them was a phone, a television set, and a couple of panels that folded out. Larry felt certain one of them would be a small bar. Air-conditioning hummed softly. The car was nice enough and large enough to live in.

He looked across the seat at the man in black, who was extending his hand. They shook. The man in black said, "Just call me James, Mr. Melford."

"Fine. This is about . . . writing? Mooney said he could give me a . . . connection. I mean, I have work, plenty of it. Four novels, a couple of dozen short stories, a novella—of course I know that length is a dog to sell, but . . ."

"None of that matters," James said.

"This *is* about writing?"

"This is about bestsellers, Mr. Melford. That is what you want, isn't it? To be a bestselling author?"

"More than anything."

"Then you're our man and we're your organization."

Herman had eased in behind the wheel. James leaned forward over the seat and said firmly, "Drive us around." Leaning back, James touched a button on the door panel and a thick glass rose out of the seat in front of them and clicked into place in a groove in the roof.

"Now," James said, "shall we talk?"

As they drove, James explained, "I'm the agent assigned to you, and it's up to me to see if I can convince you to join our little gallery. But, if you should sign on with us, we expect you to remain loyal. You must consider that we offer a service that is unique, unlike any offered anywhere. We can guarantee that you'll hit the bestseller list once a year, every year, as long as you're with us.

"Actually, Mr. Melford, we're not a real old organization, though I have a hard time remembering the exact year we were founded—it predated the Kennedy assassination by a year."

"That would be sixty-two," Larry said.

"Yes, yes, of course. I'm terrible at years. But it's only lately that we've come into our own. Consider the bad state of publishing right now, then consider the fact that our clients have each had a bestseller this year—and they will next year, no matter how bad publishing may falter. Our clients may be the only ones with books, but each of their books will be a bestseller, and their success will, as it does every year, save the industry."

"You're a packager?"

"No. We don't actually read the books, Mr. Melford, we just make sure they're bestsellers. You can write a book about the Earth being invaded by giant tree toads from the moon, if you like, and we will guarantee it will be a bestseller."

"My God, you are connected."

"You wouldn't believe the connections we have."

"And what does your organization get out of this? How much of a percentage?"

"We don't take a dime."

"What?"

"Not a dime. For our help, for our guarantee that your books will be bestsellers, we ask only one thing. A favor. One favor a year. A favor for each bestseller."

"What's the favor?"

"We'll come to that in a moment. But before we do, let me make sure you understand what we have to offer. I mean, if you were successful—and I mean no offense by this—then you wouldn't be talking to me now. You need help. We can offer help. You're in your mid-thirties, correct? Yes, I thought so. Not really old, but a bit late to start a new career plan. People do it, but it's certainly no piece of cake, now, is it?"

Larry found that he was nodding in agreement.

"So," James continued, "what we want to do is give you success. We're talking money in the millions of dollars, Mr. Melford. Fame. Respect. Most anything you'd want would be at your command. Exotic foods and wines? A snap of the fingers. Books? Cars? Women? A snap of the fingers. Anything your heart desires and it's yours."

"But I have to make a small, initial investment, right?"

"Ah, suspicious by nature, are you?"

"Wouldn't you be? My God, you're offering me the world."

"So I am. But no . . . no investment. Picture this, Mr. Melford. You might get lucky and sell the work, might even have a bestseller. But the slots are getting smaller and smaller for new writers. And one reason for that is that our writers, our clients, are filling those slots, Mr. Melford. If it's between your book and one of our clients', and yours is ten times better written, our client will still win out. Every time."

"What you're saying is, the fix is in?"

"A crude way of putting it, but rather accurate. Yes."

"What about talent, craftsmanship?"

"I wouldn't know about any of that. I sell success, not books."

"But it's the public that puts out its money for these books. They make or break an author. How can you know what they'll buy?"

"Our advertising system is the best in the world. We know how to reach the public and how to convince. We also use subliminals, Mr. Melford. We flash images on television programs, theater films; we hide them in the art of wine and cigarette ads. Little things below conscious perception, but images that lock tight to the subconscious mind. People who would not normally pick up a book will buy our bestsellers."

"Isn't that dishonest?"

"Who's to tell in this day and age what's right and wrong? It's relative, don't you think, Mr. Melford?"

Larry didn't say anything.

"Look. The public pictures writers as rich, all of them. They don't realize that the average full-time writer barely makes a living. Most of them are out there starving, and for what? Get on the winning side for a change, Mr. Melford. Otherwise, spend the rest of your life living in roach motels and living off the crumbs tossed you by the publishing world. And believe me, Mr. Melford, if you fail to join up with us, crumbs are all you'll get. If you're lucky."

The limousine had returned to the 7-Eleven parking lot. They were parked next to Larry's car.

"I suppose," James said, "we've come to that point that the bullfighters call 'the moment of truth.' You sign on with us and you'll be on Easy Street for the rest of your life."

"But we haven't talked terms."

"No, we haven't. It's at this point that I must ask you to either accept or turn down our offer, Mr. Melford. Once I've outlined the terms, you must be in full agreement with us."

"Accept before I hear what this favor you've talked about is?"

"That's correct. Bestseller or Bohemian, Mr. Melford. Which is it? Tell me right now. My time is valuable."

Larry paused only a moment. "Very well. Count me in. In for a penny, in for a pound. What's the favor?"

"Each year, you assassinate someone for us."

Larry dove for the door handle, but it wouldn't open. It had been locked electronically. James grabbed him by the wrist and held him tightly, so tightly Larry thought his bones would shatter.

"I wouldn't," James said. "After what I've told you, you step out of this car and they'll find you in a ditch this afternoon, obviously the victim of some hit-and-run driver."

"That's . . . that's murder."

"Yes, it is," James said. "Listen to me. You assassinate whomever we choose. We're not discriminating as far as sex, color, religion, or politics goes. Anyone who gets in our way dies. Simple as that. You see, Mr. Melford, we are a big organization. Our goal is world domination. You, and all our clients, are little helpers toward that goal. Who is more respected than a bestselling author? Who is allowed in places where others would not be allowed? Who is revered by public figures and the general public alike? An author—a bestselling author."

"But . . . it's murder."

"There will be nothing personal in it. It'll just be your part of the contract. One assassination a year that we'll arrange."

"But if you're so connected . . . why do it this way? Why not just hire a hit man?"

"In a sense, I have."

"I'm not an assassin. I've never even fired a gun."

"The amateur is in many ways better than the professional. He doesn't fall into a pattern. When the time comes, we will show you what you have to do. If you decide to be with us, that is."

"And if not?"

"I told you a moment ago. The ditch. The hit-and-run driver."

Suddenly, Herman was standing at the door, his hand poised to open it.

"Which is it, Mr. Melford? I'm becoming impatient. A ditch or a bestseller? And if you have any ideas about going to the police, don't. We have friends there, and you might accidentally meet one. Now, your decision."

"I'm in," Larry said, softly. "I'm in."

"Good," James said, taking Larry's hand. "Welcome aboard. You get one of those books of yours out, pick out a publisher, and mail it in. And don't bother with return postage. We'll take care of the rest. Congratulations."

James motioned to Herman. The door opened. Larry got out. And just before the door closed, James said, "If you should have trouble coming up with something, getting something finished, just let me know and we'll see that it gets written for you."

Larry stood on the sidewalk, nodding dumbly. Herman returned to the driver's seat, and a moment later the tan limo from Bestsellers Guaranteed whispered away.

*   *   *

James was as good as his word. Larry mailed off one of his shopworn novels, a thriller entitled *Texas Backlash*, and a contract for a half million dollars came back, almost by return mail.

Six months later, the book hit the bestseller list and rode there for a comfortable three months. It picked up a two-million-dollar paperback sale and a big shot movie producer purchased it for twice that amount.

Larry now had a big mansion outside of Nacogdoches, Texas, with a maid, a cook, two secretaries and a professional yard man. Any type of food he wanted was his for the asking. Once he had special seafood flown in from the East Coast to Houston and hauled from there to his door by refrigerated truck.

Any first edition book he wanted was now within his price range. He owned four cars, two motorcycles, a private airplane, and a yacht.

He could own anything—even people. They hopped at his every word, his most casual suggestion. He had money, and people wanted to satisfy those with money. Who knows, maybe it would rub off on them.

And there were women. Beautiful women. There was even one he had grown to care for, and believed cared for him instead of his money and position. Lovely Luna Malone.

But in the midst of all this finery, there was the favor. The thought of it rested on the back of his mind like a waiting vulture. And when a year had gone by, the vulture swooped in.

On a hot August day, the tan limo from Bestsellers Guaranteed pulled up the long, scenic drive to Larry's mansion. A moment later, Larry and James were in Larry's study and Herman stood outside the closed door with his arms akimbo, doing what he did best. Waiting silently.

James was dressed in black again. He still wore the thick-framed sun shades. "You know what I've come for, don't you?"

Larry nodded. "The favor."

"On March fifteenth, Bestsellers Guaranteed will arrange for an autograph party in Austin for your new bestseller, whatever that may be. At eleven-fifteen, you will excuse yourself to go upstairs to the men's room. Next door to it is a janitor's lounge. It hasn't been used in years. It's locked but we will provide you with the key.

"At the rear of the lounge is a restroom. Lift off the back of the commode and you will discover eight small packages taped to the inside. Open these and fit them together and you'll have a very sophisticated air rifle. One of the packages will contain a canister of ice, and in the middle, dyed red, you will find a bullet-shaped projectile of ice. The air gun can send that projectile through three inches of steel without the ice shattering.

"You will load the gun, go to the window, and at exactly eleven twenty-five, the Governor will drive by in an open car in the midst of the parade. A small hole has been cut in the restroom window. It will exactly accommodate the barrel of the rifle and the scope will fit snugly against the glass. You will take aim, and in a manner of seconds, your favor for this year will be done."

"Why the Governor?"

"That is our concern."

"I've never shot a rifle."

"We'll train you. You have until March. You won't need to know much more than how to put the rifle together and look through the scope. The weapon will do the rest."

"If I refuse?"

"The bestselling author of *Texas Backlash* will be found murdered in his home by a couple of burglars, and a couple of undesirables will be framed for the crime. Don't you think that has a nicer ring to it than the hit-and-run program I offered you before? Or perhaps, as a warning, we'll do something to your lady friend. What's her name, Luna?"

"You wouldn't!"

"If it would offer incentive or achieve our desired goals, Mr. Melford, we would do anything."

"You bastard!"

"That'll be quite enough, Mr. Melford. You've reaped the rewards of our services, and now we expect to be repaid.

"It seems a small thing to ask for your success—and certainly you wouldn't want to die at the hands of other bestselling authors, the ones who will ultimately be your assassins."

In spite of the air-conditioning, Larry had begun to sweat. "Just who are you guys, really?"

"I've told you. We're an organization with big plans. What we sponsor more than anything else, Mr. Melford, is moral corruption. We feed on those who thrive on greed and ego; put them in positions of power and influence. We belong to a group, to put it naively, who believe that once the silly concepts of morality and honor break down, then we, who really know how things work, can take control and make them work to our advantage. To put it even more simply, Mr. Melford, we will own it all."

"I . . . I can't just cold-bloodedly murder someone."

"Oh, I think you can. I've got faith in you. Look around you, Mr.

Melford. Look at all you've got. Think of what you've got to lose, then tell me if you can murder from a distance someone you don't even know. I'll wait outside with Herman for your answer. You have two minutes."

From the March fifteenth edition of *The Austin Statesman*, a front-page headline: "GOVERNOR ASSASSINATED, ASSASSIN SOUGHT."

From the same issue, page 4B: "BESTSELLING AUTHOR, LARRY MELFORD, SIGNS BOOKS."

Six months later, in the master bedroom of Larry Melford's estate, Larry was sitting nude in front of the dresser mirror, clipping unruly nose hairs. On the bed behind him, nude, dark, luscious, lay Luna Malone. There was a healthy glow of sweat on her body as she lay with two pillows propped under her head; her raven hair was like an explosion of ink against their whiteness.

"Larry," she said, "you know, I've been thinking . . . I mean there's something I've been wanting to tell you, but haven't said anything about it because . . . well, I was afraid you might get the wrong idea. But now that we've known each other awhile, and things look solid . . . Larry, I'm a writer."

Larry quit clipping his nose hairs. He put the clipper on the dresser and turned very slowly. "You're what?"

"I mean, I want to be. And not just now, not just this minute. I've always wanted to be. I didn't tell you, because I was afraid you'd laugh, or worse, think I'd only got to know you so you could give me an *in*, but I've been writing for years and have sent book after book, story after story in, and just know I'm good, and well . . ."

"You want me to look at it?"

"Yeah, but more than that, Larry. I need an *in*. It's what I've always wanted. To write a bestseller. I'd kill for . . ."

"Get out! Get the hell out!"

"Larry, I didn't meet you for that reason . . ."

"Get the hell out or I'll throw you out."

"Larry . . ."

"Now!" He stood up from the chair, grabbed her dressing gown. "Just go. Leave everything. I'll have it sent to you. Get dressed and never let me see you again."

"Aren't you being a little silly about this? I mean . . ."

Larry moved as fast as an eagle swooping down on a field mouse. He grabbed her shoulder and jerked her off the bed onto the floor.

"All right, you bastard, all right." Luna stood. She grabbed the robe and slipped into it. "So I did meet you for an *in;* what's wrong with that? I bet you had some help along the way. It sure couldn't have been because you're a great writer. I can hardly force myself through that garbage you write."

He slapped her across the cheek so hard she fell back on the bed.

Holding her face, she got up, gathered her clothes and walked stiffly to the bathroom. Less than a minute later, she came out dressed, the robe over her shoulder.

"I'm sorry about hitting you," Larry said. "But I meant what I said about never wanting to see you again."

"You're crazy, man. You know that? Crazy. All I asked you for was an *in,* just . . ."

Luna stopped talking. Larry had lifted his head to look at her. His eyes looked as dark and flat as the twin barrels of a shotgun.

"Don't bother having Francis drive me home. I'll call a cab from downstairs, Mr. Bigshot Writer."

She went out, slamming the bedroom door. Larry got up and turned off the light, went back to the dresser chair and sat in the darkness for a long time.

Nearly a year and a half later, not long after completing a favor for Bestsellers Guaranteed, and acquiring a somewhat rabid taste for alcoholic beverages, Larry was in the Houston airport waiting to catch a plane for Hawaii for a long vacation when he saw a woman in the distance who looked familiar. She turned and he recognized her immediately. It was Luna Malone. Still beautiful, a bit more worldly looking, and dressed to the hilt.

She saw him before he could dart away. She waved. He smiled. She came over and shook hands with him. "Larry, you aren't still mad, are you?"

"No, I'm not mad. Good to see you. You look great."

"Thanks."

"Where're you going?"

"Italy. Rome."

"Pope country," Larry said with a smile, but at his words, Luna jumped.

"Yes . . . Pope country."

The announcer called for the flight to Rome, Italy. Luna and Larry shook hands again and she went away.

To kill time, Larry went to the airport bookstores. He found he couldn't even look at the big cardboard display with his latest bestseller in it. He didn't like to look at bestsellers by anyone. But something did catch his eye. It was the cardboard display next to his. The book was called *The Little Storm*, and appeared to be one of those steamy romance novels. But what had caught his eye was the big, emblazoned name of the author—LUNA MALONE.

Larry felt like a python had uncoiled inside of him. He felt worse than he had ever felt in his life.

"Italy, Rome," she had said.

"Pope country," he had said, and she jumped.

Larry stumbled back against the rack of his book, and his clumsiness knocked it over. The books tumbled to the floor. One of them slid between his legs and when he looked down he saw that it had turned over to its back. There was his smiling face looking up at him. Larry Melford, big name author, bestseller, a man whose books found their way into the homes of millions of readers.

Suddenly, Hawaii was forgotten and Larry was running, running to the nearest pay phone. What had James said about moral corruption? "We feed on those who thrive on greed and ego . . . once silly concepts of morality and honor break down . . . we will own it all."

The nightmare had to end. Bestsellers Guaranteed had to be exposed. He would wash his hands with blood and moral corruption no more. He would turn himself in.

With trembling hand, he picked up the phone, put in his change, and dialed the police.

From today's *Houston Chronicle*, front page headline: "POPE ASSASSINATED."

From the same edition, the last page before the Want Ads, the last paragraph: "BESTSELLING AUTHOR MURDERED IN HOME." The story follows: "Police suspect the brutal murder of author Larry Melford occurred when he surprised burglars in the act. Thus far, police have been unable to . . ."

This is one of those Twilight Zone stories for the modern reader, of the kind I used to write for the magazine, but it is of recent vintage.

I have a martial arts student who was working for the forestry service, and we were joking him one day about his job being a replacement for the fire dog.

That night I dreamed about looking for a job, perhaps the insecurity of the writer's life picking at the scab of uncertainty, and this was there when I awoke.

Or most of it was. I wrote about two thirds of it, and it died.

I was asked by Golden Gryphon to do a story for an anthology, and turned it down, being overwhelmed with work. But the more I thought about it, the more I wanted to do it, and I remembered this one. I took it out, thought it over, and the rest of it came to me in a rush.

I sent it to Gary Turner at Golden Gryphon. He liked it.

And here it is.

Fire Dog

WHEN JIM APPLIED FOR THE DISPATCHER JOB the fire department turned him down, but the Fire Chief offered him something else.

"Our fire dog, Rex, is retiring. You might want that job. Pays good and the retirement is great."

"Fire dog?" Jim said.

"That's right."

"Well, I don't know . . ."

"Suit yourself."

Jim considered. "I suppose I could give it a try—"

"Actually, we prefer greater dedication than that. We don't just want someone to give it a try. Being fire dog is an important job."

"Very well," Jim said. "I'll take it."

"Good."

The Chief opened a drawer, pulled out a spotted suit with tail and ears, pushed it across the desk.

"I have to wear this?"

"How the hell you gonna be the fire dog, you don't wear the suit?"

"Of course."

Jim examined the suit. It had a hole for his face, his bottom, and what his mother had called his pee-pee.

"Good grief," Jim said. "I can't go around with my . . . well, you know, my stuff hanging out."

"How many dogs you see wearing pants?"

"Well, Goofy comes to mind."

"Those are cartoons. I haven't got time to screw around here. You either want the job, or you don't."

"I want it."

"By the way. You sure Goofy's a dog?"

"Well, he looks like a dog. And he has that dog, Pluto."

"Pluto, by the way, doesn't wear pants."

"You got me there."

"Try on the suit, let's see if it needs tailoring."

The suit fit perfectly, though Jim did feel a bit exposed. Still, he had to admit there was something refreshing about the exposure. He wore the suit into the break room, following the Chief.

Rex, the current fire dog, was sprawled on the couch watching a cop show. His suit looked worn, even a bit smoke stained. He was tired around the eyes. His jowls drooped.

"This is our new fire dog," the Chief said.

Rex turned and looked at Jim, said, "I'm not out the door, already you got a guy in the suit?"

"Rex, no hard feelings. You got what, two, three days? We got to be ready. You know that."

Rex sat up on the couch, adjusted some pillows and leaned into them. "Yeah, I know. But, I've had this job nine years."

"And in dog years that's a lot."

"I don't know why I can't just keep being the fire dog. I think I've done a good job."

"You're our best fire dog yet. Jim here has a lot to live up to."

"I only get to work nine years?" Jim said.

"In dog years you'd be pretty old, and it's a decent retirement."

"Is he gonna take my name too?" Rex said.

"No," the Chief said, "of course not. We'll call him Spot."

"Oh, that's rich," said Rex. "You really worked on that one."

"It's no worse than Rex."

"Hey, Rex is a good name."

"I don't like Spot," Jim said. "Can't I come up with something else?"

"Dogs don't name themselves," the Chief said. "Your name is Spot."

"Spot," Rex said, "don't you think you ought to get started by coming over here and sniffing my butt?"

The first few days at work Spot found riding on the truck to be uncomfortable. He was always given a tool box to sit on so that he could be seen, as this was the fire department's way. They liked the idea of the fire dog in full view, his ears flapping in the wind. It was very promotional for the mascot to be seen.

Spot's exposed butt was cold on the tool box, and the wind not only blew his ears around, it moved another part of his anatomy about. That was annoying.

He did, however, enjoy the little motorized tail-wagging device he activated with a touch of a finger. He found that got him a lot of snacks from the fire men. He was especially fond of the liver snacks.

After three weeks on the job, Spot found his wife Shella to be very friendly. After dinner one evening, when he went to the bedroom to remove his dog suit, he discovered Shella lying on their bed wearing a negligee and a pair of dog ears attached to a hair band.

"Feel frisky, Spot?"

"Jim."

"Whatever. Feel frisky?"

"Well, yeah. Let me shed the suit, take a shower . . . "

"You don't need a shower . . . And baby, leave the suit on, will you?"

They went at it.

"You know how I want it," she said.

"Yeah. Doggie style."

"Good boy."

After sex, Shella liked to scratch his belly and behind his ears. He used the tail-wagging device to show how much he appreciated it. This wasn't so bad, he thought. He got less when he was a man.

Though his sex life had improved, Spot found himself being put outside a lot, having to relieve himself in a corner of the yard while his wife looked in the other direction, her hand in a plastic bag, ready to use to pick up his deposits.

He only removed his dog suit now when Shella wasn't around. She liked it on him at all times. At first he was insulted, but the sex was so good, and his life was so good, he relented. He even let her call him Spot all the time.

When she wasn't around, he washed and dried his suit carefully, ironed it. But he never wore anything else. When he rode the bus to work, everyone wanted to pet him. One woman even asked if he liked poodles because she had one.

At work he was well respected, and enjoyed being taken to schools with the Fire Chief. The Chief talked about fire prevention. Spot wagged his tail, sat up, barked, looked cute by turning his head from side to side.

He was even taken to his daughter's class once. He heard her say proudly to a kid sitting next to her, "That's my Daddy. He's the fire dog."

His chest swelled with pride. He made his tail wag enthusiastically.

The job really was the pip. You didn't have fires every day, so Spot laid around all day most days, on the couch sometimes, though some of the fireman would run him off and make him lie on the floor when they came in. But the floor had rugs on it and the television was always on, though he was not allowed to change the channels. Some kind of rule, a union thing. The fire dog can not and will not change channels.

He did hate having to take worm medicine, and the annual required trips to the vet were no picnic either. Especially the thermometer up the ass part.

But, hell, it was a living, and not a bad one. Another plus was after several months of trying, he was able to lick his balls.

At night, when everyone was in their bunks and there were no fires, Spot would read from Call of the Wild, White Fang, Dog Digest, or such, or lie on his back with all four feet in the air, trying to look cute.

He loved it when the firemen came in and caught him that way and ooohheeed and ahhhhhed and scratched his belly or patted his head.

This went on for just short of nine years. Then, one day, while he was lying on the couch, licking his ass—something he cultivated after three years on the job—the Fire Chief and a guy in a dog suit came in.

"This is your replacement, Spot," the Chief said.

"What?"

"Well, it has been nine years."

"You didn't tell me. Has it been? You're sure? Aren't you supposed to warn me? Rex knew his time was up. Remember?"

"Not exactly. But if you say so. Spot, meet Hal."

"Hal? What kind of dog's name is that? Hal?"

But it was no use. By the end of the day he had his personal dog biscuits, pinups from Dog Digest, and his worm-away medicine packed. There was also a spray can the firemen used to mist on his poop to keep him from eating it. The can of spray didn't really belong to him, but he took it anyway.

*   *   *

He picked up his old clothes, went into the changing room. He hadn't worn anything but the fire dog suit in years, and it felt odd to try his old clothes on. He could hardly remember ever wearing them. He found they were a bit moth-eaten, and he had gotten a little too plump for them. The shoes fit, but he couldn't tolerate them.

He kept the dog suit on.

He caught the bus and went home.

"What? You lost your job?" his wife said.

"I didn't lose anything. They retired me."

"You're not the fire dog?"

"No. Hal is the fire dog."

"I can't believe it. I give you nine great years—"

"We've been married eleven."

"I only count the dog years. Those were the good ones, you know."

"Well, I don't have to quit being a dog. Hell, I am a dog."

"You're not the fire dog. You've lost your position, Spot. Oh, I can't even stand to think about it. Outside. Go on. Git. Outside."

Spot went.

After a while he scratched on the door, but his wife didn't let him in. He went around back and tried there. That didn't work either. He looked in the windows, but couldn't see her.

He laid down in the yard.

That night it rained, and he slept under the car, awakened just in time to keep his wife from backing over him on her way to work.

That afternoon he waited, but his wife did not return at the usual time. Five o'clock was when he came home from the fire house, and she was always waiting, and he had a feeling it was at least five o'clock, and finally the sun went down and he knew it was late.

Still, no wife.

Finally, he saw headlights and a car pulled into the drive. Shella got out. He ran to meet her. To show he was interested, he hunched her leg.

She kicked him loose. He noticed she was holding a leash. Out of the car came Hal.

"Look who I got. A real dog."

Spot was dumbfounded.

"I met him today at the fire house, and well, we hit it off."

"You went by the fire house?"

"Of course."

"What about me?" Spot asked.

"Well, Spot, you are a little old. Sometimes, things change. New blood is necessary."

"Me and Hal, we're going to share the house?"

"I didn't say that."

She took Hal inside. Just before they closed the door, Hal slipped a paw behind Shella's back and shot Spot the finger.

When they were inside, Spot scratched on the door in a half-hearted way. No soap.

Next morning Shella hustled him out of the shrubbery by calling his name. She didn't have Hal with her.

Great! She had missed him. He bounded out, his tongue dangling like a wet sock. "Come here, Spot."

He went. That's what dogs did. When the master called, you went to them. He was still her dog. Yes sirree, Bob.

"Come on boy." She hustled him into the car.

As he climbed inside on the back seat and she shut the door, he saw Hal come out of the house stretching. He looked pretty happy. He walked over to the car and slapped Shella on the butt.

"See you later, baby."

"You bet, you dog you."

Hal walked down the street to the bus stop. Spot watched him by turning first to the back glass, then rushing over to the side view glass.

Shella got in the car.

"Where are we going?" Spot asked.

"It's a surprise," she said.

"Can you roll down the window back here a bit?"

"Sure."

Spot stuck his head out as they drove along, his ears flapping, his tongue hanging.

They drove down a side street, turned and tooled up an alley. Spot thought he recognized the place.

Why yes, the vet. They had come from another direction and he hadn't spotted it right off, but that's where he was.

He unhooked the little tag that dangled from his collar. Checked the dates of his last shots.

No. Nothing was overdue.

They stopped and Shella smiled. She opened the back door and took hold of the leash. "Come on, Spot."

Spot climbed out of the car, though carefully. He wasn't as spry as he once was.

Two men were at the back door. One of them was the doctor. The other an assistant.

"Here's Spot," she said.

"He looks pretty good," said the doctor.

"I know. But . . . Well, he's old and has his problems. And I have too many dogs."

She left him there.

The vet checked him over and called the animal shelter. "There's nothing really wrong with him," he told the attendant that came for him. "He's just old, and well, the woman doesn't want to care for him. He'd be great with children."

"You know how it is, Doc," said the attendant. "Dogs all over the place."

Later, at the animal shelter he stood on the cold concrete and smelled the other dogs. He barked at the cats he could smell. Fact was, he found himself barking anytime anyone came into the corridor of pens.

Sometimes men and woman and children came and looked at him.

None of them chose him. The device in his tail didn't work right, so he couldn't wag as ferociously as he liked. His ears were pretty droopy and his jowls hung way too low.

"He looks like his spots are fading," said one woman whose little girl had stuck her fingers through the grating so Spot could lick her hand.

"His breath stinks," she said.

As the days went by, Spot tried to look perky all the time. Hoping for adoption.

But one day, they came for him, wearing white coats and grim faces, brandishing a leash and a muzzle and a hypodermic needle.

I've been fascinated by the West since I was a kid. First the Western movies, then Western legend and history, and finally Western fiction.

As I studied the West, I was amazed at how much of a contribution was made by blacks. This was never part of the movies or books I read, and they were seldom mentioned in the history books. The more I researched, the more I realized that much of the Indian fighting was left to black regiments, and that it was black soldiers that actually took San Juan Hill for Teddy Roosevelt. He acknowledged this early on, but by election time the blacks' contribution to this event suddenly became less important.

Anyway, I've always thought it was a shame that this part of our history has had so little attention. It has had some, and that attention is growing. But when I wrote this, nothing much had been said.

There's very little to the story. I think that maybe I was just getting something off my chest.

Cowboy

I GOT OFF THE PLANE AT ATLANTA AND CAUGHT the shuttle to what I thought was my hotel. But there was some kind of mix-up, and it wasn't my hotel at all. They told me I could go out to the curb and catch this other shuttle and it would take me over to another hotel in their chain, and that it was a short walk from there to where I wanted to go. I thought that was okay, considering I had gotten on the wrong shuttle in the first place.

I sat outside the hotel on a bench and waited for the shuttle. It was October and kind of cool, but not really uncomfortable. The air felt damp.

I had a Western paperback and I got it out of my coat pocket and read a few pages. From time to time I looked up for the shuttle, then at my watch, then back at the paperback. It wasn't a very good Western.

While I was sitting there a little black boy on skates with an empty toy pistol scabbard strapped around his waist went by. He looked at me. His head was practically shaved and his snap-button cowboy shirt was ripped in front. I guess he was about eleven.

I looked back at my book and started reading, then I heard him skate over in front of me. I looked up and saw that he was looking at the picture on the front of the paperback.

"That a cowboy book?" he said.

I told him it was.

"It any good?"

"I don't care much for it. It's a little too much like the last three or four I read."

"I like cowboy books and movies but they don't get some things right."

"I like them too."

"I'm a cowboy," he said, and his tone was a trifle defiant.

"You are?"

"You was thinking niggers can't be cowboys."

"I wasn't thinking that. Don't call yourself that."

"Nigger? It's okay if I'm doing it. I wouldn't want you to say that."

"I wouldn't."

"Anyone says that they got me to fight."

"I don't want to fight. Where's your pistol?"

He didn't answer that. "A black boy can be a cowboy, you know."

"I'm sure of it."

"They weren't all cooks."

"Course not."

"That's way the movies and books got it. There any black cowboys in that book?"

"Not so far."

"There gonna be?"

"I don't know," I said. But I did know. I'd read a lot of cowboy books.

"White boys at school said there weren't any black cowboys. They said no nigger cowboys. They said we couldn't fight Indians and stuff."

"Don't listen to them."

"I'm not going to. I went over to the playground at the school and they took my pistol. There was three of them."

It came clear to me then. His shirt being ripped and the gun missing.

"I'm sorry. That wasn't nice."

"They said a nigger didn't need no cowboy gun. Said I needed me a frying pan or a broom. I used to ride the range and rope steers and stuff. They don't know nothing."

"Is that all you did on the range, rope steers?"

"I did all kinds of things. I did everything cowboys do."

"Was it hard work?"

"It was so hard you wouldn't believe it. I did all kinds of things. Cowboys don't call one another nigger."

"Do your mom and dad work on the range with you?"

"No, my mama has a job. She does clean-up work. My daddy he got killed in Vietnam. He got some medals and stuff. He wasn't a cowboy like me."

I looked up and saw the shuttle. I picked up my suitcase and stood.

"I got to go now," I said. "I hope you get your gun back. Lot of good cowboys lose fights from time to time."

"There was three of them."

"There you are. *Adios*." As an afterthought I gave him the Western book.

"It hasn't got any black cowboys in it I bet," he said, and gave it back to me. "I want one with black cowboys in it. I'm not reading any more of 'em unless they got black cowboys in them."

"I'm sure there are some," I said.

"There ought to be."

I got on the shuttle and it carried me to the other hotel. I got off and walked to where I was supposed to be, and on the way over there I put the book in one of those wire trash baskets that line the streets.

I did this one for Roger Zelazny. It was the last anthology he edited. It was a martial arts anthology, and I was proud to be in it. I love the martial arts and have been a student of the arts all my life. To know about this, check out www.joerlansdale.com, and click on THE MASK OF SHEN CHUAN.

He wrote a nice intro praising my writing, and it made my day. I loved his work, especially the shorter pieces and they had influenced me early on.

He was a nice man, too.

He got a bum deal. Cancer got him. And just when we were starting to be friends.

I got a bum deal in that way. He was a hell of a guy.

Master of Misery

SIX O'CLOCK IN THE MORNING, RICHARD WAS crossing by ferry from the Hotel on the Quay to Christiansted with a few other early-bird tourists, when he turned, looked toward shore, and saw a large ray leap from the water, its blue-gray hide glistening in the morning sunlight like gunmetal, its devil-tail flicking to one side as if to slash.

The ray floated there in defiance of gravity, hung in the sky between the boat and the shore, backgrounded by the storefronts and dock as if it were part of a painting, then splashed almost silently into the purple Caribbean, leaving in its wake a sun-kissed ripple.

Richard turned to see if the other passengers had noticed. He could tell from their faces they had not. The ray's leap had been a private showing, just for him, and he relished it. Later, he would think that perhaps it had been some kind of omen.

Ashore, he walked along the dock past the storefronts, and in front of the Anchor Inn Restaurant, the charter fishing boat was waiting.

A man and a woman were on board already. The man was probably fifty, perhaps a little older, but certainly in good shape. He had an aura of invincibility about him, as if the normal laws of mortality and time did not apply to him.

He was about five-ten with broad shoulders and, though he was a little thick in the middle, it was a hard thickness. It was evident, even beneath the black, loose, square-cut shirt he was wearing, he was a muscular man, perhaps first by birth, and second by exercise. His skin was as dark and leathery as an old bull's hide, his hair like frost on scorched grass. He was wearing khaki shorts and his dark legs were corded with muscle and his shins had a yellow shine to them that brought to mind weathered ivory.

He stood by the fighting chair bolted to the center of the deck, and looked at Richard standing on the dock with his little paper bag containing lunch and suntan lotion. The man's crow-colored eyes studied Richard as if he were a pile of dung that might contain some kernel of rare and undigested corn a crow might want.

The man's demeanor bothered Richard immediately. There was about him a cockiness. A way of looking at you and sizing you up and letting you know he wasn't seeing much.

The woman was quite another story. She was very much the bathing beauty type, aged beyond competition, but still beautiful, with a body by Nautilus. She was at least ten years younger than the man. She wore shoulder-length blond hair bleached by sun and chemicals. She had a heart-shaped face and a perfect nose and full lips. There was a slight cleft in her chin and her eyes were a faded blue. She was willowy and big breasted and wore a loose, white T-shirt over her black bathing suit, one of the kind you see women wear in movies, but not often on the beach. She had the body for it. A thong, or string, Richard thought the suits were called. Sort of thing where the strap in the back slid between the buttocks and covered them not at all. The top of the suit made a dark outline beneath her white T-shirt. She moved her body easily, as if she were accustomed to and not bothered by scrutiny, but there was something about her eyes that disturbed Richard.

Once, driving at night, a cat ran out in front of his car and he hit it, and when he stopped to see if there was hope, he found the cat mashed and dying, the eyes glowing hot and savage and terrified in the beam of his flashlight. The woman's eyes were like that.

She glanced at him quickly, then looked away. Richard climbed on board.

Richard extended his hand to the older man. The man smiled and took his hand and shook it. Richard cursed himself as the man squeezed hard. He should have expected that. "Hugo Peak," the older man said, then moved his head to indicate the woman behind him. "My wife, Margo."

Margo nodded at Richard and almost smiled. Richard was about to give his name, when the captain, Bill Jones, came out of the cabin grinning. He was a lean, weathered fellow with a face that was all nose and eyes the color of watered meat gravy. He was carrying a couple cups of coffee. He gave one to Margo, the other to Hugo. He said, "Richard, how are you, my man."

"Wishing I'd stayed in bed," Richard said. "I can't believe I let you talk me into this, Jones."

"Hey, fishing's not so bad," said the captain.

"Off the bank at home in Texas it might be all right. But all this water. I hate it."

This was true. Richard hated the water. He could swim, had even earned lifeguard credentials as a Boy Scout, some twenty-five years ago, back when he was thirteen, but he had never learned to like the water. Especially deep water. The ocean.

He realized he had let Jones talk him into this simply because he wanted to convince himself he wasn't phobic. So, okay, he wasn't phobic, but he still didn't like the water. The thought of soon being surrounded by it, and it being deep, and above them there being nothing but hot blue sky, was not appealing.

"I'll get you some coffee and we'll shove off," Jones said.

"I thought it took five for a charter?" Richard said.

Jones looked faintly embarrassed. "Well, Mr. Peak paid the slack. He wanted to keep it down to three. More time in the chair that way, we hit something."

Richard turned to Peak. "I suppose I should split the difference with you."

"Not at all," Peak said. "It was my idea."

"That's kind of you, Hugo," Richard said.

"Not at all. And if it doesn't sound too presumptuous, I don't much prefer to be called by my first name, unless it's by my wife. If I'm not fucking the person, I want them to call me Mr. Peak. Or Peak. That all right with you?"

Richard saw Margo turn her face toward the sea, pretend to be watching the gulls in the distance. "Sure," Richard said.

"I'll get the coffee," Jones said, and disappeared into the cabin. Peak yelled after him. "Let's shove off."

The sea was calm until they reached the Atlantic. The water there was blue-green, and the rich purple color of the Caribbean stood in stark contrast against it, reaching out with long purple claws into the great ocean, as if it might tug the Atlantic to it. But the Atlantic was too mighty, and it would not come.

The little fishing boat chugged out of the Caribbean and onto the choppier waters of the Atlantic, on out and over the great depths, and above them the sky was blue, with clouds as white as the undergarments of the Sacred Virgin.

The boat rode up and the boat rode down, between wet valleys of ocean and up their sides and down again. The cool spray of the ocean splattered on the deck and the diesel engine chugged and blew its exhaust across it and onto Richard, where he sat on the supply box. The movement of the water and the stench of the diesel made him queasy.

After a couple of hours of pushing onward, Jones slowed the engine, and finally killed it. "You're up, Mr. Peak," Jones said, coming down from his steering. He got a huge, metallic chest out of the cabin and dragged it onto the deck and opened it. There were a number of small black fish inside, packed in ice. Sardines, maybe. Jones took one and cut it open, took loose one of the rods strapped to the side of the cabin, stuck the fish on the great hook. He gave the rod to Peak.

Peak took the rod and tossed the line expertly and it went way out. He sat down in the fighting chair and fastened the waist belt and shoulder straps and put the rod butt in the gimbal. He looked relaxed and professional. The boat bobbed beneath the hot sunlight and the minutes crawled by.

Margo removed her T-shirt and leaned against the side of the boat. The bathing suit top barely managed to cover her breasts. It was designed primarily to shield her nipples. The top and sides of her bathing suit bottom revealed escaped pubic hair, a darker blond than the hair on her head.

She got a tube of suntan lotion out of a little knit bag on the deck, pushed the lotion into her palm, and began to apply it, slowly and carefully from her ankles up. Richard tried not to watch her run her hand over her tanned legs and thighs, finally over her belly and the tops of her breasts. He would look away, but always his eyes would come back.

He had not made love to a woman in a year, and for the first six months of the year had not wanted to. Now, looking at Margo Peak, it was all he could think about.

Richard glanced at Peak. He was studying the ocean. Jones was in the doorway of the cabin, trying not to be too obvious as he observed the woman. Richard could see that Jones's Adam's apple rode high in his throat. Margo seemed unaware or overly accustomed to the attention. She was primarily concerned with getting the suntan lotion even. Or so it seemed.

Then the line on the rod began to sing.

Richard looked toward the ocean and the line went straight and taut as the fish hit. The line sang louder as it jerked again and cut the air.

"I'm gonna hit him," Peak said. He tightened the drag, jerked back on the rod, and the rod bent slightly. "Now I've got him."

The fish cut to the right and the line moved with him, and Peak hit him again, said, "He's not too big. He's nothing."

Peak rapidly cranked the fish on deck. It was a barracuda. Jones took hold of a metal bar and whacked the flopping barracuda in the head. He got a pair of heavy shears off the deck and opened them and put them against the barracuda's head, and snapped down hard. The head came part of the way off. Jones popped the head again, and this time the head hung by a strand. He cut the head the rest of the way off, tossed it in the ocean, put the decapitated barracuda in the huge ice chest. "Some of the restaurants buy them," he said. "Probably sell them as tuna or something."

"Good catch," Richard said.

"A barracuda," Peak said. "That's no kinda fish. That's not worth a damn."

"Sometimes that's all you hit," Jones said. "Last party I took out, that was it. Three barracuda, back to back. You're next, Mrs. Peak."

Jones baited the hook and cast the line and Margo strapped herself into the fighting chair and slipped the rod into the gimbal. They drifted for an hour and finally Jones moved the boat, letting the line troll, but nothing hit right away. It was twenty minutes later and they were all having a beer, when suddenly the gimbal cranked forward and the line whizzed so fast and loud it sent goose bumps up Richard's back.

Margo dropped the beer and grabbed the rod. The beer foamed out of the can and ran over the deck, beneath Richard's tennis shoes. The line went way out. Jones cut the engine back plenty, and the line continued to sing and go far out into the water.

"Hit him, Margo," Peak said. "Hit him. He's not stuck, he's just got the bait and the line. You don't hit, the son of a bitch is gone."

Margo tightened the drag, pushed her feet hard against the chair's footrests, and jerked back viciously on the line. The line went taut and the rod bent forward and Margo was yanked hard against the straps.

"Loosen the goddamn drag," Peak said, "or he'll snap it."

Margo loosened the drag. The line sang and the fish went wide to starboard. Jones leaped to the controls and reversed the boat and slowed the speed, gave the fish room to run. The line slacked and the pole began to straighten.

"Hit him again," Peak said, and Margo tried, but it was some job, and Richard could see that the fish was putting a tremendous strain on her. The sun had not so much as caused her tanned body to break a sweat, but the fish had given her sweat beads on her forehead and cheeks and under the nose. The muscles in her arms and legs coiled as if being braided. She pressed her feet hard against the footrests.

"It's too big for her," Richard said.

"Mind your own business, Mr. Young," Peak said.

Young? How had Peak known his last name? He was pondering that, and was about to ask, when suddenly the fish began to run. Peak yelled, "Hit him, Margo, goddamn you! Hit him!"

Margo had been working the drag back and forth, and it was evident she had done this before, but the fish was too much for her, anyone could see that, and now she hit the big fish again, solid, and it leaped. It leaped high and pretty, full of color, fastened itself to the sky, then dived like an arrow into the water and out of sight. It was a great swordfish, and Richard thought: when we drag him onto the deck, immediately it will begin to lose its color and die. It will become nothing more than a dull, gray, dead fish to harden in some taxidermist's shop, later to be hung on a wall above a couch. It seemed a shame, and Richard suddenly felt shamed for coming out here, for wanting to fish at all. At home, on the banks, he caught a fish, it got eaten. Here, there was no point to the fishing but to garner a trophy.

"I want him, Margo," Peak said. "You hear me, you don't lose this fish. I mean it, goddamnit."

"I'm trying," Margo said. "Really."

"You know how it goes, you screw it up," Peak said. "You know how it works."

"Hugo . . . I can't hold him. I'm hurting."

"You'll hold him, or wish you had," Peak said. "You just think you're hurting."

"Hey," Richard said, "that's ridiculous. You want the goddamn fish, take over."

Peak, who was standing on the other side of Margo, looked at Richard and smiled. "She'll land it. It's her fish, and she'll land it."

"It's ripping her apart," Richard said. "She's just not big enough."

"Please, Hugo," Margo said. "You can have it. It could have been me caught the barracuda."

"Look to the fish," Peak said.

Margo watched the water and her face went tight; she suddenly looked much older than she had looked. Peak reached out and laid a hand on Margo's breast and looked at Richard, said, "I say she does something, she does it. That's the way a wife does. Her husband says she does something, she does it."

Peak ran his hand over Margo's breast, nearly popping her top aside. Richard turned away from them and called up to Jones. "Cut this out. Let's go in."

Jones didn't answer.

"He does what I want," Peak said. "I pay him enough to do what I want."

The boat slowed almost to a stop, and the great fish began to sound. It went down and they waited. The rod was bent into a deep bow. Margo was beginning to shake. Her eyes looked as if they might roll up in her head. She was stretched forward in the straps so that her back was exposed to Richard, and he could see the cords of muscle there; they were as wadded and tight as the Gordian knot.

"She can't take much more of this," Richard said. "I'll take the fish, if you won't."

"You won't do a goddamn thing, Mr. Young. She can take it, and she will. She'll land it. She caught it, she'll bring it in."

"Hugo," Margo said. "I feel faint. Really."

Peak was still holding his beer, and he poured it over Margo's head. "That'll freshen you."

Margo shook beer from her hair. She began to cry silently. The rod began to bob up and down and the line on the reel was running out. The fish went down again.

Jones appeared from the upper deck. "I've killed the engine. The fish will sound and keep sounding."

"I know that," Peak said. "It'll sound until this bitch gives up, which she won't, or until she hauls it in, which she will."

Richard looked at Jones. The watered gravy eyes looked away. Richard realized now that not only was Jones a paid lackey, he had actually made sure he, Richard Young, was on this boat with Hugo Peak. He had known Jones a short time, since he'd been staying on St. Croix, and they had drunk a few together, and maybe he'd told Jones too much. Not that any of it mattered under normal circumstances, but now some things came clear, and Richard wished he had never known this Captain Jones.

Until now, he had considered Jones decent company. Had told him he was staying in the Caribbean for a few months to rest, really to get past some disappointments. And over one too many loaded fruit drinks, had told him more. For a brief time, two defenses, he had been the Heavyweight Kickboxing Champion of the World.

Trained in Kenpo and Tae Kwon Do, he had gone into kickboxing late, at thirty, and had worked his way up to the championship by age thirty-five, going at a slow rate due to lack of finances to chase all the tournaments. It wasn't like professional kickboxing paid all that much. But he had, by God, been the champion.

And on his second defense, against Manuel Martinez, it had gone wrong. Martinez was good. Real good. He gave Richard hell, and Richard lost sight of the rules in a pressed moment, snapped an elbow into the side of Martinez's temple. Martinez went down and never got up. The blow had been illegal and just right, and Martinez was dead and Richard was shamed and pained at what he had done.

He had the whole thing on videocassette. And at night, back home, when he was drunk or depressed, he sometimes got out the cassette and tormented himself with it. He had done what he had done on purpose, but he had never intended for it to kill. It was an instinctive action from years and years of self-defense training, especially Kenpo, which was fond of elbow strikes. He had lost his willpower and had killed.

He had told this to Jones, and obviously, Jones, most likely under the influence of drink, had told this to Peak, and Peak was the kind of man who would want to know a man who had killed someone. He would want to know someone like that to test himself against him. He would see killing a man in the ring as positive, a major macho achievement.

And those glowing yellow shins of Peak's. Callus. Thai boxers built their shins up to be impervious to pain. Used herbs on them to deaden feeling, so they could slam their legs against trees until they bled and scabbed and finally callused over. Peak wore those shins like a badge of honor.

Yeah, it was clear now. Peak had wanted to meet him and let it lead up to something. And Jones had made at least part of that dream possible. He had supplied Richard, lured him like an unsuspecting goat to the slaughter.

Richard began to feel sick. Not only from the tossing of the sea and the smell of the diesel, but from the fact that he had been handily betrayed, and that he had to see such a thing as a man abuse his wife over a fish, over the fact that Peak had caught a lowly barracuda, and his wife, through chance, had hooked a big one.

Richard moved to the side of the boat and threw up. He threw up hard and long. When he was finished, he turned and looked at Peak, who had slid his hand under Margo's top and was massaging her breast, his head close to her ear, whispering something. Margo no longer looked tan; she was pale and her mouth hung slack and tears ran down her face and dripped from her chin.

Richard turned back to look at the sea and saw a school of some kind of fish he couldn't identify, leaping out of the water and back in again. He looked at the deck and saw the bloodstained shears Jones had used on the barracuda. As he picked them up, and turned, the line on the rod went out fast again, finishing off the reel. Peak began to curse Margo and tell her what to do. Richard walked quickly over to the rod, reached up with the clippers, and snapped the line in two. The rod popped up, the line snapped away, drifted and looped, then it was jerked beneath the waves with the fish. Margo fell back in the chair and sighed, the harness creaking loosely against her.

Tossing the shears aside, Richard glared at Peak, who glared back. "To hell with you," Richard said.

Two days later Richard moved out of the Hotel on the Quay. Too expensive, and his savings were dwindling. He got a room over a fish market overlooking the dock and the waters of the Caribbean. He had planned to go home by now, back to Tyler, Texas, but somehow the thought of it made him sick.

Here, he seemed outside of the world he had known, and therefore, at least much of the time, outside of the event that had brought him here.

The first night in his little room, he lay fully dressed on the bed and smelled the fish smell that still lingered from the closed-up shop below. Above him, the ceiling fan beat at the hot air as if stirring chunky soup, and he watched the shadows the moonlight made off the blades of the fan, and the shadows whirled across him like some kind of alien, rotating spider.

After a time, he could lie there no more. He rose and began to move up and down the floor beside the bed, doing a Kenpo form, adjusting and varying it to suit the inconvenience of the room's size, the bed, and the furniture, which consisted of a table and two hard-back chairs.

He snapped at the air with his fists and feet, and the fan moved, and the smell of the fish was strong, and through the open window came the noise of drunks along the dock.

His body became coated with sweat, and, pausing only long

enough to remove his drenched shirt, he moved into new forms, and finally he lay down on the bed to try and sleep again, and he was almost there, when there was a knock on his door.

He went to the door, said through it: "Who is it?"

"Margo Peak."

Richard opened the door. She stood beneath the hall light, which was low down and close to her head. The bugs circling below the light were like a weird halo for her, a halo of little winged demons. She wore a short summer dress that showed her tan legs to advantage and revealed the tops of her breasts. Her face looked rough. Both eyes were blacked and there was a cut on her upper lip and her cheeks had bruises the color and size of ripe plums.

"May I come in?" she asked.

"Yes." He let her in and turned on the bare bulb that grew out of a tall floor lamp in the corner.

"Could we do without that?" she said. "I don't feel all that presentable."

"Peak?" he asked, turning off the light.

She sat on the edge of the bed, bounced it once, as if to test the springs. The moonlight came through the window and settled down on her like something heavy. "He hit me some."

Richard leaned against the wall. "Over the fish?"

"That. And you. You embarrassed him in front of me and Captain Jones by cutting the line on the fish. He felt belittled. For a moment he lost power over me. I might have been better off you'd stayed out of it and let me land the fish."

"Sorry. All things considered, you shouldn't be here. Why are you here?"

"You didn't work out like he wanted you to."

"I don't get it."

"He wants to fight you."

"Well, I got that much. I figured that's why Jones got me on the boat. Peak had plans for a match. He knows about me, I know that much. He knew my last name."

"He admires your skill. He has videos of your fights. It excites him you killed a man in the ring. He wants to fight a man who's killed a man. He thought he could antagonize you into something."

"A boat's no place to fight."

"He doesn't care where he fights. Actually, he wanted to get you mad enough to agree to come to his island. He has a little island not far out. Owns the whole thing."

"He thinks he can take me?"

"He wants to find out . . . Yes, he thinks he can."

"Tell him I think he can, too. I'll mail him one of my trophies when I get home."

"He wants it his way."

"He's out of luck."

"He sent me here. He wanted you to see what he'd done to me. He wanted me to tell you, if you don't come to the island, he'll do it again. He told me to tell you that he can be a master of misery. If not to you, then to me."

"That's your problem. Don't go back. You go back, you're a fool."

"He's got a lot of money."

"I'm not impressed with his money, or you. You're a fool, Margo."

"It's all I've got, Richard. He's not nearly as bad as my family was. He at least gives me money, attention. Being an attractive trophy is better than being your father's plaything, if you know what I mean. Hugo got me off drugs. I'm not turning tricks anymore. He did that."

"Just so he'd have a healthy punching bag. A good-looking trophy. Course, he's not treating you so good right now, is he? Listen, Margo, it's your life. Turn it around, you don't like it. Don't come to me like it's my fault you're getting your ass kicked."

"I could leave a man like Peak, I had another man to go to."

"You sound like you're shopping for cars. You see what kind of money I got. You'd leave Peak for this? You want a dump like this? A shared toilet?"

"You could do better. You've got the skill. The name. You've got the looks to get into movies. Martial arts guys can make lots of money. Look at Chuck Norris. Christ, you actually killed somebody. The media would eat that up. You're the real McCoy."

"You know, you and Peak deserve each other. Why don't you just paint bull's-eyes on yourself, give Peak spots to go for next time he gets pissed."

"He knows the spots already."

"Sorry, Margo, but goodbye."

He opened the door. Margo stood and studied him. She moved through the doorway and into the hall and turned to face him. Once again the bugs made a halo above her head. "He wants you to come out to his island. He'll have Captain Jones bring you. Jones is taking me back now, but he'll be back for you. It's a short trip where you need to go. Hugo told me to give you this."

She reached into a loose pocket on her dress and brought out a piece of folded paper, shoved it toward him. Richard took it but did not look at it. He said, "I'm not coming."

"You don't, he'll take it out on me. He'll treat me rough. You see my face. You should see my breasts. Between my legs. He did things there. He can do worse. He's done worse. What have you got to lose? You used to do it for a living. We could do all right together, you and me."

"We don't even know each other."

"We could fix that. We could start knowing one another now. We knew each other, you might not want to let me go."

She moved toward him and her arms went around his neck. He reached out and held her waist. She felt solid, small, and warm.

Richard said, "I've said it. I say it again. You can leave anytime you like."

"He'd have me followed to the ends of the Earth."

"I'd rather run like a dog, than heel like one."

"You just don't know," she said, pushing away from him. "You don't know anything."

"I know you're still turning tricks, and Peak's a kind of pimp, and you're not even aware of it."

"You don't know a goddamn thing."

"All right. Good luck."

Margo didn't move. She held her place with the bugs swarming above her head. Richard stepped inside his room, and closed the door.

Richard lay on the bed with the note in his hand. He lay that way for a full fifteen minutes. Finally, he rolled on his side and unfolded the note and read it in the moonlight.

MR. YOUNG:

COME TO THE DOCK AND TAKE JONES'S BOAT BY MID-NIGHT. HE'LL BRING YOU OUT TO MY ISLAND. WE'LL FIGHT. NO RULES. WE FIGHT, IT'S BEST FOR MARGO. YOU WIN, I'LL GIVE YOU TEN THOUSAND DOLLARS. I'LL GIVE YOU MARGO. I'LL GIVE YOU A RESTAURANT COUPON FOR FIVE DOLLARS OFF. YOU DONT COME, MARGO WILL BE UNHAPPY. I'LL BE UNHAPPY AND THE COUPON WILL EXPIRE. AND YOU'LL NEVER KNOW IF YOU COULD HAVE BEAT ME.

HUGO PEAK

Richard dropped the note on the floor, rolled onto his back. *It's that simple for Peak*, Richard thought. *He says come, and he thinks I'll come. He's nuts. Margo's nuts. She thinks I owe her something and I don't even know her. I don't want to know her. She's a gold digger. It's not my problem she hasn't the strength to do what she should do. It's not my fault he'll kick her head in. She's a grown woman and she has to make her own decisions. I'm no hero. I'm not a knight on a white charger. I killed a man once by accident, by not staying with the rules, and I'll not fight another man without rules on purpose. The goddamn son of a bitch must think he's a James Bond villain. I won't have anything to do with him. I will never fight a man for sport again.*

Richard lay in the dark and watched the fan. The shadows the fan cast were growing thicker. Soon there would be no shadows at all, only darkness, because the moonlight was fading behind clouds. A cool, wet wind came through the open window. The smell of the fish market below was not as strong now because the smell of the sea and the damp earth had replaced it. Richard held his arm up so that he could see his watch. The luminous dial told him it was just before ten o'clock. He closed his eyes and slept.

When he awoke, rain was blowing in through the window and onto the bed. The rain felt good. He didn't get up to shut the window. He thought about Hugo Peak, waiting. He looked at his watch. It was 11:35.

Peak would be starting to warm up now. Anticipating. Actually thinking he might come. Peak would believe that because he would consider Richard weak. He would think he was weak in that he wanted to protect a woman who had no urge to protect herself. He would think Richard's snipping the fishing line was a sign of weakness. He wouldn't think Richard had done it to make things easier on Margo. He would think he did it as some sort of spiteful attack, and that Richard really wanted to fight him. That was what Peak would be thinking.

And Richard knew, deep down, Peak was not entirely wrong.

He thought: *If I were to go, I could make it to the boat in ten minutes. It's not that far. I could be there in ten minutes easy, I walked fast. But I'm not going, so it doesn't matter.*

He sat on the side of the bed and let the rain slice into him. He got up and went around the bed and opened the closet and got out his martial arts bag. He unzipped and opened it. The mouthpiece and safety gear were there. He zipped it back up. He put it in the closet and closed the door. He sat on the side of the bed. He picked the note up and read it again. He tore it into little pieces and dropped the pieces on the floor, frightening a roach. He tried not to think about anything, but he thought about Margo. The way her face had looked, what she said Peak had done to her breasts, between her legs. He remembered the eyes of that dying cat, and he remembered Margo's eyes. The same eyes, only she wasn't dying as fast. She was going slowly, piece by piece, committing suicide. He remembered the horror of killing the man in the ring, and he remembered, in some hidden, primitive compartment of himself, the pleasure. It was a scary thing inside of him; inside of humankind, especially mankind, this thing about killing. This need. This desire. Maybe, he got home, he'd go deer hunting this year. He hadn't been in over ten years, but he might go now. He might ought to go.

Richard got up and took off his clothes and rubbed his body down with ICY-HOT and took six aspirin and downed them with a glass of water. He put on a jockstrap and cup and loose workout pants and pulled a heavy sweatshirt on. He put on his white tennis shoes without socks and laced them tight. He got his bag out of the closet. He walked to the door and turned around and looked at the room. It looked as if no one had ever lived here. He looked at his watch. He had exactly ten minutes. He opened the door and went out.

As he walked, the ICY-HOT began to heat up and work its way into his muscles. The smell of it was strong in his nostrils. Another fifteen minutes, and the aspirin would take effect, loosen his body further. The rain came down hard as steel pellets and washed his hair into his face, but he kept walking, and finally he began to run.

He ran fast until he came to the Anchor Inn Restaurant. He slowed there and went around the corner, and there was Jones's fishing boat. He looked at his watch. He was right on time. He walked up to the fishing boat and called out.

Jones appeared on the deck in rain hat and slicker. Water ran off the hat and fell across his face like a beaded curtain. He helped Richard aboard. Jones said, "It's just that I needed the money. I owe on the boat. I don't pay on the boat, they're gonna take it away from me."

"Everyone needs something," Richard said. "Take me out, Jones, and listen up. After this, you better hope I go home to Texas. I'm here, walking around, I see you on the dock, anywhere, you better start running. Got me?"

Jones nodded.
"Take me out."

The wind picked up and so did the rain. Richard's stomach began to turn over. He tried to stay in the cabin, but he found that worse. He rushed outside and puked over the side. Finally, he strapped himself into the fighting chair and rode the boat like a carnival ride, taking great waves of water full blast and watching lightning stitch the sky and dip down and touch the ocean in spots, as if God were punishing it.

It wasn't long before the lights of the boat showed land. Jones moved them in slowly to the little island, finally came to a dock and tied them up. When Richard went to get his bag out of the cabin, Jones came down from the wheel and said, "Here, take this. You'll need it for strength, all that pukin' you done."

It was a thick strip of jerky. "No thanks," Richard said.

"You don't like me, and I don't blame you. Take the jerky though. You got to have some kind of energy."

"All right," Richard said, took it and ate. Jones gave him a drink of water in a paper cup. When Richard was finished, he said, "Water and jerky don't change anything."

"I know," Jones said. "I'm going back to St. Croix before it gets worse. I'd rather be docked there. I think it's a little better protected for boats."

"And how do I get back?"

"Good luck," Jones said.

"So that's how it is? You're all through?"

"Soon as you get off the boat." Jones stepped back a step and produced a little .38 from somewhere under his shirt. "It's nothing personal. It's just the money. Margo was pretty convincing too. Peak likes her to be convincing. But it was the money did it. Margo was just a fringe benefit. The money was enough."

"He really wants to fight to the death, doesn't he?"

"I don't ask about much of what he wants. You got to see it from my side, taking big shots out in boats all the time, getting by on their tips. It costs to take out a charter, wear and tear on the boat. I'm thinking about doing something else, going somewhere else. I might hire some goon like me to take me out fishing. I might go somewhere where the biggest pool of water around is in a glass."

"You're that easy for money?"

"You bet. And remember, I didn't make you come. Get off."

Richard went out of the cabin and climbed down to the dock.

When he looked up through the driving rain, he could see Jones looking down at him from the boat, the .38 pointed at him.

"You go up the dock there, toward the flagstones. Follow those. They lead around a curve through the rocks and trees. Where you need to go is back there. You'll see it. Now, go on so I can cast off. And good luck. I mean it."

"Yeah, I know. Nothing personal. Well, you know what you can do with your luck." Richard turned and started up the dock.

The directions led him up through a cut in the rocks and around a curve, and there, built into the side of the mountain, was a huge house of great weathered lumber, glass, and stone. The house seemed like part of the island itself. Richard figured, you were inside, standing at one of the great windows, on a good day, you could look out and clearly see fish swimming deep in the clear Caribbean waters, see them some distance off.

He followed the trail, tried to get his mind on what it was he was going to do. He tried to think about Thai boxers and how they fought. He was sure this was how Peak had trained. Peak's shins were a giveaway, but that didn't mean he hadn't done other things. He might like grappling too, ground work. He had to think about all this, but mostly, he had to think about the Thai boxing. Thai boxers were not fancy kickers like Karataka, or Kung Fu people, but they were devastating because of the way they trained. The way they trained was more important than what they knew. They trained hard, for endurance. They trained themselves to take and accept and fuel themselves off pain. They honed their main weapons, their shins, until the best of them could kick through the thick end of a baseball bat. He had to think about that. He had to think that Peak would be in good condition, and that, unlike himself, he hadn't taken off a few years from rigorous training. Oh, he wasn't all washed-up. He practiced the moves and did exercises and his stomach was flat and his reflexes were good, but he hadn't sparred against anyone since that time he had killed a man in the ring. He had to think about all that. He had to not let the bad part of what he was thinking get him down, but he had to know what was bad about himself and what was good. He had to think of some strategy to deal with Peak before Peak threw a punch or kick. He had to think about the fact that Peak might want to kill him. He had to not think too hard about what kind of fool he'd been for coming here. He had to not think about how predictable he had been to Peak. He had to hope that he was not predictable when they fought. He had to realize that he could kill a man if he wanted to, if the opening was there. He'd already done it once, not meaning to. Now he had to mean to.

At the top of the slope there was an overhang porch of stone, and a warm orange light glowed behind the glass positioned in the thick oak door. Before Richard could touch the buzzer, the door opened, and there stood Margo. She had on the dress she had worn earlier. Her hair was pinned up now. She looked at him with those dying cat eyes. The wind and the sea howled behind him.

"Thanks," she said.

Richard stepped past her, inside, dripping water.

The house was tall as a cathedral, furnished in thick wood, leather furniture, and the heads of animals, the bodies of fish. They were everywhere. It looked like a taxidermist's shop.

Margo closed the door against the rain and wind. She said, "He's waiting for you."

"I should hope so," Richard said.

He dripped on the floor as he walked. She took him into a large, lushly furnished bedroom. She went into an adjacent bathroom and came out with a beach towel and a pair of blue workout pants and kicking shoes. "He wants you to wear these. He wants to see you right away, unless you feel you need to rest first."

"I came here to do it," Richard said. "So, the sooner the better." He took the towel and dried, removed his clothes, except for the jock, and, paying Margo no mind, dried again. He put on the pants and shoes.

Margo led him to a gymnasium. It was a wonderful and roomy gym with one wall made of thick glass overlooking rocks and sea; the windows he had seen from the trail. There was little light in there, just illumination from glow strips around the wall. Hugo Peak sat on a stool looking out one of the windows. He was dressed in red workout pants and kicking shoes. His back, turned to Richard, held shadows in the valley of its muscles.

"He's waiting," Margo said, and faded back into the shadows and leaned against the wall.

Richard turned and looked at her, a shape in the darkness. He said, "I just want you to know, I'm not doing this for you. I'm doing this for me."

"And for the money?" she said.

"That's icing. I get it, that's good. I'll even take you with me, get you away from here, you want to go. But I won't argue with you to go."

"You win, I might go. But ten thousand dollars isn't a lot of money. Not considering the way I can live now."

"You're right. Keep that in mind. Keep in mind that the ten thousand isn't yours. None of it is. I said I'd take you with me, but that means as far as the island, after that, you're on your own. I don't owe you anything."

"I can make a man happy."

"I got to be happy somewhere else besides below the belt."

"It's not fair. You win, I go with you, I don't get any of your money, and I don't get Hugo's."

"Then you better root for Hugo."

Richard left Margo in the shadows, went over and stood near Peak, and looked out the glass. The sea foamed high and dark with whitecaps against the rocks. Richard saw that the dock he had walked along was gone. The sea had picked it up and carried it away. Or most of it. A few boards were broken and twisted on the shore, lodged between rocks. The great windows vibrated slightly.

"There's going to be a hurricane," Peak said, not looking at Richard. "I believe that's appropriate."

"I want you to write the ten-thousand-dollar check now," Richard said. "Let Margo hold it. I lose, she can tear it up. I win, we'll see someone gets us off the island. Jones isn't coming back, so it'll have to be someone else."

"I'll write the check," Peak said, still looking out the window, "but you won't need to worry about getting off the island. This is your last stop, Mr. Young. You see that prominent rock closest to the house, on the left side of the trail."

"Yeah. What about it?"

Peak sat silent for a long time. Not answering. "Did you know, in the Orient, some places like Thailand, India, they have death matches? I studied there. I studied Thai boxing and Bando when I was stationed there in the army. I've fought some tough matches. People brought here from Thailand, champion Thai boxers. They came here to win money, and they went home hurt. Some of them crippled. I never killed anyone though. I've never fought anyone that's killed anyone. You'll be the first. You know I intend for this one to go all the way?"

"What's that got to do with the rock?" Richard said.

"Oh, my mind wandered. At the base of it, Hero is buried. He was my dog. A German shepherd. He understood me. That's something I miss, Mr. Young. Being understood."

"You're certainly breaking my heart."

"I think maybe, since you came here, on some level, you understand me. That's something worth having. Knowing a worthy opponent understands you. There aren't many like you and me left."

"Whatever you say."

"Death, it's nothing. You know what Hemingway said about death, don't you? He called it a gift."

"Yeah, well, I haven't noticed it being such a popular present. Shall we do it, or what? You were so all-fired wanting to do it, so let's do it."

"Warm up, and we shall. While you start, I'll get a check."

Richard began to stretch and Peak came back with the check. He showed it to Richard. Richard said, "How do I know it's good?"

"You don't. But you don't really care. This isn't about money, is it?"

"Give it to Margo to hold."

Peak did that, then he began to stretch. Fifteen minutes later, Peak said, "It's time."

They met in the center of the gym, began to move in a circular fashion, each looking for an opening. Peak stuck out a couple of jabs, and Richard moved his head away from them. He gave Peak a couple with the same results. Then they went together.

Peak threw hard Thai round kicks to the outside of Richard's right thigh, tried to spring off those for higher kicks to the neck, but Richard faded away from those. Thai boxers were famous for breaking the neck, Richard knew that. He was amazed at how hard the kicks were thrown. They were simple and looked almost stiff, but even though he managed to lift his leg to get some give in the strike, they still hurt.

Richard tried a couple of side kicks, and both times Peak blocked them by kneeing Richard's shin as the kicks came in, and the second time Peak blocked, he advanced and swung an elbow and hit Richard on the jaw. It was an elbow strike like the one Richard had used when he killed Martinez. It hit pretty hard, and Richard felt it all the way down to his heels. When he moved back to regroup, he looked at Peak and saw that he was grinning.

Then they really went to it. Richard threw a front kick to get in close, nothing great, just a front kick, more of a forward stomp to the groin, really, and this brought him into Peak's kill zone, and he tried a series of hand attacks, from backfist to the head, reverse punch to the solar plexus, an uppercut up under Peak's arm, solid to the ribs. It was like hitting a hot water heater.

Peak hit him with another elbow shot, jumped, grabbed Richard's hair, jerked his head down, brought his knee up fast and high. Richard turned his head and the knee hit him hard on the shoulder and the pain went all the way down Richard's arm, such pain that Richard couldn't maintain a fist. His hand flew open like a greedy child reaching for candy.

Richard swung his other arm outside and back and broke the grab on his hair, but lost some hair in the process. He kicked Peak in the knee, a glancing blow, but it got him in to use a double swinging elbow on either side of Peak's head, and for a moment, he thought he was in good, but Peak took the shots and did a jumping knee lift, hit Richard on the elbow, and drove him back with a series of fast round kicks and punches.

Richard felt blood gushing from his nose and over his lips and down his chin. He had to be careful not to slip in the blood when it got on the floor. Damn, the man could hit, and he was fast. Richard already felt tired, and he could tell his nose was broken. It was hot and throbbing. He had been a fool to do this. This wasn't any match. There wasn't going to be any bell. He had to finish this or be finished.

Richard kicked twice to Peak's legs. Once off the front leg, followed with a kick off the rear leg. Both landed, but Peak twisted so he took them on his shins. It was like kicking a tree. Richard began to see the outcome of this. He was going to manage to hit Peak a lot, but Peak was going to hit him a lot too, and in the long run, Peak would win because of the conditioning, because he could take full contact blows better to the body and the shins.

Richard faded back a bit, shook his injured arm. It felt a little better. He could make a solid fist again. The storm outside had gotten busy. The windows were starting to shake. The floor beneath them vibrated. Richard began to bob and weave. Peak held his hands up high, Thai boxer style, closed fists palm forward, set that way to throw devastating elbows.

Richard came in with a series of front kicks and punches, snapped his fingers to Peak's eyes. Managed to flick them, make them water. That was his edge, a brief one, but he took it, and suddenly he was in with a grab to Peak's ear. He got hold of it, jerked, heard it rip like rotten canvas. Blood flew all over Richard's face.

Peak screamed and came in with a blitz of knees and elbows. Richard faded clockwise, away from the brunt of the attack. When Peak stopped, breathing hard, Richard opened his fist. He held Peak's ear in his hand. He smiled at Peak. He put the ear between his teeth and held it there. He bobbed and weaved toward Peak. Richard understood something now. Thai boxers trained hard. They had hard bodies, and if you tried to work by their methods, fists and feet, and you weren't in the same condition, they would wear you down, take you.

But that was the advantage that a system like karate had. He was trained to use his fingers, use specific points, not just areas you could slam with kicks and elbows. True, anywhere Peak kicked or hit him hurt, but no matter how tough Peak was, he had soft eyes, ears, and throat. The groin would normally be a soft target, but like himself, Richard figured he had on a cup. That wouldn't make it so good to hit, and there was the fact a trained fighter could actually take a groin shot pretty well, and there was that rush of adrenaline a groin blow could give a foe, a few seconds of fired energy before the pain took over. It was like a shot of speed. Sometimes, that alone could whip you.

Okay, watch yourself—don't get cocky. He can still take you out and finish you with one solid blow. Richard glanced toward Margo. She was just a shape in the shadows.

Richard spit the ear out and they came together again. A flurry. Richard didn't have time to try anything sophisticated. He was too busy minimizing Peak's attack. He tied Peak up, trapped his hands down, but Peak shot his head forward and caught Richard a meaty one in the upper lip. Richard's lip exploded. Richard shifted, twisted his hip into Peak, turned and flipped him. Peak tumbled across the floor and came up on his feet.

And then Richard heard the great windows rattling like knucklebones in a plastic cup. He glanced out of the corner of his eye. The hurricane was raging. It was like the house was in a mixer. The glass cracked open in a couple of spots and rain blew in.

"None of that matters," Peak said. "This is the storm that matters." He moved toward Richard. The side of his head leaking blood, one of his eyes starting to close.

Richard thought, *Okay, I do better when I don't play his game. I'll look as if I'm going to play his game, then I won't.* Then suddenly he remembered the ray. How it had leaped out of the water and flicked its tail. It was an image that came to him, and then he knew what to do. The ray's tail reminded him of a flying reverse heel kick. In a real fight, the jump kick wasn't something you actually used much. No matter what the movies showed, you tried to stay on the ground, and you kicked low, and Peak would know that. He would know it so strongly he might not expect what Richard could do.

Richard threw a low front kick off the front leg, followed with a jab as he closed, followed with a reverse punch, and then he threw his back leg forward, as if about to execute a leaping knee, but he used the knee to launch himself, twisted hard, took to the air, whipped his back leg around into a jump heel kick, whipped it hard and fast the way the ray had whipped its tail.

He caught Peak on the side of the head, above the temple, felt the bones in Peak's skull give way to his heel. Peak fell sideways like a dipping second hand, hit the floor.

As Richard stepped in and kicked Peak with all he had in the throat, the windows blew in and shards of glass hit Richard, and a wall of water took the room and all its occupants, carried them through the other wall as if it were wet cardboard. Richard felt a blow to his head, a timber striking him, and then the water carried him away and everything was dark.

When Richard awoke he was in darkness, and he was choking to death. He was in the sea. Under it. He swam up, hard, but he couldn't seem to make it. The water kept pushing him down. He continued kicking, fighting, and finally, when he thought his lungs would explode, he broke up and got a gulp of air and went under again. But not so far this time. A long, dark, beam of wood hit him in the head, and he got hold of it. It had been an overhead beam in the gym. It was thick, but it floated just fine. He realized the storm had struck and moved on, like a hit-and-run driver, leaving in its wake stormy seas, but an oddly clear sky lit up by a cool, full moon that looked like a smudgy spotlight.

Richard looked down the length of the beam and shuddered. The beam had broken off to a point down there, and the point was stuck through Margo's chest, dead center, had her pinned like an insect to a mounting board. Her head was nodding to one side, and as the water jumped and the wind lashed, her head rolled on her neck as if on a ball bearing, rolled way too far and high to the left, then back to the right. It was like one of those bobbing, toy dog heads you see in the back of cars. Her tongue hung out of her mouth as if trying to lick the last drop of something sweet. Her hair was washed back from her bruised face. A shard of glass was punched deep into her cheek. Her arms washed back and forth and up and down, as if she might be frantically signaling.

The beam rolled and Richard rolled with it. When he came out of the water and got a grip on it again, Margo's head was under the waves and her legs were sticking up, spread wide, bent at the knees, flopping, showing her panties to the moonlight.

Richard looked for the island, but didn't see it. The waves were too high and choppy. Maybe the damn island was underwater.

Maybe he was washed way away from it. He had probably gone down below and fought his way up a dozen times, but just didn't remember. All reflex action. God, he hated the sea.

And then he saw Peak. Peak was clinging to a door. He was hanging on the door with one hand, gripping the doorknob. The door was tilted toward him, and Peak looked weak. His other arm hung by his side, floated and thrashed in the water, obviously broken. He didn't see Richard. His back was to him. He was about ten feet away. Or he was every few seconds. Waves would wash him a little farther away, then bring him back.

Richard timed it. When the waves washed Peak away, Richard let go of the beam and swam toward him, then when the waves washed him back, Richard was there. He came up behind Peak, slipped an arm around Peak's neck, and used his other to tighten the choke. It was the kind of choke that cut the blood off to the brain, didn't affect the wind.

Peak tried to hang on to the door, but he let go to grab Richard's arm. The waves took them under, but still Richard clung. They washed up into the moonlight and Richard rolled onto his back, keeping Peak on top of him. He held his head out of the water with effort. Peak's hand fluttered weakly against Richard's arm.

"You know what Hemingway said about death," Richard said. "That it's a gift. Well, I give it to you."

In a moment, Peak's hand no longer fluttered, and Richard let him go. Peak went directly beneath the waves and out of sight.

Richard swam, got on top of the door, clung to the knob, and bucked with the waves. He looked for the beam with Margo on it. He spotted it far out, on the rise of a wave, Margo's legs dangling like a broken peace symbol. The beam rolled and Margo's head came up, then it rolled again, went down into a valley of waves and out of sight. Nearby, Richard saw the check Peak had written ride up on a wave like a little flat fish, shine for a moment in the moonlight, then go down, and not come up.

Richard laughed. He no longer felt frightened of the sea, of anything. The waves rolled over him with great pressure, the door cracked and shifted, started to break up, then the knob came away in his hand.

Three thousand copies of this book have been printed by the Maple-Vail Book Manufacturing Group, Binghamton, NY, for Golden Gryphon Press, Urbana, Il. The typeset is Electra with Ruach display, printed on 55# Sebago. Typesetting by The Composing Room, Inc., Kimberly, WI.